VISIONS OF
POE

Edgar Allan Poe c. 1845.
Photographer unidentified.

VISIONS OF POE

A PERSONAL SELECTION OF EDGAR ALLAN POE'S STORIES AND POEMS

WITH PHOTOGRAPHS AND AN INTRODUCTION BY
SIMON MARSDEN

Webb & Bower

MICHAEL JOSEPH

For Skye Atalanta Marsden

First published in Great Britain 1988 by
Webb & Bower (Publishers) Limited
9 Colleton Crescent, Exeter, Devon EX2 4BY
in association with Michael Joseph Limited
27 Wright's Lane, London W8 5TZ

Designed by Vic Giolitto

Production by Nick Facer/Rob Kendrew

Copyright © 1988 Simon Marsden

British Library Cataloguing in Publication Data

Poe, Edgar Allan
    Visions of Poe : a personal selection of
    Edgar Allan Poe's stories and poems.
    I. Title II. Marsden, Simon
    818′ .309 PS2603

ISBN 0-86350-180-X

Typeset in Great Britain by Scribes Typesetting,
Exeter, Devon

Duotone reproduction by Peninsular Reproduction Services,
Exeter, Devon

Printed and bound in Italy by New Interlitho

CONTENTS

INTRODUCTION

'To be buried while alive is, beyond question, the most terrific of these extremes which has ever fallen to the lot of mere mortality. That it has frequently, very frequently, so fallen will scarcely be denied by those who think. The boundaries which divide Life from Death are at best shadowy and vague. Who shall say where the one ends, and where the other begins?'

(extract taken from *The Premature Burial* by EA Poe)

SELDOM, if ever, in the history of literature can there have existed a more mysterious, controversial and influential writer than Edgar Allan Poe. Unfortunately he has too often been portrayed as a drunken, drug-addicted madman but he cannot be so easily classified. His life and works have long been argued over by both his detractors and admirers alike, but what nobody can deny is the great and profound influence that the writings of this ill-fated genius have exerted over so many other distinguished writers, poets and artists since his tragic and premature death at the age of forty.

Poe is best known for his 'darker' works, some of the most macabre and terrifying horror stories in the English language, but there was far more to this highly sensitive and intelligent man's literary talents. He also wrote many romantic and haunting poems of exquisite beauty which his great admirer Baudelaire once described as 'deep and shimmering as dreams, mysterious and perfect as crystal'. Add to these his 'black humour', which produced stories that were chiefly written for magazines and portray the dry and sardonic wit that served him so well in adversity throughout his turbulent life. He was a man of strong convictions, and this combined with the inevitable artist's ego meant that his astute and sometimes cruel literary criticisms, which were widely read, in turn made him many enemies in literary circles. It is ironic that these manuscripts have now become the most valuable of all American writers.

Poe was also a prophet and pioneer of science fiction, taking a strong interest in the inventions of his age and he integrated them in several of his tales. He is also credited with constructing and writing the first detective story, *The Murders in the Rue Morgue*. He wrote two longer works, a travel novel *The Narrative of Arthur Gordon Pym of Nantucket*, an account of mutiny, murder and cannibalism on the high seas, which he liked to call 'a voyage of discovery', and also what he felt was his greatest work, the philosophical essay *Eureka*, a treatise on the 'creation of the universe'.

But it is for his tales of terror, written in the 'Gothic' tradition, and his magnificent poetry that Poe will be best remembered, for he possessed that unique talent of the 'true' artist; an ability to write 'from the soul', to literally confront the tragedies that so cruelly befell him and to create his art from them. However, to understand his obsession with death and the 'shroud of mystery' that surrounded him from almost the moment of his birth to the bizarre manner of his death, one must first study the 'tortured' life of this much maligned American writer.

Edgar Poe was born in Boston, Massachusetts on 19th January 1809 of itinerant actor parents. His English mother, Elizabeth Arnold Hopkins, was a beautiful and strong-willed young woman, but his American father of Irish descent, David Poe, was an alcoholic cursed with a fiery temper who deserted his wife soon after Poe's birth. Both his parents were to die of the terrible wasting disease tuberculosis before he had reached the age of three. The death of Poe's mother at the tender age of twenty-one in fact marked the beginning of the end for the small boy, but even he could never have dreamt of the nightmares to come.

Edgar, his sister Rosalie and his elder brother Henry were all adopted by different families. John Allan, a well-to-do merchant and his wife Frances, who were childless, were to be Poe's foster-parents and from that time onwards he became known as Edgar Allan Poe. The Allan family home was in Richmond, Virginia, and he spent the first years of his childhood there. Frances Allan adored the poor orphan but her husband began to resent his presence in the house from the start, and he was to grow ever more bitter over the years. In 1815 Allan decided to take his family to England to establish a branch of his business there and here Poe was sent to several private schools to begin his education as a gentleman. The first of these was in Scotland but Frances Allan, who Poe now called his beloved 'Ma', implored her husband to place him elsewhere because of it's bleak position and disciplinarian atmosphere.

In the autumn of 1817 Poe was sent to the Manor House school of the Reverend Bransby at Stoke Newington in London. His time spent here must have made a great impression on him as the school and it's headmaster featured later in his story *William Wilson*. There is no reliable record of his achievements during this time but his education

John Allan.

must have been responsible for the European setting of several of his stories as this was his only visit to Europe during his brief life. After five years in London John Allan's business was making no progress and he decided to return with his family to America.

Poe continued his schooling in Richmond and was described at the time as a beautiful, head-strong but rather sensitive youth who excelled at his studies and possessed some of the arrogance of a typical 'southern gentleman'. It was around this time that be began to write poetry and many of these lyrical verses were dedicated to the adolescent girls who were attracted to this handsome and intriguing young man.

It was during this period too that he first fell in love. It was with the mother of one of his school friends, Mrs Jane Stanard; but like so many of his relationships it was to end in tragedy for, apart from their difference in age, Mrs Stanard, like his own mother, was dying of tuberculosis. Within a short while another young lady, Elmira Royston, began receiving Poe's amorous approaches. At home John Allan was beginning to resent his adopted son's philandering and his lack of interest in the family business and so decided to send him to university in Charlottesville, but only providing him with a pittance to survive on.

At university Poe began to gamble to supplement his meagre income but he soon ran up large debts. To make matters worse Elmira's father disapproved of him and intercepted his letters to his daughter. Elmira lost heart and married another, Poe was inconsolable and began to drink for the first time. On hearing of his debts John Allan withdrew him from university and Poe returned to Richmond where, to his horror, he found Mrs Allan was now wasting away with consumption; it must have seemed to him that every chance of happiness was being cruelly snatched away from him.

Relations had now become so strained between Poe and his foster-father that after one particularly ferocious and bitter row Poe stormed out of the house and fled to Boston by ship without a cent in his pocket. He later wrote to Allan begging him to send on his clothes and a little money, but the reply coldly berated him as a 'wastrel' and he was left to fend for himself. By a rare piece of good fortune he then met a young printer called Calvin Thomas who befriended him and offered to publish a slender volume of his poems titled, *Tamerlane and other poems*, but it did not sell. Some time later, close to starvation, he enlisted in the army under a false name. For eighteen months he was a model soldier, keeping himself amused by writing poetry, but his prospects of becoming a commissioned officer appeared bleak and so be began writing to his stepfather again pleading for assistance to enter West Point, the officer training academy. Allan never replied to any of these letters.

Poe returned to Richmond on 2nd March 1829 to find his foster-mother already buried. In a sudden act of contrition John Allan agreed to pay his discharge from the army and to help him enroll at West Point, but the money he offered was barely enough for him to exist on and so he went to Baltimore to stay at the home of his aunt Maria Clemm. Mrs Clemm had two children, a son Henry and a daughter Virginia, who was destined to become his wife. Poe's elder brother, William Henry Poe, was also living in the house but was slowly dying of chronic alcoholism and consumption. He had a second volume of poems published at this time under the title *Al Aaraaf, Tamerlane and minor poems*.

Later, through John Allan's influence, Poe gained a place at West Point but by now he had begun to gain in confidence as a poet and it did not take him long to tire of the regimented and disciplined life of the academy. Once more he tried writing to John Allan, who by now had married again, begging for his permission to resign, but again he received no reply, and so he began to neglect his duties until in 1831 he was finally dismissed. He then visited New York where he succeeded in finding a publisher to issue another short volume of his poems.

Following a cold and miserable month in New York he decided to return to his aunt's house in Baltimore but within a short time of his arrival his brother died. Mrs Clemm now thought of Poe as her own son and referred to him as her 'darling Eddie'. The beautiful and delicate Virginia was now nine years old and she and her aunt had come to represent the family that he craved for, he called them his 'Muddy' and 'Sis'. The Clemm household was desperately poor and he began to write prose for the first time, in the hope of being able to provide some income. In July 1832 he submitted five tales to the *Baltimore Saturday Visitor* and won first prize with *MS found in a bottle*. This was to prove to be one of the few literary acclaims he would receive during his lifetime.

Poe then made one last desperate appeal to his foster-father, who was now on his death-bed, for financial help but none was forthcoming and on Allan's eventual death he was cut completely out of his will. He was now on his

own and knew that he must somehow earn a living. He unwillingly left Baltimore for the position as assistant editor of *The Southern Literary Messenger* in Richmond, but was desperately unhappy and lonely without his newly found 'family' and took to the bottle for comfort. Then in October 1835 he moved Mrs Clemm and Virginia to Richmond and on the 16th May 1836 he married his 'child-bride' and cousin, three months before her fourteenth birthday.

Poe's marriage to Virginia became the centre of much gossip and slander and this greatly affected his sensitive nature, but on the whole their marriage was a success and the next few years were to prove happy and productive for him although there were rumours that the marriage was never consummated and that he had only married Virginia so that he could remain close to his aunt, who was in reality for him the perfect 'substitute' mother. In January 1837 he severed his ties with *The Southern Literary Messenger* and the three of them travelled to New York and then Philadelphia with Poe moving from one editorial job to another with a considerable degree of success; he was, for all his faults, a very hard worker. They had very little money at this time but they had each other and 'Eddie' was writing. During their six years in Philadelphia Poe wrote some thirty-one stories which he published under the title *Tales of the Grotesque and Arabesque* and these included some of his most famous tales such as *The Fall of the House of Usher, Ligeia* and *The Gold Bug*. It was also during this productive period that Poe began to nurture a burning ambition, to edit and publish his own literary magazine to be titled *The Stylus*, but this was to remain merely a dream.

Then in 1842 tragedy struck. Virginia ruptured a blood vessel whilst singing one evening for visitors and to Poe's horror the doctors diagnosed that she too was dying of consumption. He was devastated and could only watch her slow death over the following five years, frequently turning to the bottle for relief but always comforted in his grief by the loyal 'Muddy'. Somehow through all this pain he wrote prolifically in a battle to retain his sanity, and his output included the horrific *The Pit and the Pendulum* and *The Tell-Tale Heart*. In the spring of 1845 his poem *The Raven* was published and he became an over-night success, but even as his name was on everyone's lips Poe could be found the same morning stumbling through the streets of Manhattan, staggering from bar to bar quite unable to come to terms with this sudden, and to him quite 'unreal' situation. He received only $8 from the publisher for what has been described as 'the most perfectly constructed poem in the English language'.

By the summer of 1846 he sensed that Virginia's health was rapidly declining and he decided to move the 'family' to a small cottage at Fordham, then a semi-rural area outside New York, where they could hide away and the country air would be beneficial to Virginia's health. Winter came and they found themselves short of money yet again. A friend who visited the cottage was moved to write a description of Virginia's plight:

> 'There was nothing on the bed, but a snow white counterpane and sheets. The weather was cold, and the sick lady had the dreadfull chills that accompany the hectic fever of consumption. She lay on the straw bed, wrapped in her husbands great coat, with a large tortoiseshell cat on her bosom. The wonderful cat seemed conscious of her great usefulness. The coat and the cat were the sufferer's only means of warmth.'

Virginia died on 30th January 1847 and Poe collapsed into a stupour of grief. Later writing of the effect of Virginia's death on him, he said:

> 'I became insane, with long intervals of horrible sanity. During these fits of absolute unconsciousness I drank, God only knows how often and how much. As a matter of course, my enemies referred the insanity to the drink, rather than the drink to the insanity.'

Poe was nursed through this hell by the ever faithful Mrs Clemm. Somehow she gave him the inspiration to go on living and often her weary figure could be seen tramping through the streets of New York trying to sell his poetry, for it was the only reason she knew that he had left to live for. Poe claimed that during this period, 'He dreamt away whole months', but was still moved to write the atmospheric poems *The Bells* and the beautiful and haunting *Annabel Lee*. Then in perhaps a desperate attempt to reconcile himself for death he threw himself into composing the mystical *Eureka*.

Poe's behaviour was now becoming ever more erratic and distraught, as if he sensed the end was close at hand. He frequently travelled to give readings and lectures of his work, and in a desperate attempt to erase the memory of Virginia he would make overtures of marriage to other women only to then destroy these relationships in a frenzy of

Virginia Clemm Poe.
A drawing by AG Learned.

alcohol and drugs as if his conscience were punishing him. Finally, in Richmond, he accidently met his childhood sweetheart Elmira Royston, now a wealthy widow, and plans were made for them to marry. It must have seemed to him that it would solve all his problems and that at last he could publish his own magazine.

On September 27th he took a boat to Baltimore so as to return to New York to make preparations for the wedding. What transpired during the next five days remains a mystery but on October 3rd an old acquaintance of Poe's, Dr Snodgrass, received a brief note which read:

'There is a gentleman, rather the worse for wear, at Ryan's 4th ward polls, who goes under the cognomen of Edgar A Poe, and who appears in great distress, and says he is acquainted with you, and I assure you he is in need of immediate assistance'.

Because he had been found in Lombard Street near a polling booth, October 3rd was election day in Baltimore, the story arose that he had been plied with drink and used as a repeating voter, a common practise in those days, but there is no proof of this and it is unlikely that he needed any encouragement to drink on what he must have somehow known was his last 'spree'. What is certain is that he was found in a semi-conscious state, dirty and dressed in clothes that were not his own. He was rushed to Washington College Hospital where he fluctuated between delirium and rambling consciousness for four days. When he came to he was observed to talk 'to spectral and imaginary objects on the walls'. Then on the night of October 6th he began calling out for one 'Reynolds', now believed to be Jeremiah Reynolds the explorer whose feats had inspired him to write *The Narrative of Arthur Gordon Pym*, but this has proved to be just one more unexplained riddle in Poe's life. Finally at 3 am on Sunday morning October 7th he became quiet, whispering 'Lord help my poor soul', and died.

Is it then any wonder that so many of Poe's tales are written as if from the 'dark of the tomb', full of desperation and fore-boding? For it was not just the heart of this sensitive and romantic man that had been so ravaged, but his very soul, and from this feeling of 'impending doom' he could find no lasting relief. One is left with the uneasy feeling that he was not merely using his imagination to pen these tales of terror, but that they were inspired by his own horrific experiences and nightmares. So many of his stories include the same themes; madness, disease, death and entombment, and so many of the character's life's are decimated by 'cruel twists of fate'. It seemed as if by writing these stories he was exacting some form of revenge on a world that had caused him so much pain and misery.

Poor Poe, the incurable romantic; almost every woman he ever loved had died tragically and he could never escape the ghost of his beautiful young mother, the image of her pale, emaciated skin as she lay wasting-away in the cramped boarding house in Richmond, and this theme of 'necrophilia' runs through his work. His waking hours too must have been peopled by images of grotesque gargoyles that watched over every step that he took along this lonely and fated path. His death has been described as a 'long, slow suicide' and the mystery surrounding it as powerful as any of his own tales, for he had paid dearly for immortality, he had released uncontrollable fantasies from the very depths of his sub-conscious mind.

But even after death the unfortunate Poe was not left to rest in peace, his bad luck was to follow him beyond the grave. Whilst alive he had been a poor judge of character and had appointed an influential editor, the Rev Rufus W Griswold, who he believed to have been his friend and admirer, to be his literary executor. It transpired that he could not have made a worse choice for Griswold was deeply jealous of Poe's literary prowess and proceeded to publish several subtle but bitter attacks on him before the poor author's body had had time to grow cold. The first of these was an obituary in the *New York Daily Tribune* and was falsely signed 'Ludwig'. This piece was to tarnish Poe's reputation for years to come, and although a number of eminent people came to his defense, it was not until the French poet Charles Baudelaire (1821–1867) took up his cause and translated his works, that the truth began to emerge.

When Baudelaire first came across Poe's writing, shortly after his death, he was instantly and profoundly impressed, saying that ideas and sentences that he himself had been only thinking and dreaming of, Poe had put into words twenty years earlier; he felt that he had discovered a 'spiritual' twin. During the following years he became obsessed with Poe and proceeded to painstakingly translate his works into French, which not only won him great acclaim, but stand today among the finest literary translations in any language. Baudelaire also wrote several fine essays on Poe and before long the American writer was held in higher esteem in Western Europe than in his own country.

Because of Baudelaire's patronage Poe's writings proved influential in the development of the 'Symbolist' move-

Charles Baudelaire c. 1863.
Photographed by Etienne Carjat.

ment in France. Stéphane Mallarmé described him as 'the absolute literary phenomena' and added that he learnt English simply to be able to read Poe. His influence also inspired the decadents and the pre-surrealists and many other writers, artists and composers through to the present day. Amongst his impressive list of admirers are: Verlaine, Rimbaud, Paul Valéry, Lautremont, JK Huysmans, Debussy, Ravel, Rackmananoff, Odilon Redon, Edouard Manet, Strindberg, Dostoevsky, André Breton, Walt Whitman, RL Stevenson, HP Lovecraft, WB Yeats, Victor Hugo (who described him as 'the prince of American literature'), Borges and Vladimir Nabokov.

Naturally Poe had his detractors too, DH Lawrence described *The Fall of the House of Usher* as 'an overdone and vulgar fantasy', and Henry James and TS Eliot were unconvinced of his literary merits, although even the disdainful Eliot had to concede 'and yet one cannot be sure that one's writing has not been influenced by Poe'. But these critics remain out-numbered and the lasting quality of Poe's writings and criticisms are still as influential today as any American writer's, dead or alive.

After his beloved Virginia was laid in the grave Poe was left a sad and haunted man. He blamed himself for her death because of their poverty and he could be found on frozen winter's nights keeping vigil by the side of her tomb, weeping uncontrollably until Mrs Clemm would come and help him back to their cottage. He never liked to be alone and so Mrs Clemm would sit up with him while he wrote. Then he would write all night until the first morning light for he was afraid to go to bed with Virginia's ghost.

Let us try to imagine Poe's frail figure sitting at his desk in this cramped cottage in Fordham towards the end of his life, dreaming of his lost love while he labours over stories and criticisms that he never wanted to write, but which will pay him a pittance so that he can survive in a world that appears to have rejected him. For Poe this is time wasted, if only he could be allowed to finish what he considers to be his most important work, *Eureka*. Wearily he puts on his cloak, picks up his walking cane and begins the long trek into the city of New York. He delivers his finished work and receives his payment but he feels no elation, it is an impersonal act and merely serves to re-inforce his views on the 'commerciality' of American society of the time, it's apparent indifference to art and the artist's search for truth. He feels trapped in a country where money is the only God and where romance and literature are insupportable.

With a heavy heart he begins the arduous journey home feeling alienated and alone. The sun begins to set as he crosses the bridge over the Hudson river, the sky glowing with the red and purple hue of an opium inspired dream. Some distance further on he passes a bar with it's provocative lights and the intriguing lure of the 'low-life', a place where he can lose himself amongst strangers for a while, unfortunate souls, fellow sufferers who can identify with his torment. He hesitates on approaching the door knowing that a perverse pattern is about to repeat itself, but he is powerless to resist and so, with the artist's weakness for self-destruction, he enters the bar. All around him are strange faces, the lights are dim and the room is full of smoke. He orders a drink whilst staring at the rows of bright, luminous bottles that line the shelves in front of him. He drinks nervously and a mixture of release and exhilaration begins to envelop him, at last he feels in control of his own destiny.

Later somebody engages him in conversation and he voices his opinions on life, politics and art. Then as others gather round, fascinated by this strange figure dressed in black and the intensity of his speech, he realises that at last he has an audience for his views after so many solitary hours spent in the remote cottage, they seem to understand his plight and so he drinks more and buys his audience drinks too. Then others approach the circle their faces less sympathetic, by now he is shouting lines from *Eureka* to make himself heard above the crowd. Hours later he awakes to find himself lying in the street, his clothes torn and his money gone, but he has no memory of the events.

Much has been written about this 'darker' side of Poe's character, usually to the detriment of his finer points. He has been sensationally 'caricaturised' as a demented alcoholic and a hopeless drug addict, but this is not an accurate portrayal. That he experimented with opium was not unusual in those days as it could be bought openly over the counter, and there is no denying that he drank to excess, but not constantly, rather he would indulge in the frenzied and barbarous 'binges' of the 'dipsomaniac' or not at all. His apologists say that he had a weak head for alcohol, one glass of wine was enough to produce in him 'the passionate urge to drink to oblivion', and it is thought that he suffered from diabetes which would go some way towards explaining this condition. They also say that he could never have written so much if he had drunk so much; but the evidence is there in his stories, the paranoia of the drunk, the hallucinations of the opium-eater and the desperation of both to find some form of peace in the only haven left — the grave.

If ever a man had reason to find solace in drink and drugs then Poe was that man, but he was also intelligent enough to be aware of his plight and there are many references to it in his letters. Towards the end of his life he wrote:

'I have absolutely no pleasure in the stimulants in which I sometimes so madly indulge. It has not been in pursuit of pleasure that I have periled life and reputation and reason. It has been in the desperate attempt to escape from torturing memories, from a sense of insupportable loneliness, and a dread of some strange impending doom'.

I first came across Poe's works around the age of ten in the form of an *Illustrated Classics* comic. It included three of his better known stories and I was immediately obsessed by these nightmarish tales. Over the following years I read many such macabre books in the genre but it was always Poe who came back to haunt me, and in particular the illustrations in that original comic. About five years ago a friend suggested that I should consider compiling a book taking extracts from Poe's fiction and poetry and illustrating them with my photographs. At first I was dubious, feeling somewhat overawed by the idea of associating my own work with that of such an eminent literary figure, but gradually, on re-reading the stories and poems and selecting the photographs to illustrate them, I began to see that there was a poetic theme that we shared, a timeless melancholy and a feeling of isolation from the world.

In due course my travels took me to America where I photographed Poe's various homes and his grave in Baltimore. During this time I met many interesting and devoted admirers of the man and I in turn became fascinated by his extraordinary life and the variety of his literary talents. The more I discovered about him the more I felt I could identify with him; with his romanticism, being only too aware myself that society rarely tolerates a romantic in its midst, preferring to ridicule them as 'unrealistic' and 'immature'; with his contempt for the mindless greed and arrogance of the mass, their obsession with money and their ignorant pursuit of material possessions at the expense of nature, art and the originality of the individual. I also admired his strength of character that enabled him to go straight to the 'heart of the matter' in his work, to explore the fundamental fears of mankind in spite of all the misery and despair of his own existence. In the final analysis Poe appeared to me as an honourable, sensitive and enthusiastic man who had destroyed himself not only because of the many personal tragedies that he had had to endure but because of an overpowering frustration with what he saw as an imperfect and unjust world, and the feeling of immense sadness that accompanies such a sense of alienation.

In this book I have illustrated a number of my favourite stories and poems from Poe's works with some of my own photographs, to try and capture in images something of the world as he envisaged it in his romantic but tortured imagination, for Poe was a master at creating images with words. It is of interest to note that photography was invented during Poe's life-time and that he took great interest in this, being one of the first Americans to have his daguerreotype portrait taken. The locations for the photographs were chosen for various reasons. France, because of Baudelaire's importance to Poe; England and Scotland for the formative years that he spent there as a child; America his homeland, and Ireland because of his Irish ancestry, his grandfather was born in Londonderry. The images are those that must have obsessed him during his insufferable existence: tombs, horrific gargoyles, mysterious landscapes, Gothic houses and abbeys, all symbols of the fantasy world that he created.

I did not set out to try and illustrate the stories and poems exactly, but instead have attempted to create an 'atmosphere' to compliment the writing in the hope that the reader will use their imagination too. Obviously it is difficult to do justice to such a great man in so brief an introduction or by the small number of his works that are included here, he wrote over fifty poems and seventy short stories during his brief life, but my hope is that it will be appreciated as a new way of trying to shed more light on this unique literary figure.

Poe's stories and poems have a 'timeless' quality, and they gain in perpetuity because they are so divorced from reality. It was necessary for him to invent a fantasy world to live in, a world peopled by images more terrible and frightening than those that haunted his own life. He had ventured to the very 'edge' where few have dared to follow, he was in his own words from his masterful poem *The Raven*, 'dreaming dreams no mortals ever dared to dream before'.

The tomb of Edgar Allan Poe,
Westminster Cemetery, Baltimore.

ALONE

From childhood's hour I have not been
As others were—I have not seen
As others saw—I could not bring
My passions from a common spring.
From the same source I have not taken
My sorrow; I could not awaken
My heart to joy at the same tone;
And all I lov'd, *I* lov'd alone.
Then—in my childhood—in the dawn
Of a most stormy life—was drawn
From ev'ry depth of good and ill
The mystery which binds me still:
From the torrent, or the fountain,
From the red cliff of the mountain,
From the sun that 'round me roll'd
In its autumn tint of gold
From the lightning in the sky
As it pass'd me flying by—
From the thunder and the storm,
And the cloud that took the form
(When the rest of Heaven was blue)
Of a demon in my view.

THE MASQUE OF THE RED DEATH

THE 'red death' had long devastated the country. No pestilence had ever been so fatal, or so hideous. Blood was its Avatar and its seal — the redness and the horror of blood. There were sharp pains, and sudden dizziness, and then profuse bleeding at the pores, with dissolution. The scarlet stains upon the body and especially upon the face of the victim, were the pest ban which shut him out from the aid and from the sympathy of his fellow-men. And the whole seizure, progress, and termination of the disease, were the incidents of half an hour.

But the Prince Prospero was happy and dauntless and sagacious. When his dominions were half depopulated, he summoned to his presence a thousand hale and light-hearted friends from among the knights and dames of his court, and with these retired to the deep seclusion of one of his castellated abbeys. This was an extensive and magnificent structure, the creation of the prince's own eccentric yet august taste. A strong and lofty wall girdled it in. This wall had gates of iron. The courtiers, having entered, brought furnaces and massy hammers and welded the bolts. They resolved to leave means neither of ingress nor egress to the sudden impulses of despair or of frenzy from within. The abbey was amply provisioned. With such precautions the courtiers might bid defiance to contagion. The external world could take care of itself. In the meantime it was folly to grieve, or to think. The prince had provided all the appliances of pleasure. There were buffoons, there were improvisatori, there were ballet-dancers, there were musicians, there was Beauty, there was wine. All these and security were within. Without was the 'Red Death'.

It was toward the fifth or sixth month of his seclusion, and while the pestilence raged most furiously abroad, that the Prince Prospero entertained his thousand friends at a masked ball of the most unusual magnificence.

It was a voluptuous scene, that masquerade. But first let me tell of the rooms in which it was held. There were seven — an imperial suite. In many palaces, however, such suites form a long and straight vista, while the folding doors slide back nearly to the walls on either hand, so that the view of the whole extent is scarcely impeded. Here the case was very different; as might have been expected from the duke's love of the *bizarre*. The apartments were so irregularly disposed that the vision embraced but little more than one at a time. There was

a sharp turn at every twenty or thirty yards, and at each turn a novel effect. To the right and left, in the middle of each wall, a tall and narrow Gothic window looked out upon a closed corridor which pursued the windings of the suite. These windows were of stained glass whose colour varied in accordance with the prevailing hue of the decorations of the chamber into which it opened. That at the eastern extremity was hung, for example, in blue — and vividly blue were its windows. The second chamber was purple in its ornaments and tapestries, and here the panes were purple. The third was green throughout, and so were the casements. The fourth was furnished and lighted with orange — the fifth with white — the sixth with violet. The seventh apartment was closely shrouded in black velvet tapestries that hung all over the ceiling and down the walls, falling in heavy folds upon a carpet of the same material and hue. But in this chamber only, the colour of the windows failed to correspond with the decorations. The panes here were scarlet — a deep blood colour. Now in no one of the seven apartments was there any lamp or candelabrum, amid the profusion of golden ornaments that lay scattered to and fro or depended from the roof. There was no light of any kind emanating from lamp or candle within the suite of chambers. But in the corridors that followed the suite, there stood, opposite to each window, a heavy tripod, bearing a brazier of fire, that projected its rays through the tinted glass and so glaringly illumined the room. And thus were produced a multitude of gaudy and fantastic appearances. But in the western or black chamber the effect of the fire-light that streamed upon the dark hangings through the blood-tinted panes was ghastly in the extreme, and produced so wild a look upon the countenances of those who entered, that there were few of the company bold enough to set foot within its precincts at all.

It was in this apartment, also, that there stood against the western wall, a gigantic clock of ebony. Its pendulum swung to and fro with a dull, heavy, monotonous clang; and when the minute-hand made the circuit of the face, and the hour was to be stricken, there came from the brazen lungs of the clock a sound which was clear and loud and deep and exceedingly musical, but of so peculiar a note and emphasis that, at each lapse of an hour, the musicians of the orchestra were constrained to pause, momentarily, in their performance, to hearken to the sound; and thus the waltzers perforce ceased their evolutions; and there was a brief disconcert of the whole gay company; and, while the chimes of the clock yet rang, it was observed that the giddiest grew pale, and the more aged and sedate passed their hands over their brows as if in confused revery or meditation. But when the echoes had fully ceased, a light laughter at once pervaded the assembly; the musicians looked at each other and smiled as if at their own nervousness and folly, and made whispering vows, each to the other, that the next chiming of the clock should produce in them no similar emotion; and then, after the lapse of sixty minutes (which embrace three thousand and six hundred seconds of the Time that flies), there came yet another chiming of the clock, and then were the same disconcert and tremulousness and meditation as before.

But, in spite of these things, it was a gay and magnificent revel. The tastes of the duke were peculiar. He had a fine eye for colours and effects. He disregarded the *decora* of mere fashion. His plans were bold and fiery, and his conceptions glowed with barbaric lustre. There are some who would have thought him mad. His followers felt that he was not. It was necessary to hear and see and touch him to be *sure* that he was not.

He had directed, in great part, the movable embellishments of the seven chambers, upon occasion of this great *fête*; and it was his own guiding taste which had given character to the masqueraders. Be sure they were grotesque. There were much glare and glitter and piquancy and phantasm — much of what has been since seen in 'Hernani.' There were arabesque figures with unsuited limbs and appointments. There were delirious fancies such as the madman fashions. There were much of the beautiful, much of the wanton, much of the *bizarre*, something of the terrible, and not a little of that which might have excited disgust. To and fro in the seven chambers there stalked, in fact, a multitude of dreams. And these — the dreams — writhed in and about, taking hue from the rooms, and causing the wild music of the orchestra to seem as the echo of their steps. And, anon, there strikes the ebony clock which stands in the hall of the velvet. And then, for a moment, all is still, and all is silent save the voice of the clock. The dreams are stiff-frozen as they stand. But the echoes of the chime die away — they have endured but an instant — and a light, half-subdued laughter floats after them as they depart. And now again the music swells, and the dreams live, and writhe to and fro more merrily than ever, taking hue from the many-tinted windows through which stream the rays from the tripods. But to the chamber which lies most westwardly of the seven there are now none of the maskers who venture; for the night is waning away; and there flows a ruddier light through the blood-coloured panes; and the blackness of the sable drapery appals; and to him whose foot falls upon the sable carpet, there comes from the near clock of ebony a muffled peal more solemnly emphatic than any which reaches

their ears who indulge in the more remote gaieties of the other apartments.

But these other apartments were densely crowded, and in them beat feverishly the heart of life. And the revel went whirlingly on, until at length there commenced the sounding of midnight upon the clock. And then the music ceased, as I have told; and the evolutions of the waltzers were quieted; and there was an uneasy cessation of all things as before. But now there were twelve strokes to be sounded by the bell of the clock; and thus it happened, perhaps that more of thought crept, with more of time, into the meditations of the thoughtful among those who revelled. And thus too, it happened, perhaps, that before the last echoes of the last chime had utterly sunk into silence, there were many individuals in the crowd who had found leisure to become aware of the presence of a masked figure which had arrested the attention of no single individual before. And the rumour of this new presence having spread itself whisperingly around, there arose at length from the whole company a buzz, or murmur, expressive of disapprobation and surprise — then, finally, of terror, of horror, and of disgust.

In an assembly of phantasms such as I have painted, it may well be supposed that no ordinary appearance could have excited such sensation. In truth the masquerade license of the night was nearly unlimited; but the figure in question had out-Heroded Herod, and gone beyond the bounds of even the prince's indefinite decorum. There are chords in the hearts of the most reckless which cannot be touched without emotion. Even with the utterly lost, to whom life and death are equally jests, there are matters of which no jest can be made. The whole company, indeed, seemed now deeply to feel that in the costume and bearing of the stranger neither wit nor propriety existed. The figure was tall and gaunt, and shrouded from head to foot in the habiliments of the grave. The mask which concealed the visage was made so nearly to resemble the countenance of a stiffened corpse that the closest scrutiny must have had difficulty in detecting the cheat. And yet all this might have been endured, if not approved, by the mad revellers around. But the mummer had gone so far as to assume the type of the Red Death. His vesture was dabbled in *blood* — and his broad brow, with all the features of the face, was besprinkled with the scarlet horror.

When the eyes of Prince Prospero fell upon this spectral image (which, with a slow and solemn movement, as if more fully to sustain its *rôle*, stalked to and fro among the waltzers) he was seen to be convulsed, in the first moment with a strong shudder either of terror or distaste; but, in the next, his brow reddened with rage.

'Who dares' — he demanded hoarsely of the courtiers who stood near him — 'who dares insult us with this blasphemous mockery? Seize him and unmask him — that we may know

whom we have to hang, at sunrise, from the battlements!'

It was in the eastern or blue chamber in which stood the Prince Prospero as he uttered these words. They rang throughout the seven rooms loudly and clearly, for the prince was a bold and robust man, and the music had become hushed at the waving of his hand.

It was in the blue room where stood the prince, with a group of pale courtiers by his side. At first, as he spoke, there was a slight rushing movement of this group in the direction of the intruder, who, at the moment was also near at hand, and now, with deliberate and stately step, made closer approach to the speaker. But from a certain nameless awe with which the mad assumptions of the mummer had inspired the whole party, there were found none who put forth hand to seize him; so that, unimpeded, he passed within a yard of the prince's person; and, while the vast assembly, as if with one impulse, shrank from the centres of the rooms to the walls, he made his way uninterruptedly, but with the same solemn and measured step which had distinguished him from the first, through the blue chamber to the purple — through the purple to the green — through the green to the orange — through this again to the white — and even thence to the violet, ere a decided movement had been made to arrest him. It was then, however, that the Prince Prospero, maddening with rage and the shame of his own momentary cowardice, rushed hurriedly through the six chambers, while none followed him on account of a deadly terror that had seized upon all. He bore aloft a drawn dagger, and had approached, in rapid impetuosity, to within three or four feet of the retreating figure, when the latter, having attained the extremity of the velvet apartment, turned suddenly and confronted his pursuer. There was a sharp cry — and the dagger dropped gleaming upon the sable carpet, upon which, instantly afterward, fell prostrate in death the Prince Prospero. Then, summoning the wild courage of despair, a throng of the revellers at once threw themselves into the black apartment, and, seizing the mummer, whose tall figure stood erect and motionless within the shadow of the ebony clock, gasped in unutterable horror at finding the grave cerements and corpse-like mask, which they handled with so violent a rudeness, untenanted by any tangible form.

And now was acknowledged the presence of the Red Death. He had come like a thief in the night. And one by one dropped the revellers in the blood-bedewed halls of their revel, and died each in the despairing posture of his fall. And the life of the ebony clock went out with that of the last of the gay. And the flames of the tripods expired. And Darkness and Decay and the Red Death held illimitable dominion over all.

MESMERIC REVELATION

WHATEVER doubt may still envelop the *rationale* of mesmerism, its startling *facts* are now almost universally admitted. Of these latter, those who doubt, are your mere doubters by profession — an unprofitable and disreputable tribe. There can be no more absolute waste of time than the attempt to *prove*, at the present day, that man, by mere exercise of will, can so impress his fellow, as to cast him into an abnormal condition, in which the phenomena resemble very closely those of *death*, or at least resemble them more nearly than they do the phenomena of any other normal condition within our cognizance; that, while in this state, the person so impressed employs only with effort, and then feebly, the external organs of sense, yet perceives, with keenly refined perception, and through channels supposed unknown, matters beyond the scope of the physical organs; that, moreover, his intellectual faculties are wonderfully exalted and invigorated; that his sympathies with the person so impressing him are profound; and, finally, that his susceptibility to the impression increases with its frequency, while, in the same proportion, the peculiar phenomena elicited are more extended and more *pronounced*.

I say that these — which are the laws of mesmerism in its general features — it would be supererogation to demonstrate; nor shall I inflict upon my readers so needless a demonstration to-day. My purpose at present is a very different one indeed. I am impelled, even in the teeth of a world of prejudice, to detail, without comment, the very remarkable substance of a colloquy occurring between a sleep-walker and myself.

I had been long in the habit of mesmerizing the person in question (Mr Vankirk), and the usual acute susceptibility and exaltation of the mesmeric perception had supervened. For many months he had been laboring under confirmed phthisis, the more distressing effects of which had been relieved by my manipulations; and on the night of Wednesday, the fifteenth instant, I was summoned to his bedside.

The invalid was suffering with acute pain in the region of the heart, and breathed with great difficulty, having all the ordinary symptoms of asthma. In spasms such as these he had usually found relief from the application of mustard to the nervous centres, but to-night this had been attempted in vain.

As I entered his room he greeted me with a cheerful smile, and although evidently in much bodily pain, appeared to be, mentally, quite at ease.

'I sent for you to-night,' he said, 'not so much to administer to my bodily ailment, as to satisfy me concerning certain psychal impressions which, of late, have occasioned me much anxiety and surprise. I need not tell you how sceptical I have hitherto been on the topic of the soul's immortality. I cannot deny that there has always existed, as if in that very soul which I have been denying, a vague half-sentiment of its own existence. But this half-sentiment at no time amounted to conviction. With it my reason had nothing to do. All attempts at logical inquiry resulted, indeed, in leaving me more sceptical than before. I had been advised to study Cousin. I studied him in his own works as well as in those of his European and American echoes. The 'Charles Elwood' of Mr Brownson, for example, was placed in my hands. I read it with profound attention. Throughout I found it logical, but the portions which were not *merely* logical were unhappily the initial arguments of the disbelieving hero of the book. In his summing up it seemed evident to me that the reasoner had not even succeeded in convincing himself. His end had plainly forgotten his beginning, like the government of Trinculo. In short, I was not long in perceiving that if man is to be intellectually convinced of his own immortality, he will never be so convinced by the mere abstractions which have been so long the fashion of the moralists of England, of France, and of Germany. Abstractions may amuse and exercise, but take no hold on the mind. Here upon earth, at least, philosophy, I am persuaded, will always in vain call upon us to look upon qualities as things. The will may assent — the soul — the intellect, never.

'I repeat, then, that I only half felt, and never intellectually believed. But latterly there has been a certain deepening of the feeling, until it has come so nearly to resemble the acquiescence of reason, that I find it difficult to distinguish between the two. I am enabled, too, plainly to trace this effect to the mesmeric influence. I cannot better explain my meaning than by the hypothesis that the mesmeric exaltation enables me to perceive a train of ratiocination which, in my abnormal existence, convinces, but which, in full accordance with the mesmeric phenomena, does not extend, except through its *effect*, into my normal condition. In sleep-waking, the reasoning and its conclusion — the cause and its effect — are

present together. In my natural state, the cause vanishing, the effect only, and perhaps only partially, remains.

'These considerations have led me to think that some good results might ensue from a series of well-directed questions propounded to me while mesmerized. You have often observed the profound self-cognizance evinced by the sleep-waker — the extensive knowledge he displays upon all points relating to the mesmeric condition itself; and from this self-cognizance may be deduced hints for the proper conduct of a catechism.'

I consented of course to make this experiment. A few passes threw Mr Vankirk into the mesmeric sleep. His breathing became immediately more easy, and he seemed to suffer no physical uneasiness. The following conversation then ensued: — V in the dialogue representing the patient, and P myself.

P Are you asleep?

V Yes — no; I would rather sleep more soundly.

P [*After a few more passes.*] Do you sleep now?

V Yes.

P How do you think your present illness will result?

V [*After a long hesitation and speaking as if with effort.*] I must die.

P Does the idea of death afflict you?

V [*Very quickly.*] No — no!

P Are you pleased with the prospect?

V If I were awake I should like to die, but now it is no matter. The mesmeric condition is so near death as to content me.

P I wish you would explain yourself, Mr Vankirk.

V I am willing to do so, but it requires more effort than I feel able to make. You do not question me properly.

P What then shall I ask?

V You must begin at the beginning.

P You know that the beginning is God. [*This was said in a low, fluctuating tone, and with every sign of the most profound veneration.*]

P What, then, is God?

V [*Hesitating for many minutes.*] I cannot tell.

P Is not God spirit?

V While I was awake I knew what you meant by 'spirit,' but now it seems only a word — such, for instance, as truth, beauty — a quality, I mean.

P Is not God immaterial?

V There is no immateriality; it is a mere word. That which is not matter, is not at all — unless qualities are things.

P Is God, then, material?

V No. [*This reply startled me very much.*]

P What, then, is he?

V [*After a long pause, and mutteringly.*] I see — but it is a thing difficult to tell. [*Another long pause.*] He is not spirit, for he exists. Nor is he matter, *as you understand it.* But there are *gradations* of matter of which man knows nothing; the grosser impelling the finer, the finer pervading the grosser. The atmosphere, for example, impels the electric principle, while the

electric principle permeates the atmosphere. These gradations of matter increase in rarity or fineness, until we arrive at a matter *unparticled* — without particles — indivisible — *one*; and here the law of impulsion and permeation is modified. The ultimate or unparticled matter not only permeates all things, but impels all things; and thus *is* all things within itself. This matter is God. What men attempt to embody in the word 'thought,' is this matter in motion.

P The metaphysicians maintain that all action is reducible to motion and thinking, and that the latter is the origin of the former.

V Yes; and I now see the confusion of idea. Motion is the action of *mind*, not of *thinking*. The unparticled matter, or God, in quiescence, is (as nearly as we can conceive it) what men call mind. And the power of self-movement (equivalent in effect to human volition) is, in the unparticled matter, the result of its unity and omni-prevalence; *how*, I know not, and now clearly see that I shall never know. But the unparticled matter, set in motion by a law or quality existing within itself, is thinking.

P Can you give me no more precise idea of what you term the unparticled matter?

V The matters of which man is cognizant escape the senses in gradation. We have, for example, a metal, a piece of wood, a drop of water, the atmosphere, a gas, caloric, electricity, the luminiferous ether. Now, we call all these things matter, and embrace all matter in one general definition; but in spite of this, there can be no two ideas more essentially distinct than that which we attach to a metal, and that which we attach to the luminiferous ether. When we reach the latter, we feel an almost irresistible inclination to class it with spirit, or with nihility. The only consideration which restrains us is our conception of its atomic constitution; and here, even, we have to seek aid from our notion of an atom, as something possessing in infinite minuteness, solidity, palpability, weight. Destroy the idea of the atomic constitution and we should no longer be able to regard the ether as an entity, or, at least, as matter. For want of a better word we might term it spirit. Take, now, a step beyond the luminiferous ether; conceive a matter as much more rare than the ether, as this ether is more rare than the metal, and we arrive at once (in spite of all the school dogmas) at a unique mass — an unparticled matter. For although we may admit infinite littleness in the atoms themselves, the infinitude of littleness in the spaces between them is an absurdity. There will be a point — there will be a degree of rarity at which, if the atoms are sufficiently numerous, the interspaces must vanish, and the mass absolutely coalesce. But the consideration of the atomic constitution being now taken away, the nature of the mass inevitably glides into what we conceive of spirit. It is clear, however, that it is as fully matter as before. The truth is, it is impossible to conceive spirit, since it is impossible to imagine what is not. When we flatter ourselves that we have formed its conception, we have merely deceived our understanding by the consideration of infinitely rarified matter.

P There seems to me an insurmountable objection to the idea of absolute coalescence;—and that is the very slight resistance experienced by the heavenly bodies in their revolutions through space—a resistance now ascertained, it is true, to exist in *some* degree, but which is, nevertheless, so slight as to have been quite overlooked by the sagacity even of Newton. We know that the resistance of bodies is, chiefly, in proportion to their density. Absolute coalescence is absolute density. Where there are no interspaces, there can be no yielding. An ether, absolutely dense, would put an infinitely more effectual stop to the progress of a star than would an ether of adamant or of iron.

V Your objection is answered with an ease which is nearly in the ratio of its apparent unanswerability.—As regards the progress of the star, it can make no difference whether the star passes through the ether *or the ether through it*. There is no astronomical error more unaccountable than that which reconciles the known retardation of the comets with the idea of their passage through an ether; for, however rare this ether be supposed, it would put a stop to all sidereal revolution in a very far briefer period than has been admitted by those astronomers who have endeavored to slur over a point which they found it impossible to comprehend. The retardation actually experienced is, on the other hand, about that which might be expected from the *friction* of the ether in the instantaneous passage through the orb. In the one case, the retarding force is momentary and complete within itself—in the other it is endlessly accumulative.

P But in all this—in this identification of mere matter with God—is there nothing of irreverence? [*I was forced to repeat this question before the sleep-waker fully comprehended my meaning.*]

V Can you say *why* matter should be less reverenced than mind? But you forget that the matter of which I speak is, in all respects, the very 'mind' or 'spirit' of the schools, so far as regards its high capacities, and is, moreover, the 'matter' of these schools at the same time. God, with all the powers attributed to spirit, is but the perfection of matter.

P You assert, then, that the unparticled matter, in motion, is thought.

V In general, this motion is the universal thought of the universal mind. This thought creates. All created things are but the thoughts of God.

P You say, 'in general.'

V Yes. The universal mind is God. For new individualities, *matter* is necessary.

P But you now speak of 'mind' and 'matter' as do the metaphysicians.

V Yes—to avoid confusion. When I say 'mind,' I mean the

unparticled or ultimate matter; by 'matter,' I intend all else.

P You were saying that 'for new individualities matter is necessary.'

V Yes; for mind, existing unincorporate, is merely God. To create individual, thinking beings, it was necessary to incarnate portions of the divine mind. Thus man is individualized. Divested of corporate investiture, he were God. Now the particular motion of the incarnated portions of the unparticled matter is the thought of man; as the motion of the whole is that of God.

P You say that divested of the body man will be God?

V [*After much hesitation.*] I could not have said this; it is an absurdity.

P [*Referring to my notes.*] You *did* say that 'divested of corporate investiture man were God.'

V And this is true. Man thus divested *would be* God— would be unindividualized. But he can never be thus divested—at least never *will be*—else we must imagine an action of God returning upon itself—a purposeless and futile action. Man is a creature. Creatures are thoughts of God. It is the nature of thought to be irrevocable.

P I do not comprehend. You say that man will never put off the body?

V I say that he will never be bodiless.

P Explain.

V There are two bodies—the rudimental and the complete, corresponding with the two conditions of the worm and the butterfly. What we call 'death,' is but the painful metamorphosis. Our present incarnation is progressive, preparatory, temporary. Our future is perfected, ultimate, immortal. The ultimate life is the full design.

P But of the worm's metamorphosis we are palpably cognizant.

V *We,* certainly—but not the worm. The matter of which our rudimental body is composed, is within the ken of the organs of that body; or, more distinctly, our rudimental organs are adapted to the matter of which is formed the rudimental body; but not to that of which the ultimate is composed. The ultimate body thus escapes our rudimental senses, and we perceive only the shell which falls, in decaying, from the inner form; not that inner form itself; but this inner form, as well as the shell, is appreciable by those who have already acquired the ultimate life.

P You have often said that the mesmeric state very nearly resembles death. How is this?

V When I say that it resembles death, I mean that it resembles the ultimate life; for when I am entranced the senses of my rudimental life are in abeyance, and I perceive external things directly, without organs, through a medium which I shall employ in the ultimate, unorganized life.

P Unorganized?

V Yes; organs are contrivances by which the individual is

brought into sensible relation with particular classes and forms of matter, to the exclusion of other classes and forms. The organs of man are adapted to his rudimental condition, and to that only; his ultimate condition, being unorganized, is of unlimited comprehension in all points but one — the nature of the volition of God — that is to say, the motion of the unparticled matter. You will have a distinct idea of the ultimate body by conceiving it to be entire brain. This it is *not*; but a conception of this nature will bring you near a comprehension of what it *is*. A luminous body imparts vibration to the luminiferous ether. The vibrations generate similar ones within the retina; these again communicate similar ones to the optic nerve. The nerve conveys similar ones to the brain; the brain, also, similar ones to the unparticled matter which permeates it. The motion of this latter is thought, of which perception is the first undulation. This is the mode by which the mind of the rudimental life communicates with the external world; and this external world is, to the rudimental life, limited, through the idiosyncrasy of its organs. But in the ultimate, unorganized life, the external world reaches the whole body, (which is of a substance having affinity to brain, as I have said,) with no other intervention than that of an infinitely rarer ether than even the luminiferous; and to this ether — in unison with it — the whole body vibrates, setting in motion the unparticled matter which permeates it. It is to the absence of idiosyncratic organs, therefore, that we must attribute the nearly unlimited perception of the ultimate life. To rudimental beings, organs are the cages necessary to confine them until fledged.

P You speak of rudimental 'beings.' Are there other rudimental thinking beings than man?

V The multitudinous conglomeration of rare matter into nebulæ, planets, suns, and other bodies which are neither nebulæ, suns, nor planets, is for the sole purpose of supplying *pabulum* for the idiosyncrasy of the organs of an infinity of rudimental beings. But for the necessity of the rudimental, prior to the ultimate life, there would have been no bodies such as these. Each of these is tenanted by a distinct variety of organic, rudimental, thinking creatures. In all, the organs vary with the features of the place tenanted. At death, or metamorphosis, these creatures, enjoying the ultimate life — immortality — and cognizant of all secrets but *the one*, act all things and pass every where by mere volition: — indwelling, not the stars, which to us seem the sole palpabilities, and for the accommodation of which we blindly deem space created — but that SPACE itself — that infinity of which the truly substantive vastness swallows up the star-shadows — blotting them out as non-entities from the perception of the angels.

P You say that 'but for the *necessity* of the rudimental life, there would have been no stars.' But why this necessity?

V In the inorganic life, as well as in the inorganic matter generally, there is nothing to impede the action of one simple *unique* law — the Divine Volition. With the view of producing impediment, the organic life and matter (complex, substantial, and law-encumbered) were contrived.

P But again — why need this impediment have been produced?

V The result of law inviolate is perfection — right — negative happiness. The result of law violate is imperfection, wrong, positive pain. Through the impediments afforded by the number, complexity, and substantiality of the laws of organic life and matter, the violation of law is rendered, to a certain extent, practicable. Thus pain, which in the inorganic life is impossible, is possible in the organic.

P But to what good end is pain thus rendered possible?

V All things are either good or bad by comparison. A sufficient analysis will show that pleasure, in all cases, is but the contrast of pain. *Positive* pleasure is a mere idea. To be happy at any one point we must have suffered at the same. Never to suffer would have been never to have been blessed. But it has been shown that, in the inorganic life, pain cannot be; thus the necessity for the organic. The pain of the primitive life of Earth, is the sole basis of the bliss of the ultimate life of Heaven.

P Still, there is one of your expressions which I find it impossible to comprehend — 'the truly *substantive* vastness of infinity.'

V This, probably, is because you have no sufficiently generic conception of the term '*substance*' itself. We must not regard it as a quality, but as a sentiment: — it is the perception, in thinking beings, of the adaptation of matter to their organization. There are many things on the Earth, which would be nihility to the inhabitants of Venus — many things visible and tangible in Venus, which we could not be brought to appreciate as existing at all. But to the inorganic beings — to the angels — the whole of the unparticled matter is substance; that is to say, the whole of what we term 'space,' is to them the truest substantiality; — the stars, meantime, through what we consider their materiality, escaping the angelic sense, just in proportion as the unparticled matter, through what we consider its immateriality, eludes the organic.

As the sleep-waker pronounced these latter words, in a feeble tone, I observed on his countenance a singular expression, which somewhat alarmed me, and induced me to wake him at once. No sooner had I done this, than, with a bright smile irradiating all his features, he fell back upon his pillow and expired. I noticed that in less than a minute afterward his corpse had all the stern rigidity of stone. His brow was of the coldness of ice. Thus, ordinarily, should it have appeared, only after long pressure from Azrael's hand. Had the sleep-waker, indeed, during the latter portion of this discourse, been addressing me from out the region of the shadows?

WILLIAM WILSON

What say of it? what say CONSCIENCE *grim*
That spectre in my path?

Chamberlain *Pharronida*

LET me call myself, for the present, William Wilson. The fair page now lying before me need not be sullied with my real appellation. This has been already too much an object for the scorn—for the horror—for the detestation of my race. To the uttermost regions of the globe have not the indignant winds bruited its unparalleled infamy? Oh, outcast of all outcasts most abandoned!—to the earth art thou not for ever dead? to its honours, to its flowers, to its golden aspirations?—and a cloud, dense, dismal, and limitless, does it not hang eternally between thy hopes and heaven?

I would not, if I could, here or to-day, embody a record of my later years of unspeakable misery, and unpardonable crime. This epoch—these later years—took unto themselves a sudden elevation in turpitude, whose origin alone it is my present purpose to assign. Men usually grow base by degrees. From me, in an instant, all virtue dropped bodily as a mantle. From comparatively trivial wickedness I passed, with the stride of a giant, into more than the enormities of an Elah-Gabalus. What chance—what one event brought this evil thing to pass, bear with me while I relate. Death approaches; and the shadow which foreruns him has thrown a softening influence over my spirit. I long, in passing through the dim valley, for the sympathy—I had nearly said for the pity—of my fellow men. I would fain have them believe that I have been, in some measure, the slave of circumstances beyond human control. I would wish them to seek out for me, in the details I am about to give, some little oasis of *fatality* amid a wilderness of error. I would have them allow—what they cannot refrain from allowing—that, although temptation may have erewhile existed as great, man was never *thus*, at least, tempted before—certainly, never *thus* fell. And is it therefore that he has never thus suffered? Have I not indeed been living in a dream? And am I not now dying a victim to the horror and the mystery of the wildest of all sublunary visions?

I am the descendant of a race whose imaginative and easily excitable temperament has at all times rendered them remarkable; and, in my earliest infancy, I gave evidence of having fully inherited the family character. As I advanced in years it was more strongly developed; becoming, for many reasons, a cause of serious disquietude to my friends, and of positive injury to myself. I grew self-willed, addicted to the wildest caprices, and a prey to the most ungovernable passions. Weak-minded, and beset with constitutional infirmities akin to my own, my parents could do but little to check the evil propensities which distinguished me. Some feeble and ill-directed efforts resulted in complete failure on their part, and, of course, in total triumph on mine. Thenceforward my voice was a household law; and at an age when few children have abandoned their leading-strings, I was left to the guidance of my own will, and became, in all but name, the master of my own actions.

My earliest recollections of a school-life, are connected with a large, rambling, Elizabethan house, in a misty-looking village of England, where were a vast number of gigantic and gnarled trees, and where all the houses were excessively ancient. In truth, it was a dream-like and spirit-soothing place, that venerable old town. At this moment, in fancy, I feel the refreshing chilliness of its deeply-shadowed avenues, inhale the fragrance of its thousand shrubberies, and thrill anew with undefinable delight, at the deep hollow note of the church-bell, breaking, each hour, with sullen and sudden roar, upon the stillness of the dusky atmosphere in which the fretted Gothic steeple lay imbedded and asleep.

It gives me, perhaps, as much of pleasure as I can now in any manner experience, to dwell upon minute recollections of the school and its concerns. Steeped in misery as I am—misery, alas! only too real—I shall be pardoned for seeking relief, however slight and temporary, in the weakness of a few rambling details. These, moreover, utterly trivial, and even ridiculous in themselves, assume, to my fancy, adventitious importance, as connected with a period and a locality when and where I recognize the first ambiguous monitions of the destiny which afterward so fully overshadowed me. Let me then remember.

The house, I have said, was old and irregular. The grounds were extensive, and a high and solid brick wall, topped with a bed of mortar and broken glass, encompassed the whole. This prison-like rampart formed the limit of our domain; beyond it we saw but thrice a week—once every Saturday afternoon, when, attended by two ushers, we were permitted to take brief walks in a body through some of the neighbouring fields—and twice during Sunday, when we were paraded in the same formal manner to the morning and evening service in the one church of the village. Of this church the principal of our school was pastor. With how deep a spirit of wonder and perplexity was I wont to regard him from our remote pew in the gallery, as, with step solemn and slow, he ascended the pulpit! This reverend man, with countenance so demurely benign, with robes so glossy and so clerically flowing, with wig so minutely powdered, so rigid and so vast, — could this be he who, of late, with sour visage, and in snuffy habiliments, administered, ferule in hand, the Draconian Laws of the academy? Oh, gigantic paradox, too utterly monstrous for solution!

At an angle of the ponderous wall frowned a more ponderous gate. It was riveted and studded with iron bolts, and surmounted with jagged iron spikes. What impressions of deep awe did it inspire! It was never opened save for the three periodical egressions and ingressions already mentioned; then, in every creak of its mighty hinges, we found a plenitude of mystery — a world of matter for solemn remark, or for more solemn meditation.

The extensive enclosure was irregular in form, having many capacious recesses. Of these, three or four of the largest constituted the play-ground. It was level, and covered with fine hard gravel. I well remember it had no trees, nor benches, nor any thing similar within it. Of course it was in the rear of the house. In front lay a small parterre, planted with box and other shrubs, but through this sacred division we passed only upon rare occasions indeed — such as a first advent to school or final departure thence, or perhaps, when a parent or friend having called for us, we joyfully took our way home for the Christmas or Midsummer holidays.

But the house! — how quaint an old building was this! — to me how veritably a palace of enchantment! There was really no end to its windings — to its incomprehensible subdivisions. It was difficult, at any given time, to say with certainty upon which of its two stories one happened to be. From each room to every other there were sure to be found three or four steps either in ascent or descent. Then the lateral branches were innumerable — inconceivable — and so returning in upon themselves, that our most exact ideas in regard to the whole mansion were not very far different from those with which we pondered upon infinity. During the five years of my residence here, I was never able to ascertain with precision, in what remote locality lay the little sleeping apartment assigned to myself and some eighteen or twenty other scholars.

The school-room was the largest in the house — I could not help thinking, in the world. It was very long, narrow, and dismally low, with pointed Gothic windows and a ceiling of oak. In a remote and terror-inspiring angle was a square enclosure of eight or ten feet, comprising the *sanctum*, 'during hours,' of our principal, the Reverend Dr Bransby. It was a solid structure, with massy door, sooner than open which in the absence of the 'Dominie,' we would all have willingly perished by the *peine forte et dure*. In other angles were two other similar boxes, far less reverenced, indeed, but still greatly matters of awe. One of these was the pulpit of the 'classical' usher, one of the 'English and mathematical.' Interspersed about the room, crossing and recrossing in endless irregularity, were innumerable benches and desks, black, ancient, and time-worn, piled desperately with much bethumbed books, and so beseamed with initial letters, names at full length, grotesque figures, and other multiplied efforts of the knife, as to have entirely lost what little of original form might have been their portion in days long departed. A huge bucket with water stood at one extremity of the room, and a clock of stupendous dimensions at the other.

Encompassed by the massy walls of this venerable academy, I passed, yet not in tedium or disgust, the years of the third lustrum of my life. The teeming brain of childhood requires no external world of incident to occupy or amuse it; and the apparently dismal monotony of a school was replete with more intense excitement than my riper youth has derived from luxury, or my full manhood from crime. Yet I must believe that my first mental development had in it much of the uncommon — even much of the *outré*. Upon mankind at large the events of very early existence rarely leave in mature age any definite impression. All is gray shadow — a weak and irregular remembrance — an indistinct regathering of feeble pleasures and phantasmagoric pains. With me this is not so. In childhood I must have felt with the energy of a man what I now find stamped upon memory in lines as vivid, as deep, and as durable as the *exergues* of the Carthaginian medals.

Yet in fact — in the fact of the world's view — how little was there to remember! The morning's awakening, the nightly summons to bed; the connings, the recitations; the periodical half-holidays, and perambulations; the play-ground, with its broils, its pastimes, its intrigues; — these, by a mental sorcery long forgotten, were made to involve a wilderness of sensation, a world of rich incident, an universe of varied emotion, of excitement the most passionate and spirit-stirring. '*Oh, le bon temps, que ce siècle de fer!*'

In truth, the ardour, the enthusiasm, and the imperiousness of my disposition, soon rendered me a marked character among my schoolmates, and by slow, but natural gradations, gave me an ascendency over all not greatly older than myself; — over all with a single exception. This exception was found in the person of a scholar, who, although no relation, bore the same Christian and surname as myself; — a circumstance, in fact, little remarkable; for, notwithstanding a noble descent, mine was one of those everyday appellations which seem, by prescriptive right, to have been, time out of mind, the common property of the mob. In this narrative I have therefore designated myself as William Wilson, — a fictitious title not very dissimilar to the real. My namesake alone, of those who in school phraseology constituted 'our set,' presumed to compete with me in the studies of the class — in the sports and broils of the play-ground — to refuse implicit belief in my assertions, and submission to my will — indeed, to interfere with my arbitrary dictation in any respect whatsoever. If there is on earth a supreme and unqualified despotism, it is the despotism of a mastermind in boyhood over the less energetic spirits of its companions.

Wilson's rebellion was to me a source of the greatest embarrassment; the more so as, in spite of the bravado with which in public I made a point of treating him and his pretensions, I secretly felt that I feared him, and could not help thinking the equality which he maintained so easily with myself, a proof of his true superiority; since not to be overcome, cost me a perpetual struggle. Yet this superiority — even this equality — was in truth acknowedged by no one but myself; our associates, by some unaccountable blindness, seemed not even to suspect it. Indeed, his competition, his resistance, and especially his impertinent and dogged interference with my purposes, were not more pointed than private. He appeared to be destitute alike of the ambition which urged, and of the passionate energy of mind which enabled me to excel. In his rivalry he might have been supposed actuated solely by a whimsical desire to thwart, astonish, or mortify myself; although there were times when I could not help observing, with a feeling made up of wonder, abasement, and pique, that he mingled with his injuries, his insults, or his contradictions, a certain most inappropriate, and assuredly most unwelcome *affectionateness* of manner. I could only conceive this singular behaviour to arise from a consummate self-conceit assuming the vulgar airs of patronage and protection.

Perhaps it was this latter trait in Wilson's conduct, conjoined with our identity of name, and the mere accident of our having entered the school upon the same day, which set afloat the notion that we were brothers, among the senior classes in the academy. These do not usually inquire with much strictness into the affairs of their juniors. I have before said, or should have said, that Wilson was not, in a most remote degree, connected with my family. But assuredly if we *had* been brothers we must have been twins; for, after leaving Dr Bransby's, I casually learned that my namesake was born on the nineteenth of January, 1813 — and this is a somewhat remarkable coincidence; for the day is precisely that of my own nativity.

It may seem strange that in spite of the continual anxiety occasioned me by the rivalry of Wilson, and his intolerable spirit of contradiction, I could not bring myself to hate him altogether. We had, to be sure, nearly every day a quarrel in which, yielding me publicly the palm of victory, he, in some manner, contrived to make me feel that it was he who had

deserved it; yet a sense of pride on my part, and a veritable dignity on his own, kept us always upon what are called 'speaking terms,' while there were many points of strong congeniality in our tempers, operating to awake in me a sentiment which our position alone, perhaps, prevented from ripening into friendship. It is difficult, indeed, to define, or even to describe, my real feelings toward him. They formed a motley and heterogeneous admixture; — some petulant animosity, which was not yet hatred, some esteem, more respect, much fear, with a world of uneasy curiosity. To the moralist it will be necessary to say, in addition, that Wilson and myself were the most inseparable of companions.

It was no doubt the anomalous state of affairs existing between us which turned all my attacks upon him (and there were many, either open or covert) into the channel of banter or practical joke (giving pain while assuming the aspect of mere fun) rather than into a more serious and determined hostility. But my endeavours on this head were by no means uniformly successful, even when my plans were the most wittily concocted; for my namesake had much about him, in character, of that unassuming and quiet austerity which, while enjoying the poignancy of its own jokes, has no heel of Achilles in itself, and absolutely refuses to be laughed at. I could find, indeed, but one vulnerable point, and that, lying in a personal peculiarity, arising, perhaps, from constitutional disease, would have been spared by any antagonist less at his wit's end than myself; — my rival had a weakness in the faucial or guttural organs, which precluded him from raising his voice at any time *above a very low whisper*. Of this defect I did not fail to take what poor advantage lay in my power.

Wilson's retaliations in kind were many; and there was one form of his practical wit that disturbed me beyond measure. How his sagacity first discovered at all that so petty a thing would vex me, is a question I never could solve; but having discovered, he habitually practised the annoyance. I had always felt aversion to my uncourtly patronymic, and its very common, if not plebeian praenomen. The words were venom in my ears; and when, upon the day of my arrival, a second William Wilson came also to the academy, I felt angry with him for bearing the name, and doubly disgusted with the name because a stranger bore it, who would be the cause of its twofold repetition, who would be constantly in my presence, and whose concerns, in the ordinary routine of the school business, must inevitably, on account of the detestable coincidence, be often confounded with my own.

The feeling of vexation thus engendered grew stronger with every circumstance tending to show resemblance, moral or physical, between my rival and myself. I had not then discovered the remarkable fact that we were of the same age; but I saw that we were of the same height, and I perceived that we were even singularly alike in general contour of person and

outline of feature. I was galled, too, by the rumour touching a relationship, which had grown current in the upper forms. In a word, nothing could more seriously disturb me (although I scrupulously concealed such disturbance) than any allusion to a similarity of mind, person, or condition existing between us. But, in truth, I had no reason to believe that (with the exception of the matter of relationship, and in the case of Wilson himself) this similarity had ever been made a subject of comment, or even observed at all by our schoolfellows. That *he* observed it in all its bearings, and as fixedly as I, was apparent; but that he could discover in such circumstances so fruitful a field of annoyance, can only be attributed, as I said before, to his more than ordinary penetration.

His cue, which was to perfect an imitation of myself, lay both in words and in actions; and most admirably did he play his part. My dress it was an easy matter to copy; my gait and general manner were without difficulty, appropriated; in spite of his constitutional defect, even my voice did not escape him. My louder tones were, of course, unattempted, but then the key, — it was identical; *and his singular whisper, it grew the very echo of my own.*

How greatly this most exquisite portraiture harassed me (for it could not justly be termed a caricature), I will not now venture to describe. I had but one consolation — in the fact that the imitation, apparently, was noticed by myself alone, and that I had to endure only the knowing and strangely sarcastic smiles of my namesake himself. Satisfied with having produced in my bosom the intended effect, he seemed to chuckle in secret over the sting he had inflicted, and was characteristically disregardful of the public applause which the success of his witty endeavours might have so easily elicited. That the school, indeed, did not feel his design, perceive its accomplishment, and participate in his sneer, was, for many anxious months, a riddle I could not resolve. Perhaps the *gradation* of his copy rendered it not readily perceptible; or, more possibly, I owed my security to the masterly air of the copyist, who, disdaining the letter (which in a painting is all the obtuse can see), gave but the full spirit of his original for my individual contemplation and chagrin.

I have already more than once spoken of the disgusting air of patronage which he assumed toward me, and of his frequent officious interference with my will. This interference often took the ungracious character of advice; advice not openly given, but hinted or insinuated. I received it with a repugnance which gained strength as I grew in years. Yet, at this distant day, let me do him the simple justice to acknowledge that I can recall no occasion when the suggestions of my rival were on the side of those errors or follies so usual to his immature age and seeming inexperience; that his moral sense, at least, if not his general talents and worldly wisdom, was far keener than my own; and that I might, to-day, have been a

better and thus a happier man, had I less frequently rejected the counsels embodied in those meaning whispers which I then but too cordially hated and too bitterly despised.

As it was I at length grew restive in the extreme under his distasteful supervision, and daily resented more and more openly, what I considered his intolerable arrogance. I have said that, in the first years of our connection as schoolmates, my feelings in regard to him might have been easily ripened into friendship; but, in the latter months of my residence at the academy, although the intrusion of his ordinary manner had, beyond doubt, in some measure, abated, my sentiments, in nearly similar proportion, partook very much of positive hatred. Upon one occasion he saw this, I think, and afterward avoided, or made a show of avoiding me.

It was about the same period, if I remember aright, that, in an altercation of violence with him, in which he was more than usually thrown off his guard, and spoke and acted with an openness of demeanour rather foreign to his nature, I discovered, or fancied I discovered, in his accent, in his air, and general appearance, a something which first startled, and then deeply interested me, by bringing to mind dim visions of my earliest infancy — wild, confused, and thronging memories of a time when memory herself was yet unborn. I cannot better describe the sensation which oppressed me, than by saying that I could with difficulty shake off the belief of my having been acquainted with the being who stood before me, at some epoch very long ago—some point of the past even infinitely remote. The delusion, however, faded rapidly as it came; and I mention it at all but to define the day of the last conversation I there held with my singular namesake.

The huge old house, with its countless subdivisions, had several large chambers communicating with each other, where slept the greater number of the students. There were, however (as must necessarily happen in a building so awkwardly planned), many little nooks or recesses, the odds and ends of the structure; and these the economic ingenuity of Dr Bransby had also fitted up as dormitories; although, being the merest closets, they were capable of accommodating but a single individual. One of these small apartments was occupied by Wilson.

One night, about the close of my fifth year at the school, and immediately after the altercation just mentioned, finding every one wrapped in sleep, I arose from bed, and, lamp in hand, stole through a wilderness of narrow passages, from my own bedroom to that of my rival. I had long been plotting one of those ill-natured pieces of practical wit at his expense in which I had hitherto been so uniformly unsuccessful. It was my intention, now, to put my scheme in operation and I resolved to make him feel the whole extent of the malice with which I was imbued. Having reached his closet, I noiselessly entered, leaving the lamp, with a shade over it, on the outside.

I advanced a step and listened to the sound of his tranquil breathing. Assured of his being asleep, I returned, took the light, and with it again approached the bed. Close curtains were around it, which, in the prosecution of my plan, I slowly and quietly withdrew, when the bright rays fell vividly upon the sleeper, and my eyes at the same moment, upon his countenance. I looked;—and a numbness, an iciness of feeling instantly pervaded my frame. My breast heaved, my knees tottered, my whole spirit became possessed with an objectless yet intolerable horror. Gasping for breath, I lowered the lamp in still nearer proximity to the face. Were these—*these* the lineaments of William Wilson? I saw, indeed, that they were his, but I shook as if with a fit of the ague, in fancying they were not. What *was* there about them to confound me in this manner? I gazed;—while my brain reeled with a multitude of incoherent thoughts. Not thus he appeared—assuredly not *thus*—in the vivacity of his waking hours. The same name! the same contour of person! the same day of arrival at the academy! And then his dogged and meaningless imitation of my gait, my voice, my habits, and my manner! Was it, in truth, within the bounds of human possibility, that *what I now saw* was the result, merely, of the habitual practice of this sarcastic imitation? Awe-stricken, and with a creeping shudder, I extinguished the lamp, passed silently from the chamber, and left, at once, the halls of that old academy, never to enter them again.

After a lapse of some months, spent at home in mere idleness, I found myself a student at Eton. The brief interval had been sufficient to enfeeble my remembrance of the events at Dr Bransby's, or at least to effect a material change in the nature of the feelings with which I remembered them. The truth—the tradgedy—of the drama was no more. I could now find room to doubt the evidence of my senses; and seldom called up the subject at all but with wonder at the extent of human credulity, and a smile at the vivid force of the imagination which I hereditarily possessed. Neither was this species of skepticism likely to be diminished by the character of the life I led at Eton. The vortex of thoughtless folly into which I there so immediately and so recklessly plunged, washed away all but the froth of my past hours, ingulfed at once every solid or serious impression, and left to memory only the veriest levities of a former existence.

I do not wish, however, to trace the course of my miserable profligacy here—a profligacy which set at defiance the laws, while it eluded the vigilance of the institution. Three years of folly, passed without profit, had but given me rooted habits of vice, and added, in a somewhat unusual degree, to my bodily stature, when, after a week of soulless dissipation, I invited a small party of the most dissolute students to a secret carousel in my chambers. We met at a late hour of the night; for our debaucheries were to be faithfully protracted until morning.

The wine flowed freely, and there were not wanting other and perhaps more dangerous seductions; so that the gray dawn had already faintly appeared in the east while our delirious extravagance was at its height. Madly flushed with cards and intoxication, I was in the act of insisting upon a toast of more than wonted profanity, when my attention was suddenly diverted by the violent, although partial, unclosing of the door of the apartment, and by the eager voice of a servant from without. He said that some person, apparently in great haste, demanded to speak with me in the hall.

Wildly excited with wine, the unexpected interruption rather delighted than surprised me. I staggered forward at once, and a few steps brought me to the vestibule of the building. In this low and small room there hung no lamp; and now no light at all was admitted, save that of the exceedingly feeble dawn which made its way through the semi-circular window. As I put my foot over the threshold, I became aware of the figure of a youth about my own height, and habited in a white kerseymere morning frock, cut in the novel fashion of the one I myself wore at the moment. This the faint light enabled me to perceive; but the features of his face I could not distinguish. Upon my entering, he strode hurriedly up to me, and, seizing me by the arm with a gesture of petulant impatience, whispered the words 'William Wilson' in my ear.

I grew perfectly sober in an instant.

There was that in the manner of the stranger, and in the tremulous shake of his uplifted finger, as he held it between my eyes and the light, which filled me with unqualified amazement; but it was not this which had so violently moved me. It was the pregnancy of solemn admonition in the singular, low, hissing utterance; and, above all, it was the character, the tone, the *key*, of those few, simple, and familiar, yet-*whispered* syllables, which came with a thousand thronging memories of by-gone days, and struck upon my soul with the shock of a galvanic battery. Ere I could recover the use of my senses he was gone.

Although this event failed not of a vivid effect upon my disordered imagination, yet was it evanescent as vivid. For some weeks, indeed, I busied myself in earnest enquiry, or was wrapped in a cloud of morbid speculation. I did not pretend to disguise from my perception the identity of the singular individual who thus perseveringly interfered with my affairs, and harassed me with his insinuated counsel. But who and what was this Wilson?—and whence came he?—and what were his purposes? Upon neither of these points could I be satisfied—merely ascertaining, in regard to him, that a sudden accident in his family had caused his removel from Dr Bransby's academy on the afternoon of the day in which I myself had eloped. But in a brief period I ceased to think upon the subject, my attention being all absorbed in a contemplated departure for Oxford. Thither I soon went, the uncalculating vanity of

my parents furnishing me with an outfit and annual establishment, which would enable me to indulge at will in the luxury already so dear to my heart—to vie in profuseness of expenditure with the haughtiest heirs of the wealthiest earldoms in Great Britain.

Excited by such appliances to vice, my constitutional temperament broke forth with redoubled ardour, and I spurned even the common restraints of decency in the mad infatuation of my revels. But it were absurd to pause in the detail of my extravagance. Let it suffice, that among spendthrifts I out-Heroded Herod, and that, giving name to a multitude of novel follies, I added no brief appendix to the long catalogue of vices then usual in the most dissolute university of Europe.

It could hardly be credited, however, that I had, even here, so utterly fallen from the gentlemanly estate, as to seek acquaintance with the vilest arts of the gambler by profession, and, having become an adept in his despicable science, to practice it habitually as a means of increasing my already enormous income at the expense of the weak-minded among my fellow-collegians. Such, nevertheless, was the fact. And the very enormity of this offence against all manly and honourable sentiment proved, beyond doubt, the main if not the sole reason of the impunity with which it was committed. Who, indeed, among my most abandoned associates, would not rather have disputed the clearest evidence of his senses, than have suspected of such courses, the gay, the frank, the generous William Wilson—the noblest and most liberal commoner at Oxford—him whose follies (said his parasites) were but the follies of youth and unbridled fancy—whose errors but inimitable whim—whose darkest vice but a careless and dashing extravagance?

I had been now two years successfully busied in this way, when there came to the university a young *parvenu* nobleman, Glendinning—rich, said report, as Herodes Atticus—his riches, too, as easily acquired. I soon found him of weak intellect, and, of course, marked him as a fitting subject for my skill. I frequently engaged him in play, and contrived, with the gambler's usual art, to let him win considerable sums, the more effectually to entangle him in my snares. At length, my schemes being ripe, I met him (with the full intention that this meeting should be final and decisive) at the chambers of a fellow-commoner (Mr Preston), equally intimate with both, but who, to do him justice, entertained not even a remote suspicion of my design. To give to this a better colouring, I had contrived to have assembled a party of some eight or ten, and was solicitously careful that the introduction of cards should appear accidental, and originate in the proposal of my contemplated dupe himself. To be brief upon a vile topic, none of the low finesse was omitted, so customary upon similar occasions, that it is a just matter for wonder how any are still found so besotted as to fall its victim.

We had protracted our sitting far into the night, and I had at length effected the manoeuvre of getting Glendinning as my sole antagonist. The game, too, was my favourite *écarté*. The rest of the company, interested in the extent of our play, had abandoned their own cards, and were standing around us as spectators. The *parvenu*, who had been induced by my artifices in the early part of the evening, to drink deeply, now shuffled, dealt, or played, with a wild nervousness of manner for which his intoxication, I thought, might partially, but could not altogether account. In a very short period he had become my debtor to a large amount, when, having taken a long draught of port, he did precisely what I had been coolly anticipating—he proposed to double our already extravagant stakes. With a well-feigned show of reluctance, and not until after my repeated refusal had seduced him into some angry words which gave a colour of *pique* to my compliance, did I finally comply. The result, of couse, did but prove how entirely the prey was in my toils: in less than an hour he had quadrupled his debt. For some time his countenance had been losing the florid tinge lent it by the wine; but now, to my astonishment, I perceived that it had grown to a pallor truly fearful. I say, to my astonishment. Glendinning had been represented to my eager enquiries as immeasurably wealthy; and the sums which he had as yet lost, although in themselves vast, could not, I supposed, very seriously annoy, much less so violently affect him. That he was overcome by the wine just swallowed, was the idea which most readily presented itself; and, rather with a view to the preservation of my own character in the eyes of my associates, than from any less interested motive, I was about to insist, peremptorily, upon a discontinuance of the play, when some expressions at my elbow from among the company, and an ejaculation evincing utter despair on the part of Glendinning, gave me to understand that I had effected his total ruin under circumstances which, rendering him an object for the pity of all, should have protected him from the ill offices even of a fiend.

What now might have been my conduct it is difficult to say. The pitiable condition of my dupe had thrown an air of embarrassed gloom over all; and, for some moments, a profound silence was maintained, during which I could not help feeling my cheeks tingle with the many burning glances of scorn or reproach cast upon me by the less abandoned of the party. I will even own that an intolerable weight of anxiety was for a brief instant lifted from my bosom by the sudden and extraordinary interruption which ensued. The wide, heavy folding doors of the apartment were all at once thrown open, to their full extent, with a vigorous and rushing impetuosity that extinguished, as if by magic, every candle in the room. Their light, in dying, enabled us just to perceive that a stranger had entered, about my own height, and closely muffled in a cloak. The darkness, however, was not total; and we could only *feel* that he was standing in our midst. Before any one of us could recover from the extreme astonishment into which this rudeness had thrown all, we heard the voice of the intruder.

'Gentlemen,' he said, in a low, distinct, and never-to-be-forgotten *whisper* which thrilled to the very marrow of my bones, 'Gentlemen, I make an apology for this behaviour, because in thus behaving, I am fulfilling a duty. You are, beyond doubt, uninformed of the true character of the person who has to-night won at *écarté* a large sum of money from Lord Glendinning. I will therefore put you upon an expeditious and decisive plan of obtaining this very necessary information. Please to examine, at your leisure, the inner linings of the cuff of his left sleeve, and the several little packages which may be found in the somewhat capacious pockets of his embroidered morning wrapper.'

While he spoke, so profound was the stillness that one might have heard a pin drop upon the floor. In ceasing, he departed at once, and as abruptly as he had entered. Can I—shall I describe my sensations? Must I say that I felt all the horrors of the damned? Most assuredly I had little time for reflection. Many hands roughly seized me upon the spot, and lights were immediately reprocured. A search ensued. In the lining of my sleeve were found all the court cards essential in *écarté*, and, in the pockets of my wrapper, a number of packs, facsimiles of those used at our sittings, with the single exception that mine were of the species called, technically, *arrondées*; the honours being slightly convex at the ends, the lower cards slightly convex at the sides. In this disposition, the dupe who cuts, as customary, at the length of the pack, will invariably find that he cuts his antagonist an honour; while the gambler, cutting at the breadth, will, as certainly, cut nothing for his victim which may count in the records of the game.

Any burst of indignation upon this discovery would have affected me less than the silent contempt, or the sarcastic composure, with which is was received.

'Mr Wilson,' said our host, stooping to remove from beneath his feet an exceedingly luxurious cloak of rare furs, 'Mr Wilson, this is your property.' (The weather was cold; and, upon quitting my own room, I had thrown a cloak over my dressing wrapper, putting it off upon reaching the scene of play.) 'I presume it is supererogatory to seek here (eyeing the folds of the garment with a bitter smile) for any farther evidence of your skill. Indeed, we have had enough. You will see the necessity, I hope, of quitting Oxford—at all events, of quitting instantly my chambers.'

Abased, humbled to the dust as I then was, it is probable that I should have resented this galling language by immediate personal violence, had not my whole attention been at the moment arrested by a fact of the most startling character. The cloak which I had worn was of a rare description of fur; how rare, how extravagantly costly, I shall not venture to say. Its fashion, too, was of my own fantastic invention; for I was fastidious to an absurd degree of coxcombry, in matters of this frivolous nature. When, therefore, Mr Preston reached me that which he had picked up upon the floor, and near the folding-doors of the apartment, it was with an astonishment nearly bordering upon terror, that I perceived my own already hanging on my arm (where I had no doubt unwittingly placed it), and that the one presented me was but its exact counterpart in every, in even the minutest possible particular. The singular being who had so disastrously exposed me, had been muffled, I remembered, in a cloak; and none had been worn at all by any of the members of our party, with the exception of myself. Retaining some presence of mind, I took the one offered me by Preston; placed it, unnoticed, over my own; left the apartment with a resolute scowl of defiance; and, next morning ere dawn of day, commenced a hurried journey from Oxford to the Continent, in a perfect agony of horror and of shame.

I fled in vain, My evil destiny pursued me as if in exultation, and proved, indeed, that the exercise of its mysterious dominion had as yet only begun. Scarcely had I set foot in Paris, ere I had fresh evidence of the detestable interest taken by this Wilson in my concerns. Years flew, while I experienced no relief. Villain!—at Rome, with how untimely, yet with how spectral an officiousness, stepped he in between me and my ambition! at Vienna, too—at Berlin—and at Moscow! Where, in truth, had I *not* bitter cause to curse him within my heart? From his inscrutable tyranny did I at length flee, panic-stricken, as from a pestilence; and to the very ends of the earth *I fled in vain*.

And again, and again, in secret communion with my own spirit, would I demand the questions 'Who is he?—whence came he?—and what are his objects?' But no answer was there found. And now I scrutinized, with a minute scrutiny, the forms, and the methods, and the leading traits of his impertinent supervision. But even here there was very little upon which to base a conjecture. It was noticeable, indeed, that, in no one of the multiplied instances in which he had of late crossed my path, had he so crossed it except to frustrate those schemes, or to disturb those actions; which, if fully carried out, might have resulted in bitter mischief. Poor justification this, in truth, for an authority so imperiously assumed! Poor indemnity for natural rights of self-agency so pertinaciously, so insultingly denied!

I had also been forced to notice that my tormentor, for a very long period of time (while scrupulously and with miraculous dexterity maintaining his whim of an identity of apparel with myself) had so contrived it, in the execution of his varied interference with my will, that I saw not, at any moment, the features of his face. Be Wilson what he might,

this, at least, was but the veriest of affectation, or of folly. Could he, for an instant, have supposed that, in my admonisher at Eton—in the destroyer of my honour at Oxford,—in him who thwarted my ambition at Rome, my revenge at Paris, my passionate love at Naples, or what he falsely termed my avarice in Egypt,—that in this, my arch-enemy and evil genius, I could fail to recognize the William Wilson of my shcool-boy days,—the namesake, the companion, the rival,—the hated and dreaded rival at Dr Bransby's? Impossible!—But let me hasten to the last eventful scene of the drama.

Thus far I had succumbed supinely to this imperious domination. The sentiment of deep awe with which I habitually regarded the elevated character, the majestic wisdom, the apparent omnipresence and omnipotence of Wilson, added to a feeling of even terror, with which certain other traits in his nature and assumptions inspired me, had operated, hitherto, to impress me with an idea of my own utter weakness and helplessness, and to suggest an implicit, although bitterly reluctant submission to his arbitrary will. But, of late days, I had given myself up entirely to wine; and its maddening influence upon my hereditary temper rendered me more and more impatient of control. I began to murmur,—to hesitate,—to resist. And was it only fancy which induced me to believe that, with the increase of my own firmness, that of my tormentor underwent a proportional diminution? Be this as it may, I now began to feel the inspiration of a burning hope, and at length nurtured in my secret thoughts a stern and desperate resolution that I would submit no longer to be enslaved.

It was at Rome, during the Carnival of 18—, that I attended a masquerade in the palazzo of the Neapolitan Duke Di Broglio. I had indulged more freely than usual in the excesses of the wine-table; and now the suffocating atmosphere of the crowded rooms irritated me beyond endurance. The difficulty, too, of forcing my way through the mazes of the company contributed not a little to the ruffling of my temper; for I was anxiously seeking (let me not say with what unworthy motive) the young, the gay, the beautiful wife of the aged and doting Di Broglio. With a too unscrupulous confidence she had previously communicated to me the secret of the costume in which she would be habited, and now, having caught a glimpse of her person, I was hurrying to make my way into her presence. At this moment I felt a light hand placed upon my shoulder, and that ever-remembered, low, damnable *whisper* within my ear.

In an absolute frenzy of wrath, I turned at once upon him who had thus interrupted me, and seized him violently by the collar. He was attired, as I had expected, in a costume altogether similar to my own; wearing a Spanish cloak of blue velvet, begirt about the waist with a crimson belt sustaining a rapier. A mask of black silk entirely covered his face.

'Scoundrel!' I said, in a voice husky with rage, while every syllable I uttered seemed as new fuel to my fury; 'scoundrel! imposter! accursed villain! you shall not—you *shall not* dog me unto death! Follow me, or I stab you where you stand!'—and I broke my way from the ballroom into a small antechamber adjoining, dragging him unresistingly with me as I went.

Upon entering, I thrust him furiously from me. He staggered against the wall, while I closed the door with an oath, and commanded him to draw. He hesitated but for an instant; then, with a slight sigh, drew in silence, and put himself upon his defence.

The contest was brief indeed. I was frantic with every species of wild excitement, and felt within my single arm the energy and power of a multitude. In a few seconds I forced him by sheer strength against the wainscoting, and thus, getting him at mercy, plunged my sword, with brute ferocity, repeatedly through and through his bosom.

At that instant some person tried the latch of the door. I hastened to prevent an intrusion, and then immediately returned to my dying antagonist. But what human language can adequately portray *that* astonishment, *that* horror which possessed me at the spectacle then presented to view? The brief moment in which I averted my eyes had been sufficient to produce, apparently, a material change in the arrangements at the upper or farther end of the room. A large mirror,—so at first it seemed to me in my confusion—now stood where none had been perceptible before; and as I stepped up to it in extremity of terror, mine own image, but with features all pale and dabbled in blood, advanced to meet me with a feeble and tottering gait.

Thus it appeared, I say, but was not. It was my antagonist—it was Wilson, who then stood before me in the agonies of his dissolution. His mask and cloak lay, where he had thrown them, upon the floor. Not a thread in all his raiment—not a line in all the marked and singular lineaments of his face which was not, even in the most absolute identity, *mine own!*

It was Wilson; but he spoke no longer in a whisper, and I could have fancied that I myself was speaking while he said:

'*You have conquered, and I yield. Yet henceforward art thou also dead—dead to the World, to Heaven, and to Hope! In me didst thou exist—and, in my death, see by this image, which is thine own, how utterly thou hast murdered thyself.*'

THE OVAL PORTRAIT

THE château into which my valet had ventured to make forcible entrance, rather than permit me, in my desperately wounded condition, to pass a night in the open air, was one of those piles of commingled gloom and grandeur which have so long frowned among the Apennines, not less in fact than in the fancy of Mrs Radcliffe. To all appearance it had been temporarily and very lately abandoned. We established ourselves in one of the smallest and least sumptuously furnished apartments. It lay in a remote turret of the building. Its decorations were rich, yet tattered and antique. Its walls were hung with tapestry and bedecked with manifold and multiform armorial trophies, together with an unusually great number of very spirited modern paintings in frames of rich golden arabesque. In these paintings, which depended from the walls not only in their main surfaces, but in very many nooks which the bizarre architecture of the château rendered necessary—in these paintings my incipient delirium, perhaps, had caused me to take deep interest; so that I bade Pedro to close the heavy shutters of the room—since it was already night,—to light the tongues of a tall candelabrum which stood by the head of my bed, and to throw open far and wide the fringed curtains of black velvet which enveloped the bed itself. I wished all this done that I might resign myself, if not to sleep, at least alternately to the contemplation of these pictures, and the perusal of a small volume which had been found upon the pillow, and which purported to criticise and describe them.

Long, long I read—and devoutly, devoutly I gazed. Rapidly and gloriously the hours flew by and the deep midnight came. The position of the candelabrum displeased me, and outreaching my hand with difficulty, rather than disturb my slumbering valet, I placed it so as to throw its rays more fully upon the book.

But the action produced an effect altogether unanticipated. The rays of the numerous candles (for there were many) now fell within a niche of the room which had hitherto been thrown into deep shade by one of the bedposts. I thus saw in vivid light a picture all unnoticed before. It was the portrait of a young girl just ripening into womanhood. I glanced at the painting hurriedly, and then closed my eyes. Why I did this was not at first apparent even to my own perception. But while my lids remained thus shut, I ran over in mind my reason

for so shutting them. It was an impulsive movement to gain time for thought—to make sure that my vision had not deceived me—to calm and subdue my fancy for a more sober and more certain gaze. In a very few moments I again looked fixedly at the painting.

That I now saw aright I could not and would not doubt; for the first flashing of the candles upon that canvas had seemed to dissipate the dreamy stupor which was stealing over my senses, and to startle me at once into waking life.

The portrait, I have already said, was that of a young girl. It was a mere head and shoulders, done in what is technically termed a *vignette* manner; much in the style of the favourite heads of Sully. The arms, the bosom, and even the ends of the radiant hair melted imperceptibly into the vague yet deep shadow which formed the background of the whole. The frame was oval, richly gilded and filigreed in *Moresque*. As a thing of art nothing could be more admirable than the painting itself. But it could have been neither the execution of the work, nor the immortal beauty of the countenance, which had so suddenly and so vehemently moved me. Least of all, could it have been that my fancy, shaken from its half slumber, had mistaken the head for that of a living person. I saw at once that the peculiarities of the design, of the *vignetting*, and of the frame, must have instantly dispelled such idea—must have prevented even its momentary entertainment. Thinking earnestly upon these points, I remained, for an hour perhaps, half sitting, half reclining, with my vision riveted upon the portrait. At length, satisfied with the true secret of its effect, I fell back within the bed. I had found the spell of the picture in an absolute *lifelikeliness* of expression, which, at first startling, finally confounded, subdued, and appalled me. With deep and reverent awe I replaced the candelabrum in its former position. The cause of my deep agitation being thus shut from view, I sought eagerly the volume which discussed the paintings and their histories. Turning to the number which designated the oval portrait, I there read the vague and quaint words which follow:

'She was a maiden of rarest beauty, and not more lovely than full of glee. And evil was the hour when she saw, and loved, and wedded the painter. He, passionate, studious, austere, and having already a bride in his Art: she a maiden of rarest beauty, and not more lovely than full of glee; all light

and smiles, and frolicsome as the young fawn; loving and cherishing all things; hating only the Art which was her rival; dreading only the pallet and brushes and other untoward instruments which deprived her of the countenance of her lover. It was thus a terrible thing for this lady to hear the painter speak of his desire to portray even his young bride. But she was humble and obedient, and sat meekly for many weeks in the dark high turret-chamber where the light dripped upon the pale canvas only from overhead. But he, the painter, took glory in his work, which went on from hour to hour, and from day to day. And he was a passionate, and wild, and moody man, who became lost in reveries; so that he *would* not see that the light which fell so ghastly in that lone turret withered the health and the spirits of his bride, who pined visibly to all but him. Yet she smiled on and still on, uncomplainingly, because she saw that the painter (who had high renown) took a fervid and burning pleasure in his task, and wrought day and night to depict her who so loved him, yet who grew daily more dispirited and weak. And in sooth some who beheld the portrait spoke of its resemblance in low words, as of a mighty marvel, and a proof not less of the power of the painter than of his deep love for her whom he depicted so surpassingly well. But at length, as the labor drew nearer to its conclusion, there were admitted none into the turret; for the painter had grown wild with the ardour of his work, and turned his eyes from the canvas rarely, even to regard the countenance of his wife. And he *would* not see that the tints which he spread upon the canvas were drawn from the cheeks of her who sat beside him. And when many weeks had passed, and but little remained to do, save one brush upon the mouth and one tint upon the eye, the spirit of the lady again flickered up as the flame within the socket of the lamp. And then the brush was given, and then the tint was placed; and, for one moment, the painter stood entranced before the work which he had wrought; but in the next, while he yet gazed, he grew tremulous and very pallid, and aghast, and crying with a loud voice, "This is indeed *Life* itself!" turned suddenly to regard his beloved: — *She was dead!'*

TO ONE IN PARADISE

Thou wast that all to me, love,
   For which my soul did pine—
A green isle in the sea, love,
   A fountain and a shrine,
All wreathed with fairy fruits and flowers,
   And all the flowers were mine.

Ah, dream too bright to last!
   Ah, starry Hope! that didst arise
But to be overcast!
   A voice from out the Future cries,
'On! on!'—but o'er the Past
   (Dim gulf!) my spirit hovering lies
Mute, motionless, aghast!

For, alas! alas! with me
   The light of Life is o'er!
   'No more—no more—no more—'
(Such language holds the solemn sea
   To the sands upon the shore)
Shall bloom the thunder-blasted tree,
Or the stricken eagle soar!

And all my days are trances,
   And all my nightly dreams
Are where thy dark eye glances,
   And where thy footstep gleams—
In what ethereal dances,
   By what eternal streams.

THE ANGEL OF THE ODD

AN EXTRAVAGANZA

IT WAS a chilly November afternoon. I had just consummated an unusually hearty dinner, of which the dyspeptic *truffe* formed not the least important item, and was sitting alone in the dining-room, with my feet upon the fender, and at my elbow a small table which I had rolled up to the fire, and upon which were some apologies for dessert, with some miscellaneous bottles of wine, spirit and *liqueur*. In the morning I had been reading Glover's *Leonidas*, Wilkie's *Epigoniad*, Lamartine's *Pilgrimage*, Barlow's *Columbiad*, Tuckermann's *Sicily*, and Griswold's *Curiosities*; I am willing to confess, therefore, that I now felt a little stupid. I made effort to arouse myself by aid of frequent Lafitte, and, all failing, I betook myself to a stray newspaper in despair. Having carefully perused the column of 'houses to let,' and the column of 'dogs lost,' and then the two columns of 'wives and apprentices runaway,' I attacked with great resolution the editorial matter, and, reading it from beginning to end without understanding a syllable, conceived the possibility of its being Chinese, and so re-read it from the end to the beginning, but with no more satisfactory result. I was about throwing away, in disgust,

'This folio of four pages, happy work
Which not even poets criticise,'

when I felt my attention somewhat aroused by the paragraph which follows:

'The avenues to death are numerous and strange. A London paper mentions the decease of a person from a singular cause. He was playing at "puff the dart," which is played with a long needle inserted in some worsted, and blown at a target through a tin tube. He placed the needle at the wrong end of the tube, and drawing his breath strongly to puff the dart forward with force, drew the needle into his throat. It entered the lungs, and in a few days killed him.'

Upon seeing this I fell into a great rage, without exactly knowing why. 'This thing,' I exclaimed, 'is a contemptible falsehood—a poor hoax—the lees of the invention of some pitiable penny-a-liner—of some wretched concoctor of accidents in Cocaigne. These fellows, knowing the extravagant gullibility of the age, set their wits to work in the imagination of improbable possibilities—of odd accidents, as they term them; but to a reflecting intellect (like mine,' I added, in parenthesis, putting my forefinger unconsciously to the side of my nose), 'to a contemplative understanding such as I myself possess, it seems evident at once that the marvellous increase of late in these "odd accidents" is by far the oddest accident of all. For my own part, I intend to believe nothing henceforward that has any thing of the "singular" about it.'

'Mein Gott, den, vat a vool you bees for dat!' replied one of the most remarkable voices I ever heard. At first I took it for a rumbling in my ears—such as a man sometimes experiences when getting very drunk—but, upon second thought, I considered the sound as more nearly resembling that which proceeds from an empty barrel beaten with a big stick; and, in fact, this I should have concluded it to be, but for the articulation of the syllables and words. I am by no means naturally nervous, and the very few glasses of Lafitte which I had sipped served to embolden me a little, so that I felt nothing of trepidation, but merely uplifted my eyes with a leisurely movement, and looked carefully around the room for the intruder. I could not, however, perceive any one at all.

'Humph!' resumed the voice, as I continued my survey, 'you mus pe so dronk as de pig, den, for not zee me as I zit here at your zide.'

Hereupon I bethought me of looking immediately before my nose, and there, sure enough, confronting me at the table sat a personage nondescript, although not altogether indescribable. His body was a wine-pipe, or a rum-puncheon, or something of that character, and had a truly Falstaffian air. In its nether extremity were inserted two kegs, which seemed to answer all the purposes of legs. For arms there dangled from the upper portion of the carcass two tolerably long bottles, with the necks outward for hands. All the head that I saw the monster possessed of was like a Hessian canteen with resembles a large snuff-box with a hole in the middle of the lid. This canteen (with a funnel on its top, like a cavalier cap slouched over the eyes) was set on edge upon the puncheon, with the hole toward myself; and through this hole, which seemed puckered up like the mouth of a very precise old maid, the creature was emitting certain rumbling and grumbling noises which he evidently intended for intelligible talk.

'I zay,' said he, 'you mos pe dronk as de pig, vor zit dare and not zee me zit ere; and I zay, doo, you most pe pigger vool as de goose, vor to dispelief vat iz print in de print. 'Tis de troof—dat it iz—eberry vord ob it.'

'Who are you, pray?' I said, with much dignity, although somewhat puzzled; 'how did you get here? and what is it you are talking about?'

'As vor ow I com'd ere,' replied the figure, 'dat iz none of your pizzness; and as vor vat I be talking apout, I be talk apout vat I tink proper; and as vor who I be, vy dat is de very ting I com'd here for to let you zee for yourzelf.'

'You are a drunken vagabond,' said I, 'and I shall ring the bell and order my footman to kick you into the street.'

'He! he! he!' said the fellow, 'hu! hu! hu! dat you can't do.'

'Can't do!' said I, 'what do you mean?—I can't do what?'

'Ring de pell,' he replied, attempting a grin with his little villainous mouth.

Upon this I made an effort to get up, in order to put my threat into execution; but the ruffian just reached across the table very deliberately, and hitting me a tap on the forehead with the neck of one of the long bottles, knocked me back into the arm-chair from which I had half arisen. I was utterly astounded; and, for a moment, was quite at a loss what to do. In the meantime, he continued his talk.

'You zee,' said he, 'it iz te bess vor zit still; and now you shall know who I pe. Look at me! zee! I am te *Angel ov te Odd.*'

'And odd enough, too,' I ventured to reply; 'but I was always under the impression that an angel had wings.'

'Te wing!' he cried, highly incensed, 'vat I pe do mit te wing? Mein Gott! do you take me vor a shicken?'

'No—oh, no!' I replied, much alarmed, 'you are no chicken—certainly not.'

'Well, den, zit still and pehabe yourself, or I'll rap you again mid me vist. It iz te shicken ab te wing, und te owl ab te wing, und te imp ab de wing, and te headteuffel ab te wing. Te angel ab *not* te wing, and I am te *Angel ov te Odd.*'

'And your business with me at present is—is'

'My pizzness!' ejaculated the thing, 'vy vot a low-bred puppy you mos pe vor to ask a gentleman und an angel apout his pizzness!'

This language was rather more than I could bear, even from an angel; so, plucking up courage, I seized a salt-cellar which lay within reach, and hurled it at the head of the intruder. Either he dodged, however, or my aim was inaccurate; for all I accomplished was the demolition of the crystal which protected the dial of the clock upon the mantel-piece. As for the Angel, he evinced his sense of my assault by giving me two or three hard consecutive raps upon the forehead as before. These reduced me at once to submission, and I am almost ashamed to confess that, either through pain or vexation, there came a few tears into my eyes.

'Mein Gott!' said the Angel of the Odd, apparently much softened at my distress; 'mein Gott, te man is eder ferry dronk or ferry sorry. You mos not trink it so strong—you mos put

de water in te wine. Here, trink dis, like a goot veller, und don't gry now—don't!'

Hereupon the Angel of the Odd replenished my goblet (which was about a third full of Port) with a colourless fluid that he poured from one of his hand bottles. I observed that these bottles had labels about their necks, and that these labels were inscribed 'Kirschenwasser.'

The considerate kindness of the Angel mollified me in no little measure; and, aided by the water with which he diluted my Port more than once, I at length regained sufficient temper to listen to his very extraordinary discourse. I cannot pretend to recount all that he told me, but I gleaned from what he said that he was the genius who presided over the *contretemps* of mankind, and whose business it was to bring abut the *odd accidents* which are continually astonishing the skeptic. Once or twice, upon my venturing to express my total incredulity in respect to his pretensions, he grew very angry indeed, so that at length I considered it the wiser policy to say nothing at all, and let him have his own way. He talked on, therefore, at great length, while I merely leaned back in my chair with my eyes shut, and amused myself with munching raisins and filliping the stems about the room. But, by and by, the Angel suddenly construed this behaviour of mine into contempt. He arose in a terrible passion, slouched his funnel down over his eyes, swore a vast oath, uttered a threat of some character which I did not precisely comprehend, and finally made me a low bow and departed, wishing me, in the language of the archbishop in 'Gil-Blas,' *beaucoup de bonheur et un peu plus de bon sens.*

His departure afforded me relief. The *very* few glasses of Lafitte that I had sipped had the effect of rendering me drowsy, and I felt inclined to take a nap of some fifteen or twenty minutes, as is my custom after dinner. At six I had an appointment of consequence, which it was quite indispensable that I should keep. The policy of insurance for my dwelling-house had expired the day before; and, some dispute having arisen, it was agreed that, at six, I should meet the board of directors of the company and settle the terms of a renewal. Glancing upward at the clock on the mantel-piece (for I felt too drowsy to take out my watch), I had the pleasure to find that I had still twenty-five minutes to spare. It was half-past five; I could easily walk to the insurance office in five minutes; and my usual siestas had never been known to exceed five and twenty. I felt sufficiently safe, therefore, and composed myself to my slumbers forthwith.

Having completed them to my satisfaction, I again looked toward the time-piece, and was half inclined to believe in the possibility of odd accidents when I found that, instead of my ordinary fifteen or twenty minutes, I had been dozing only three; for it still wanted seven and twenty of the appointed hour. I betook myself again to my nap, and at length a second

time awoke, when, to my utter amazement, it *still* wanted twenty-seven minutes of six. I jumped up to examine the clock, and found that it had ceased running. My watch informed me that it was half-past seven; and, of course, having slept two hours, I was too late for my appointment. 'It will make no difference,' I said; 'I can call at the office in the morning and apologize; in the meantime what can be the matter with the clock?' Upon examining it I discovered that one of the raisin-stems which I had been filliping about the room during the discourse of the Angel of the Odd had flown through the fractured crystal, and lodging, singularly enough, in the key-hole, with an end projecting outward, had thus arrested the revolution of the minute-hand.

'Ah!' said I; 'I see how it is. This thing speaks for itself. A natural accident, such as *will* happen now and then!'

I gave the matter no further consideration, and at my usual hour retired to bed. Here, having placed a candle upon a reading-stand at the bed-head, and having made an attempt to peruse some pages of the *Omnipresence of the Deity*, I unfortunately fell asleep in less than twenty seconds, leaving the light burning as it was.

My dreams were terrifically disturbed by visions of the Angel of the Odd. Methought he stood at the foot of the couch, drew aside the curtains, and, in the hollow, detestable tones of a rum-puncheon, menaced me with the bitterest vengeance for the contempt with which I had treated him. He concluded a long harangue by taking off his funnel-cap, inserting the tube into my gullet, and thus deluging me with an ocean of Kirschenwasser, which he poured, in a continuous flood, from one of the long-necked bottles that stood him instead of an arm. My agony was at length insufferable, and I awoke just in time to perceive that a rat had run off with the lighted candle from the stand, but *not* in season to prevent his making his escape with it through the hole. Very soon, a strong suffocating odor assailed my nostrils; the house, I clearly perceived, was on fire. In a few minutes the blaze broke forth with violence, and in an incredibly brief period the entire building was wrapped in flames. All egress from my chamber, except through a window, was cut off. The crowd, however, quickly procured and raised a long ladder. By means of this I was descending rapidly, and in apparent safety, when a huge hog, about whose rotund stomach, and indeed about whose whole air and physiognomy, there was something which reminded me of the Angel of the Odd,—when this hog, I say, which hitherto had been quietly slumbering in the mud, took it suddenly into his head that his left shoulder needed scratching, and could find no more convenient rubbing-post than that afforded by the foot of the ladder. In an instant I was precipitated, and had the misfortune to fracture my arm.

This accident, with the loss of my insurance, and with the more serious loss of my hair,—the whole of which had been singed off by the fire,—predisposed me to serious impressions, so that, finally, I made up my mind to take a wife. There was a rich widow disconsolate for the loss of her seventh husband, and to her wounded spirit I offered the balm of my vows. She yielded a reluctant consent to my prayers. I knelt at her feet in gratitude and adoration. She blushed, and bowed her luxuriant tresses into close contact with those supplied me, temporarily, by Grandjean. I know not how the entanglement took place, but so it was. I arose with a shining pate, wigless; she in disdain and wrath, half buried in alien hair. Thus ended my hopes of the widow by an accident which could not have been anticipated, to be sure, but which the natural sequence of events had brought about.

Without despairing, however, I undertook the siege of a less implacable heart. The fates were again propitious for a brief period; but again a trivial incident interfered. Meeting my betrothed in an avenue thronged with the *élite* of the city, I was hastening to greet her with one of my best considered bows, when a small particle of some foreign matter, lodging in the corner of my eye, rendered me, for the moment, completely blind. Before I could recover my sight, the lady of my love had disappeared—irreparably affronted at what she chose to consider my premeditated rudeness in passing her by ungreeted. While I stood bewildered at the suddenness of this accident (which might have happened, nevertheless, to any one under the sun), and while I still continued incapable of sight, I was accosted by the Angel of the Odd, who proffered me his aid with a civility which I had no reason to expect. He examined my disordered eye with much gentleness and skill, informed me that I had a drop in it, and (whatever a 'drop' was) took it out, and afforded me relief.

I now considered it high time to die (since fortune had so determined to persecute me) and accordingly made my way to the nearest river. Here, divesting myself of my clothes (for there is no reason why we cannot die as we were born), I threw myself headlong into the current; the sole witness of my fate being a solitary crow that had been seduced into the eating of brandy-saturated corn, and so had staggered away from his fellows. No sooner had I entered the water than this bird took it into its head to fly away with the most indispensable portion of my apparel. Postponing, therefore, for the present, my suicidal design, I just slipped my nether extremities into the sleeves of my coat, and betook myself to a pursuit of the felon with all the nimbleness which the case required and its circumstances would admit. But my evil destiny attended me still. As I ran at full speed, with my nose up in the atmosphere, and intent only upon the purloiner of my property, I suddenly perceived that my feet rested no longer upon *terra firma*; the fact is, I had thrown myself over a precipice, and should inevitably have been dashed to pieces but for my good fortune in grasping the end of a long guide-

rope, which depended from a passing balloon.

As soon as I sufficiently recovered my senses to comprehend the terrific predicament in which I stood or rather hung, I exerted all the power of my lungs to make that predicament known to the aeronaut overhead. But for a long time I exerted myself in vain. Either the fool could not, or the villain would not perceive me. Meantime the machine rapidly soared, while my strength even more rapidly failed. I was soon upon the point of resigning myself to my fate, and dropping quietly into the sea, when my spirits were suddenly revived by hearing a hollow voice from above, which seemed to be lazily humming an opera air. Looking up, I perceived the Angel of the Odd. He was leaning with his arms folded, over the rim of the car; and with a pipe in his mouth, at which he puffed leisurely, seemed to be upon excellent terms with himself and the universe. I was too much exhausted to speak, so I merely regarded him with an imploring air.

For several minutes, although he looked me full in the face, he said nothing. At length removing carefully his meerschaum from the right to the left corner of his mouth, he condescended to speak.

'Who pe you,' he asked, 'und what der teuffel you pe do dare?'

To this piece of impudence, cruelty, and affectation, I could reply only by ejaculating the monosyllable, 'Help!'

'Elp!' echoed the ruffian — 'not I. Dare iz te pottle — elp yourself, und pe tam'd!'

With these words he let fall a heavy bottle of Kirschenwasser which, dropping precisely upon the crown of my head, caused me to imagine that my brains were entirely knocked out. Impressed with this idea, I was about to relinquish my hold and give up the ghost with a good grace, when I was arrested by the cry of the Angel, who bade me hold on.

'Old on!' he said; 'don't pe in te urry — don't. Will you pe take de odder pottle, or ave you pe got zober yet and come to your zenzes?'

I made haste, hereupon, to nod my head twice — once in the negative, meaning thereby that I would prefer not taking the other bottle at present — and once in the affirmative, intending thus to imply that I *was* sober and *had* positively come to my senses. By these means I somewhat softened the Angel.

'Und you pelief, ten,' he inquired, 'at te last? You pelief, ten, in te possibility of te odd?'

I again nodded my head in assent.

'Und you ave pelief in *me*, te Angel ov te Odd?'

I nodded again.

'Und you acknowledge tat you pe te blind dronk and te vool?'

I nodded once more.

'Put your right hand into your left hand preeches pocket, ten, in token ov your vull zubmizzion unto te Angel ov te Odd.'

This thing, for very obvious reasons, I found it quite impossible to do. In the first place, my left arm had been broken in my fall from the ladder, and, therefore, had I let go my hold with the right hand, I must have let go altogether. In the second place, I could have no breeches until I came across the crow. I was therefore obliged, much to my regret, to shake my head in the negative — intending thus to give the Angel to understand that I found it inconvenient, just at that moment, to comply with his very reasonable demand! No sooner, however, had I ceased shaking my head than —

'Go to der teuffel, ten!' roared the Angel of the Odd.

In pronouncing these words, he drew a sharp knife across the guide-rope by which I was suspended, and as we then happened to be precisely over my own house (which, during my peregrinations, had been handsomely rebuilt), it so occurred that I tumbled headlong down the ample chimney and alit upon the dining-room hearth.

Upon coming to my senses (for the fall had very thoroughly stunned me), I found it about four o'clock in the morning. I lay outstretched where I had fallen from the balloon. My head grovelled in the ashes of an extinguished fire, while my feet reposed upon the wreck of a small table, overthrown, and amid the fragments of a miscellaneous dessert, intermingled with a newspaper, some broken glass and shattered bottles, and an empty jug of the Schiedam Kirschenwasser. Thus revenged himself the Angel of the Odd.

THE COLLOQUY OF MONOS
AND UNA

Μελλοντα ταυτα
—Sophocles—*Antig.*
'These things are in the near future.'

UNA, 'Born again?'

Monos Yes, fairest and best beloved Una, 'born again.' These were the words upon whose mystical meaning I had so long pondered, rejecting the explanation of the priesthood, until Death himself resolved for me the secret.

Una Death!

Monos How strangely, sweet Una, you echo my words! I observe, too, a vacillation in your step—a joyous inquietude in your eyes. You are confused and oppressed by the majestic novelty of the Life Eternal. Yes, it was of Death I spoke. And here how singularly sounds that word which of old was wont to bring terror to all hearts—throwing a mildew upon all pleasures!

Una Ah, Death, the spectre which sate at all feasts! How often, Monos, did we lose ourselves in speculations upon its nature! How mysteriously did it act as a check to human bliss—saying unto it 'thus far, and no farther!' That earnest mutual love, my own Monos, which burned within our bosoms—how vainly did we flatter ourselves, feeling happy in its first upspringing, that our happiness would strengthen with its strength! Alas! as it grew, so grew in our hearts the dread of that evil hour which was hurrying to separate us forever! Thus, in time, it became painful to love. Hate would have been mercy then.

Monos Speak not here of these griefs, dear Una—mine, mine forever now!

Una But the memory of past sorrow—is it not present joy? I have much to say yet of the things which have been. Above all, I burn to know the incidents of your own passage through the dark Valley and Shadow.

Monos And when did the radiant Una ask any thing of her Monos in vain? I will be minute in relating all—but at what point shall the weird narrative begin?

Una At what point?

Monos You have said.

Una Monos, I comprehend you. In Death we have both learned the propensity of man to define the indefinable. I will not say, then, commence with the moment of life's cessation—but commence with that sad, sad instant when, the fever having abandoned you, you sank into a breathless and motionless torpor, and I pressed down your pallid eyelids with the passionate fingers of love.

Monos One word first, my Una, in regard to man's general condition at this epoch. You will remember that one or two of the wise among our forefathers—wise in fact, although not in the world's esteem—had ventured to doubt the propriety of the term 'improvement,' as applied to the progress of our civilization. There were periods in each of the five or six centuries immediately preceding our dissolution, when arose some vigorous intellect, boldly contending for those principles whose truth appears now, to our disenfranchised reason, so utterly obvious—principles which should have taught our race to submit to the guidance of the natural laws, rather than attempt their control. At long intervals some masterminds appeared, looking upon each advance in practical science as a retro-gradation in the true utility. Occasionally the poetic intellect—that intellect which we now feel to have been the most exalted of all—since those truths to us were of the most enduring importance and could only be reached by that *analogy* which speaks in proof-tones to the imagination alone, and to the unaided reason bears no weight—occasionally did this poetic intellect proceed a step farther in the evolving of the vague idea of the philosophic, and find in the mystic parable that tells of the tree of knowledge, and of its forbidden fruit, death-producing, a distinct intimation that knowledge was not meet for man in the infant condition of his soul. And these men, the poets, living and perishing amid the scorn of the 'utilitarians'—of rough pedants, who arrogated to themsleves a title which could have been properly applied only to the scorned—these men, the poets, ponder piningly, yet not unwisely, upon the ancient days when our wants were not more simple than our enjoyments were keen—days when *mirth* was a word unknown, so solemnly deep-toned was happiness—holy, august and blissful days, when blue rivers ran undammed, between hills unhewn, into far forest solitudes, primeval, odourous, and unexplored.

Yet these noble exceptions from the general misrule served but to strengthen it by opposition. Alas! we had fallen upon the most evil of all our evil days. The great 'movement'—that was the cant term—went on: a diseased commotion, moral and physical. Art—the Arts—arose supreme, and, once enthroned, cast chains upon the intellect which had elevated them to power. Man, because he could not but acknowledge

the majesty of Nature, fell into childish exultation at his acquired and still-increasing dominion over her elements. Even while he stalked a God in his own fancy, an infantine imbecility came over him. As might be supposed from the origin of his disorder, he grew infected with system, and with abstraction. He enwrapped himself in generalities. Among other odd ideas, that of universal equality gained ground; and in the face of analogy and of God—in despite of the loud warning voice of the laws of *gradation* so visibly pervading all things in Earth and Heaven—wild attempts at an omni-prevalent Democracy were made. Yet this evil sprang necessarily from the leading evil—Knowledge. Man could not both know and succumb. Meantime huge smoking cities arose, innumerable. Green leaves shrank before the hot breath of furnaces. The fair face of Nature was deformed as with the ravages of some loathsome disease. And methinks, sweet Una, even our slumbering sense of the forced and of the far-fetched might have arrested us here. But now it appears that we had worked out our own destruction in the perversion of our *taste*, or rather in the blind neglect of its culture in the schools. For, in truth, it was at this crisis that taste alone—that faculty which, holding a middle position between the pure intellect and the moral sense, could never safely have been disregarded—it was now that taste alone could have led us gently back to Beauty, to Nature, and to Life. But alas for the pure contemplative spirit and majestic intuition of Plato! Alas for the μουσιχη which he justly regarded as an all sufficient education for the soul! Alas for him and for it!—since both were most desperately needed when both were most entirely forgotten or despised.[1]

Pascal, a philosopher whom we both love, has said, how truly!—'que tout notre raisonnement se réduit à céder au sentiment'; and it is not impossible that the sentiment of the natural, had time permitted it, would have regained its old ascendancy over the harsh mathematical reason of the schools. But this thing was not to be. Prematurely induced by intemperance of knowledge, the old age of the world drew on. This the mass of mankind saw not, or, living lustily although unhappily, affected not to see. But, for myself, the Earth's

records had taught me to look for widest ruin as the price of highest civilization. I had imbibed a prescience of our Fate from comparison of China the simple and enduring, with Assyria the architect, with Egypt the astrologer, with Nubia, more crafty than either, the turbulent mother of all Arts. In history[2] of these regions I met with a ray from the Future. The individual artificialities of the three latter were local diseases of the Earth, and in their individual overthrows we had seen local remedies applied; but for the infected world at large I could anticipate no regeneration save in death. That man, as a race, should not become extinct, I saw that he must be 'born again.'

And now it was, fairest and dearest, that we wrapped our spirits, daily, in dreams. Now it was that, in twilight, we discoursed of the days to come, when the Art-scarred surface of the Earth, having undergone that purification[3] which alone could efface its rectangular obscenities, should clothe itself anew in the verdure and the mountain-slopes and the smiling waters of Paradise, and be rendered at legnth a fit dwelling-place for man:—for man the Death-purged—for man to whose now exalted intellect there should be poison in knowledge no more—for the redeemed, regenerated, blissful, and now immortal, but still for the *material*, man.

Una Well do I remember these conversations, dear Monos; but the epoch of the fiery overthrow was not so near at hand as we believed, and as the corruption you indicate did surely warrant us in believing. Men lived; and died individually. You yourself sickened, and passed into the grave; and thither your constant Una speedily followed you. And though the century which has since elapsed, and whose conclusion brings us thus together once more, tortured our slumbering senses with no impatience of duration, yet, my Monos, it was a century still.

Monos Say, rather, a point in the vague infinity. Unquestionably, it was in the Earth's dotage that I died. Wearied at heart with anxieties which had their origin in the general turmoil and decay, I succumbed to the fierce fever. After some few days of pain, and many of dreamy delirium replete with ecstasy, the manifestations of which you mistook for pain, while I longed but was impotent to undeceive you—after some days there came upon me, as you have said, a breathless and motionless torpor; and this was termed *Death* by those who stood around me.

Words are vague things. My condition did not deprive me of sentience. It appeared to me not greatly dissimilar to the extreme quiescence of him, who, having slumbered long and profoundly, lying motionless and fully prostrate in a midsummer noon, begins to steal slowly back into conscious-

---

[1] 'It will be hard to discover a better [method of education] than that which the experience of so many ages has already discovered; and this may be summed up as consisting in gymnastics for the body, and *music* for the soul.'—Repub. lib. 2. 'For this reason is a musical education most essential; since it causes Rhythm and Harmony to penetrate most intimately into the soul, taking the strongest hold upon it, filling it with *beauty* and making the man *beautifully-minded*.* * * He will praise and admire *the beautiful*; will receive it with joy into his soul, will feed upon it, and *assimilate his own condition with it*.'—Ibid. lib. 3. Music μουσιχη had, however, among the Athenians, a far more comprehensive signification than with us. It included not only the harmonies of time and of tune, but the poetic diction, sentiment and creation each in its widest sense. The study of *music* was with them, in fact, the general cultivation of the taste—of that which recognizes the beautiful—in contradistinction from reason, which deals only with the true.

[2] 'History,' from Ιστορειν, to contemplate.

[3] The word '*purification*' seems here to be used with reference to its root in the Greek πυρ, fire.

ness, through the mere sufficiency of his sleep, and without being awakened by external disturbances.

I breathed no longer. The pulses were still. The heart had ceased to beat. Volition had not departed, but was powerless. The senses were unusually active, although eccentrically so—assuming often each other's functions at random. The taste and the smell were inextricably confounded, and became one sentiment, abnormal and intense. The rose-water with which your tenderness had moistened my lips to the last, affected me with sweet fancies of flowers—fantastic flowers, far more lovely than any of the old Earth, but whose prototypes we have here blooming around us. The eyelids, transparent and bloodless, offered no complete impediment to vision. As volition was in abeyance the balls could not roll in their sockets—but all objects within the range of the visual hemisphere were seen with more or less distinctness; the rays which fell upon the external retina, or into the corner of the eye, producing a more vivid effect than those which struck the front or anterior surface. Yet, in the former instance, this effect was so far anomalous that I appreciated it only as *sound*—sound sweet or discordant as the matters presenting themselves at my side were light or dark in shade—curved or angular in outline. The hearing at the same time, although excited in degree, was not irregular in action—estimating real sounds with an extravagance of precision, not less than of sensibility. Touch had undergone a modification more peculiar. Its impressions were tardily received, but pertinaciously retained ,and resulted always in the highest physical pleasure. Thus the pressure of your sweet fingers upon my eyelids, at first only recognized through vision, at length, long after their removal, filled my whole being with a sensual delight immeasurable. I say with a sensual delight. *All* my perceptions were purely sensual. The materials furnished the passive brain by the senses were not in the least degree wrought into shape by the deceased understanding. Of pain there was some little; of pleasure there was much; but of moral pain or pleasure none at all. Thus your wild sobs floated into my ear with all their mournful cadences, and were appreciated in their every variation of sad tone; but they were soft musical sounds and no more; they conveyed to the extinct reason no intimation of the sorrows which gave them birth; while the large and constant tears which fell upon my face, telling the bystanders of a heart which broke, thrilled every fibre of my frame with ecstasy alone. And this was in truth the *Death* of which these bystanders spoke reverently, in low whispers—you, sweet Una, gaspingly, with loud cries.

They attired me for the coffin—three or four dark figures which flitted busily to and fro. As these crossed the direct line of my vision they affected me as *forms*; but upon passing to my side their images impressed me with the idea of shrieks, groans, and other dismal expressions of terror, of horror, or

of woe. You alone, habited in a white robe, passed in all directions musically about me.

The day waned; and, as its light faded away, I became possessed by a vague uneasiness—an anxiety such as the sleeper feels when sad real sounds fall continuously within his ear—low distant bell tones, solemn, at long but equal intervals, and commingling with melancholy dreams. Night arrived; and with its shadows a heavy discomfort. It oppressed my limbs with the oppression of some dull weight, and was palpable. There was also a moaning sound, not unlike the distant reverberation of surf, but more continuous, which, beginning with the first twilight, had grown in strength with the darkness. Suddenly lights were brought into the room, and this reverberation became forthwith interrupted into frequent unequal bursts of the same sound, but less dreary and less distinct. The ponderous oppression was in a great measure relieved; and, issuing from the flame of each lamp (for there were many), there flowed unbrokenly into my ears a strain of melodious monotone. And when now, dear Una, approaching the bed upon which I lay outstretched, you sat gently by my side, breathing odor from your sweet lips, and pressing them upon my brow, there arose tremulously within my bosom, and mingling with the merely physical sensations which circumstances had called forth, a something akin to sentiment itself—a feeling that, half appreciating, half responded to your earnest love and sorrow; but this feeling took no root in the pulseless heart, and seemed indeed rather a shadow than a reality, and faded quickly away, first into extreme quiescence, and then into a purely sensual pleasure as before.

And now, from the wreck and the chaos of the usual senses, there appeared to have arisen within me a sixth, all perfect. In its exercise I found a wild delight—yet a delight still physical, inasmuch as the understanding in it had no part. Motion in the animal frame had fully ceased. No muscle quivered; no nerve thrilled; no artery throbbed. But there seemed to have sprung up in the brain, *that* of which no words could convey to the merely human intelligence even an indistinct conception. Let me term it a mental pendulous pulsation. It was the moral embodiment of man's abstract idea of *Time*. By the absolute equalization of this movement—or of such as this—had the cycles of the firmamental orbs themselves, been adjusted. By its aid I measured the irregularities of the clock upon the mantel, and of the watches of the attendants. Their tickings came sonorously to my ears. The slightest deviation from the true proportion—and these deviations were omni-prevalent—affected me just as violations of abstract truth are wont, on earth, to affect the moral sense. Although no two of the timepieces in the chamber struck individual seconds accurately together, yet I had no difficulty in holding steadily in mind the tones, and the respective momentary errors of each. And this—this keen, perfect, self-existing sentiment of *duration*—

this sentiment existing (as man could not possibly have conceived it to exist) independently of any succession of events—this idea—this sixth sense, upspringing from the ashes of the rest, was the first obvious and certain step of the intemporal soul upon the threshold of the temporal Eternity.

It was midnight; and you still sat by my side. All others had departed from the chamber of Death. They had deposited me in the coffin. The lamps burned flickeringly; for this I knew by the tremulousness of the monotonous strains. But, suddenly these strains diminished in distinctness and in volume. Finally they ceased. The perfume in my nostrils died away. Forms affected my vision no longer. The oppression of the Darkness uplifted itself from my bosom. A dull shock like that of electricity pervaded my frame, and was followed by total loss of the idea of contact. All of what man has termed sense was merged in the sole consciousness of entity, and in the one abiding sentiment of duration. The mortal body had been at length stricken with the hand of the deadly *Decay*.

Yet had not all of sentience departed; for the consciousness and the sentiment remaining supplied some of its functions by a lethargic intuition. I appreciated the direful change now in operation upon the flesh, and, as the dreamer is sometimes aware of the bodily presence of one who leans over him, so, sweet Una, I still dully felt that you sat by my side. So, too, when the noon of the second day came, I was not unconscious of those movements which displaced you from my side, which confined me within the coffin, which deposited me within the hearse, which bore me to the grave, which lowered me within it, which heaped heavily the mould upon me, and which thus left me, in blackness and corruption, to my sad and solemn slumbers with the worm.

And here, in the prison-house which has few secrets to disclose, there rolled away days and weeks and months; and the soul watched narrowly each second as it flew, and, without effort, took record of its flight—without effort and without object.

A year passed. The consciousness of *being* had grown hourly more indistinct, and that of mere *locality* had, in great measure, usurped its position. The idea of entity was becoming merged in that of *place*. The narrow space immediately surrounding what had been the body, was now going to be the body itself. At length, as often happens to the sleeper (by sleep and its world alone is *Death* imaged)—at length, as sometimes happened on Earth to the deep slumberer, when some flitting light half startled him into awaking, yet left him half enveloped in dreams—so to me, in the strict embrace of the *Shadow*, came *that* light which alone might have had power to startle—the light of enduring *Love*. Men toiled at the grave in which I lay darkling. They upthrew the damp earth. Upon my mouldering bones there descended the coffin of Una.

And now again all was void. That nebulous light had been extinguished. That feeble thrill had vibrated itself into quiescence. Many *lustra* had supervened. Dust had returned to dust. The worm had food no more. The sense of being had at length utterly departed, and there reigned in its stead—instead of all things—dominant and perpetual—the autocrats *Place* and *Time*. For *that* which *was not*—for that which had no form—for that which had no thought—for that which had no sentience—for that which was soulless, yet of which matter formed no portion—for all this nothingness, yet for all this immortality, the grave was still a home, and the corrosive hours, co-mates.

THE RAVEN

Once upon a midnight dreary, while I pondered, weak and weary,
Over many a quaint and curious volume of forgotten lore —
While I nodded, nearly napping, suddenly there came a tapping,
As of some one gently rapping, rapping at my chamber door.
'Tis some visitor,' I muttered, 'tapping at my chamber door —
     Only this and nothing more.'

Ah, distinctly I remember it was in the bleak December,
And each separate dying ember wrought its ghost upon the floor.
Eagerly I wished the morrow; — vainly I had sought to borrow
From my books surcease of sorrow — sorrow for the lost Lenore —
For the rare and radiant maiden whom the angels name Lenore —
     Nameless here for evermore.

And the silken sad uncertain rustling of each purple curtain
Thrilled me — filled me with fantastic terrors never felt before;
So that now, to still the beating of my heart, I stood repeating:
'Tis some visitor entreating entrance at my chamber door;
     This it is and nothing more.'

Presently my soul grew stronger; hesitating then no longer,
'Sir,' said I, 'or Madam, truly your forgiveness I implore;
But the fact is I was napping, and so gently you came rapping,
And so faintly you came tapping, tapping at my chamber door,
That I scarce was sure I heard you' — here I opened wide the door; —
     Darkness there and nothing more.

Deep into that darkness peering, long I stood there wondering, fearing,
Doubting, dreaming dreams no mortals ever dared to dream before;
But the silence was unbroken, and the stillness gave no token,
And the only word there spoken was the whispered word, 'Lenore!'
This I whispered, and an echo murmured back the word, 'Lenore!' —
     Merely this and nothing more.

Back into the chamber turning, all my soul within me burning,
Soon again I heard a tapping something louder than before.
'Surely,' said I, 'surely that is something at my window lattice;
Let me see, then, what thereat is, and this mystery explore —
Let my heart be still a moment, and this mystery explore; —
     'Tis the wind and nothing more.'

Open here I flung the shutter, when, with many a flirt and flutter,
In there stepped a stately Raven of the saintly days of yore.
Not the least obeisance made he; not a minute stopped or stayed he,
But, with mien of lord or lady, perched above my chamber door —
Perched upon a bust of Pallas just above my chamber door —
     Perched, and sat, and nothing more.

Then this ebony bird beguiling my sad fancy into smiling,
By the grave and stern decorum of the countenance it wore,
'Though thy crest be shorn and shaven, thou,' I said, 'art sure no craven,
Ghastly grim and ancient Raven wandering from the Nightly shore —
Tell me what thy lordly name is on the Night's Plutonian shore!'
     Quoth the Raven, 'Nevermore.'

Much I marvelled this ungainly fowl to hear discourse so plainly,
Though its answer little meaning — little relevancy bore;
For we cannot help agreeing that no living human being
Ever yet was blessed with seeing bird above his chamber door —
Bird or beast upon the sculptured bust above his chamber door,
     With such name as 'Nevermore.'

But the Raven, sitting lonely on that placid bust, spoke only
That one word, as if his soul in that one word he did outpour.
Nothing farther then he uttered; not a feather then he fluttered —
Till I scarcely more than muttered: 'Other friends have flown before —
On the morrow *he* will leave me as my Hopes have flown before.'
     Then the bird said, 'Nevermore.'

Startled as the stillness broken by reply so aptly spoken,
'Doubtless,' said I, 'what it utters is its only stock and store,
Caught from some unhappy master whom unmerciful Disaster
Followed fast and followed faster till his songs one burden bore —
Till the dirges of his Hope that melancholy burden bore
     Of 'Never — nevermore.'

But the Raven still beguiling all my sad soul into smiling,
Straight I wheeled a cushioned seat in front of bird and bust and door;
Then, upon the velvet sinking, I betook myself to linking
Fancy unto fancy, thinking what this ominous bird of yore —
What this grim, ungainly, ghastly, gaunt, and ominous bird of yore
     Meant in croaking 'Nevermore.'

This I sat engaged in guessing, but no syllable expressing
To the fowl whose fiery eyes now burned into my bosom's core;
This and more I sat divining, with my head at ease reclining
On the cushion's velvet lining that the lamp-light gloated o'er,
But whose velvet violet lining with the lamp-light gloating o'er
     She shall press, ah, nevermore!

Then, methought, the air grew denser, perfumed from an unseen censer
Swung by Seraphim whose foot-falls tinkled on the tufted floor.
'Wretch,' I cried, 'thy God hath lent thee — by these angels he hath sent thee
Respite — respite and nepenthe from thy memories of Lenore!
Quaff, oh quaff this kind nepenthe and forget this lost Lenore!'
     Quoth the Raven, 'Nevermore.'

'Prophet!' said I, 'thing of evil! — prophet still, if bird or devil! —
Whether Tempter sent, or whether tempest tossed thee here ashore,
Desolate, yet all undaunted, on this desert land enchanted —
On this home by Horror haunted, — tell me truly, I implore —
Is there — *is* there balm in Gilead? — tell me — tell me, I implore!'
     Quoth the Raven, 'Nevermore.'

'Prophet!' said I, 'thing of evil! — prophet still, if bird or devil!
By that heaven that bends above us — by that God we both adore —
Tell this soul with sorrow laden if, within the distant Aidenn,
It shall clasp a sainted maiden whom the angels name Lenore —
Clasp a rare and radiant maiden whom the angels name Lenore.'
     Quoth the Raven, 'Nevermore.'

'Be that word our sign of parting, bird or fiend!' I shrieked, upstarting —
'Get thee back into the tempest and the Night's Plutonian shore!
Leave no black plume as a token of that lie thy soul hath spoken!
Leave my loneliness unbroken! — quit the bust above my door!
Take thy beak from out my heart, and take thy form from off my door!'
     Quoth the Raven, 'Nevermore.'

And the Raven, never flitting, still is sitting, still is sitting
On the pallid bust of Pallas just above my chamber door;
And his eyes have all the seeming of a demon's that is dreaming,
And the lamp-light o'er him streaming throws his shadow on the floor;
And my soul from out that shadow that lies floating on the floor
     Shall be lifted — nevermore!

THE BLACK CAT

FOR the most wild yet most homely narrative which I am about to pen, I neither expect nor solicit belief. Mad indeed would I be to expect it, in a case where my very senses reject their own evidence. Yet, mad am I not—and very surely do I not dream. But to-morrow I die, and to-day I would unburden my soul. My immediate purpose is to place before the world, plainly, succinctly, and without comment, a series of mere household events. In their consequences, these events have terrified—have tortured—have destroyed me. Yet I will not attempt to expound them. To me, they have presented little but horror—to many they will seem less terrible than *baroques*. Hereafter, perhaps, some intellect may be found which will reduce my phantasm to the commonplace—some intellect more calm, more logical, and far less excitable than my own, which will perceive, in the circumstances I detail with awe, nothing more than an ordinary succession of very natural causes and effects.

From my infancy I was noted for the docility and humanity of my disposition. My tenderness of heart was even so conspicuous as to make me the jest of my companions. I was especially fond of animals, and was indulged by my parents with a great variety of pets. With these I spent most of my time, and never was so happy as when feeding and caressing them. This peculiarity of character grew with my growth, and, in my manhood, I derived from it one of my principal sources of pleasure. To those who have cherished an affection for a faithful and sagacious dog, I need hardly be at the trouble of explaining the nature or the intensity of the gratification thus derivable. There is something in the unselfish and self-sacrificing love of a brute, which goes directly to the heart of him who has had frequent occasion to test the paltry friendship and gossamer fidelity of mere *Man*.

I married early, and was happy to find in my wife a disposition not uncongenial with my own. Observing my partiality for domestic pets, she lost no opportunity of procuring those of the most agreeable kind. We had birds, gold-fish, a fine dog, rabbits, a small monkey, and a *cat*.

This latter was a remarkably large and beautiful animal, entirely black, and sagacious to an astonishing degree. In speaking of his intelligence, my wife, who at heart was not a little tinctured with superstition, made frequent allusion to the ancient popular notion, which regarded all black cats as witches in disguise. Not that she was ever *serious* upon this point—and I mention the matter at all for no better reason than that it happens, just now, to be remembered.

Pluto—this was the cat's name—was my favourite pet and playmate. I alone fed him, and he attended me wherever I went about the house. It was even with difficulty that I could prevent him from following me through the streets.

Our friendship lasted, in this manner, for several years, during which my general temperament and character—through the instrumentality of the Fiend Intemperance—had (I blush to confess it) experienced a radical alteration for the worse. I grew, day by day, more moody, more irritable, more regardless of the feelings of others. I suffered myself to use intemperate language to my wife. At length, I even offered her personal violence. My pets, of course, were made to feel the change in my disposition. I not only neglected, but ill-used them. For Pluto, however, I still retained sufficient regard to restrain me from maltreating him, as I made no scruple of maltreating the rabbits, the monkey, or even the dog, when, by accident, or through affection, they came in my way. But my disease grew upon me—for what disease is like Alcohol!—and at length even Pluto, who was now becoming old, and consequently somewhat peevish—even Pluto began to experience the effects of my ill temper.

One night, returning home, much intoxicated, from one of my haunts about town, I fancied that the cat avoided my presence. I seized him; when, in his fright at my violence, he inflicted a slight wound upon my hand with his teeth. The fury of a demon instantly possessed me. I knew myself no longer. My original soul seemed, at once, to take its flight from my body; and a more than fiendish malevolence, gin-nurtured, thrilled every fibre of my frame. I took from my waistcoat-pocket a penknife, opened it, grasped the poor beast by the throat, and deliberately cut one of its eyes from the socket! I blush, I burn, I shudder, while I pen the damnable atrocity.

When reason returned with the morning—when I had slept off the fumes of the night's debauch—I experienced a sentiment half of horror, half of remorse, for the crime of which I had been guilty; but it was, at best, a feeble and equivocal feeling, and the soul remained untouched. I again plunged into excess, and soon drowned in wine all memory of the deed.

In the meantime the cat slowly recovered. The socket of the lost eye presented, it is true, a frightful appearance, but he no longer appeared to suffer any pain. He went about the house as usual, but, as might be expected, fled in extreme terror at my approach. I had so much of my old heart left, as to be at first grieved by this evident dislike on the part of a creature which had once so loved me. But this feeling soon gave place to irritation. And then came, as if to my final and irrevocable overthrow, the spirit of PERVERSENESS. Of this spirit philosophy takes no account. Yet I am not more sure that my soul lives, than I am that perverseness is one of the primitive impulses of the human heart — one of the indivisible primary faculties, or sentiments, which give direction to the character of Man. Who has not, a hundred times, found himself committing a vile or a stupid action, for no other reason than because he knows he should *not*? Have we not a perpetual inclination, in the teeth of our best judgement, to violate that which is *Law*, merely because we understand it to be such? This spirit of perverseness, I say, came to my final overthrow. It was this unfathomable longing of the soul *to vex itself* — to offer violence to its own nature — to do wrong for the wrong's sake only — that urged me to continue and finally to consummate the injury I had inflicted upon the unoffending brute. One morning, in cold blood, I slipped a noose about its neck and hung it to the limb of a tree; — hung it with the tears streaming from my eyes, and with the bitterest remorse at my heart; — hung it *because* I knew that it had loved me, and *because* I felt it had given me no reason of offence; — hung it *because* I knew that in so doing I was committing a sin — a deadly sin that would so jeopardize my immortal soul as to place it — if such a thing were possible — even beyond the reach of the infinite mercy of the Most Merciful and Most Terrible God.

On the night of the day on which this most cruel deed was done, I was aroused from sleep by the cry of fire. The curtains of my bed were in flames. The whole house was blazing. It was with great difficulty that my wife, a servant, and myself, made our escape from the conflagration. The destruction was complete. My entire worldly wealth was swallowed up, and I resigned myself thenceforward to despair.

I am above the weakness of seeking to establish a sequence of cause and effect, between the disaster and the atrocity. But I am detailing a chain of facts — and wish not to leave even a possible link imperfect. On the day succeeding the fire, I visited the ruins. The walls, with one exception, had fallen in. This exception was found in a compartment wall, not very thick, which stood about the middle of the house, and against which had rested the head of my bed. The plastering had here, in great measure, resisted the action of the fire — a fact which I attributed to its having been recently spread. About this wall a dense crowd were collected, and many persons seemed to be examining a particular portion of it with very minute and eager attention. The words 'strange!' 'singular!' and other similar expressions, excited my curiosity. I approached and saw, as if graven in *bas-relief* upon the white surface, the figure of a gigantic *cat*. The impression was give with an accuracy truly marvellous. There was a rope about the animal's neck.

When I first beheld this apparition — for I could scarcely regard it as less — my wonder and my terror were extreme. But at length reflection came to my aid. The cat, I remembered, had been hung in a garden adjacent to the house. Upon the alarm of fire, this garden had been immediately filled by the crowd — by some one of whom the animal must have been cut from the tree and thrown, through an open window, into my chamber. This had probably been done with the view of arousing me from sleep. The falling of other walls had compressed the victim of my cruelty into the substance of the freshly-spread plaster; the lime of which, with the flames, and the *ammonia* from the carcass, had then accomplished the portraiture as I saw it.

Although I thus readily accounted to my reason, if not altogether to my conscience, for the startling fact just detailed, it did not the less fail to make a deep impression upon my fancy. For months I could not rid myself of the phantasm of the cat; and, during this period, there came back into my spirit a half-sentiment that seemed, but was not, remorse. I went so far as to regret the loss of the animal, and to look about me, among the vile haunts which I now habitually frequented, for another pet of the same species, and of somewhat similar appearance, with which to supply its place.

One night as I sat, half stupefied, in a den of more than infamy, my attention was suddenly drawn to some black object, reposing upon the head of one of the immense hogsheads of gin, or of rum, which constituted the chief furniture of the apartment. I had been looking steadily at the top of this hogshead for some minutes, and what now caused me surprise was the fact that I had not sooner perceived the object thereupon. I approached it, and touched it with my hand. It was a black cat — a very large one — fully as large as Pluto, and closely resembling him in every respect but one. Pluto had not a white hair upon any portion of his body; but this cat had a large, although indefinite splotch of white, covering nearly the whole region of the breast.

Upon my touching him, he immediately arose, purred loudly, rubbed against my hand, and appeared delighted with my notice. This, then, was the very creature of which I was in search. I at once offered to purchase it of the landlord; but this person made no claim to it — knew nothing of it — had never seen it before.

I continued my caresses, and when I prepared to go home, the animal evinced a disposition to accompany me. I permitted it to do so; occasionally stooping and patting it as I proceeded.

When it reached the house it domesticated itself at once, and became immediately a great favourite with my wife.

For my own part, I soon found a dislike to it arising within me. This was just the reverse of what I had anticipated; but—I know not how or why it was—its evident fondness for myself rather disgusted and annoyed me. By slow degrees these feelings of disgust and annoyance rose into the bitterness of hatred. I avoided the creature; a certain sense of shame, and the remembrance of my former deed of cruelty, preventing me from physically abusing it. I did not, for some weeks, strike, or otherwise violently ill use it; but gradually—very gradually—I came to look upon it with unutterable loathing, and to flee silently from its odious presence, as from the breath of a pestilence.

What added, no doubt, to my hatred of the beast, was the discovery, on the morning after I brought it home, that, like Pluto, it also had been deprived of one of its eyes. This circumstance, however, only endeared it to my wife, who, as I have already said, possessed, in a high degree, that humanity of feeling which had once been my distinguishing trait, and the source of many of my simplest and purest pleasures.

With my aversion to this cat, however, its partiality for myself seemed to increase. It followed my footsteps with a pertinacity which it would be difficult to make the reader comprehend. Whenever I sat, it would crouch beneath my chair, or spring upon my knees, covering me with its loathsome caresses. If I arose to walk it would get between my feet and thus nearly throw me down, or, fastening its long and sharp claws in my dress, clamber, in this manner, to my breast. At such times, although I longed to destroy it with a blow, I was yet withheld from so doing, partly by a memory of my former crime, but chiefly—let me confess it at once—by absolute *dread* of the beast.

This dread was not exactly a dread of physical evil—and yet I should be at a loss how otherwise to define it. I am almost ashamed to own—yes, even in this felon's cell, I am almost ashamed to own—that the terror and horror with which the animal inspired me, had been heightened by one of the merest chimeras it would be possible to conceive. My wife had called my attention, more than once, to the character of the mark of white hair, of which I have spoken, and which constituted the sole visible difference between the strange beast and the one I had destroyed. The reader will remember that his mark, although large, had been originally very indefinite; but, by slow degrees—degrees nearly imperceptible, and which for a long time my reason struggled to reject as fanciful—it had, at length, assumed a rigorous distinctness of outline. It was now the representation of an object that I shudder to name—and for this, above all, I loathed, and dreaded, and would have rid myself of the monster *had I dared*—it was now, I say, the image of a hideous—of a ghastly thing—of the GALLOWS—

oh, mournful and terrible engine of Horror and of Crime—of Agony and of Death!

And now was I indeed wretched beyond the wretchedness of mere Humanity. And *a brute beast*—whose fellow I had contemptuously destroyed—*a brute beast* to work out for *me*—for me, a man fashioned in the image of the High God—so much of insufferable woe! Alas! neither by day nor by night knew I the blessing of rest any more! During the former the creature left me no moment alone, and in the latter I started hourly from dreams of unutterable fear to find the hot breath of *the thing* upon my face, and its vast weight—an incarnate nightmare that I had no power to shake off—incumbent eternally upon my *heart!*

Beneath the pressure of torments such as these the feeble remnant of the good within me succumbed. Evil thoughts became my sole intimates—the darkest and most evil of thoughts. The moodiness of my usual temper increased to hatred of all things and of all mankind; while from the sudden, frequent, and ungovernable outbursts of a fury to which I now blindly abandoned myself, my uncomplaining wife, alas, was the most usual and the most patient of sufferers.

One day she accompanied me, upon some household errand, into the cellar of the old building which our poverty compelled us to inhabit. The cat followed me down the steep stairs, and, nearly throwing me headlong, exasperated me to madness. Uplifting an axe, and forgetting in my wrath the childish dread which had hitherto stayed my hand, I aimed a blow at the animal, which, of course, would have proved instantly fatal had it descended as I wished. But this blow was arrested by the hand of my wife. Goaded by the interference into a rage more than demoniacal, I withdrew my arm from her grasp and buried the axe in her brain. She fell dead upon the spot without a groan.

This hideous murder accomplished, I set myself forthwith, and with entire deliberation, to the task of concealing the body. I knew that I could not remove it from the house, either by day or by night, without the risk of being observed by the neighbours. Many projects entered my mind. At one period I thought of cutting the corpse into minute fragments, and destroying them by fire. At another, I resolved to dig a grave for it in the floor of the cellar. Again, I deliberated about casting it in the well in the yard—about packing it in a box, as if merchandise, with the usual arrangements, and so getting a porter to take it from the house. Finally I hit upon what I considered a far better expedient than either of these. I determined to wall it up in the cellar, as the monks of the Middle Ages are recorded to have walled up their victims.

For a purpose such as this the cellar was well adapted. Its walls were loosely constructed, and had lately been plastered throughout with a rough plaster, which the dampness of the atmosphere had prevented from hardening. Moreover, in one

of the walls was a projection, caused by a false chimney, or fireplace, that had been filled up and made to resemble the rest of the cellar. I made no doubt that I could readily displace the bricks at this point, insert the corpse, and wall the whole up as before, so that no eye could detect any thing suspicious.

And in this calculation I was not deceived. By means of a crowbar I easily dislodged the bricks, and, having carefully deposited the body against the inner wall, I propped it in that position, while with little trouble I relaid the whole structure as it originally stood. Having procured mortar, sand, and hair, with every possible precaution, I prepared a plaster which could not be distinguished from the old, and with this I very carefully went over the new brick-work. When I had finished, I felt satisfied that all was right. The wall did not present the slightest appearance of having been disturbed. The rubbish on the floor was picked up with the minutest care. I looked around triumphantly, and said to myself: "Here at least, then, my labor has not been in vain".

My next step was to look for the beast which had been the cause of so much wretchedness; for I had, at length, firmly resolved to put it to death. Had I been able to meet with it at the moment, there could have been no doubt of its fate; but it appeared that the crafty animal had been alarmed at the violence of my previous anger, and forbore to present itself in my present mood. It is impossible to describe or to imagine the deep, the blissful sense of relief which the absence of the detested creature occasioned in my bosom. It did not make its appearance during the night; and thus for one night, at least, since its introduction into the house, I soundly and tranquilly slept; aye, *slept* even with the burden of murder upon my soul.

The second and the third day passed, and still my tormentor came not. Once again I breathed as a freeman. The monster, in terror, had fled the premises for ever! I should behold it no more! My happiness was supreme! The guilt of my dark deed disturbed me but little. Some few inquiries had been made, but these had been readily answered. Even a search had been instituted—but of course nothing was to be discovered. I looked upon my future felicity as secured.

Upon the fourth day of the assassination, a party of the police came, very unexpectedly, into the house, and proceeded again to make rigorous investigation of the premises. Secure, however, in the inscrutability of my place of concealment, I felt no embarrassment whatever. The officers bade me accompany them in their search. They left no nook or corner unexplored. At length, for the third or fourth time, they descended into the cellar. I quivered not in a muscle. My heart beat calmly as that of one who slumbers in innocence. I walked the cellar from end to end. I folded my arms upon my bosom, and roamed easily to and fro. The police were thoroughly satisfied and prepared to depart. The glee at my heart was too strong to be restrained. I burned to say if but one word, by way of triumph, and to render doubly sure their assurance of my guiltlessness.

'Gentlemen,' I said at last, as the party ascended the steps, 'I delight to have allayed your suspicions. I wish you all health and a little more courtesy. By the bye, gentlemen, this—this is a very well-constructed house,' (in the rabid desire to say something easily, I scarcely knew what I uttered at all),—'I may say an *excellently* well-constructed house. These walls—are you going, gentlemen?—these walls are solidly put together'; and here, through the mere frenzy of bravado, I rapped with a cane which I held in my hand, upon that very portion of the brickwork behind which stood the corpse of the wife of my bosom.

But may God shield and deliver me from the fangs of the Arch-Fiend! No sooner had the reverberation of my blows sunk into silence, than I was answered by a voice from within the tomb!—by a cry, at first muffled and broken, like the sobbing of a child, and then quickly swelling into one long, loud, and continuous scream, utterly anomalous and inhuman—a howl—a wailing shriek, half of horror and half of triumph, such as might have arisen only out of hell, conjointly from the throats of the damned in their agony and of the demons that exult in the damnation.

Of my own thoughts it is folly to speak. Swooning, I staggered to the opposite wall. For one instant the party on the stairs remained motionless, through extremity of terror and awe. In the next a dozen stout arms were toiling at the wall. It fell bodily. The corpse, already greatly decayed and clotted with gore, stood erect before the eyes of the spectators. Upon its head, with red extended mouth and solitary eye of fire, sat the hideous beast whose craft had seduced me into murder, and whose informing voice had consigned me to the hangman. I had walled the monster up within the tomb.

BERENICE

Dicebant mihi sodales, si sepulchrum amicæ visitarem,
curas meas aliquar tulum fore levatas

— Ebn Zaiat

MISERY is manifold. The wretchedness of earth is multiform. Overreaching the wide horizon as the rainbow, its hues are as various as the hues of that arch — as distinct too, yet as intimately blended. Overreaching the wide horizon as the rainbow! How is it that from beauty I have derived a type of unloveliness? — from the covenant of peace, a simile of sorrow? But, as in ethics, evil is a consequence of good, so, in fact, out of joy is sorrow born. Either the memory of past bliss is the anguish of to-day, or the agonies which *are*, have their origin in the ecstasies which *might have been*.

My baptismal name is Egæus; that of my family I will not mention. Yet there are no towers in the land more time-honoured than my gloomy, gray, hereditary halls. Our line has been called a race of visionaries; and in many striking particulars — in the character of the family mansion — in the frescos of the chief saloon — in the tapestries of the dormitories — in the chiselling of some buttresses in the armoury — but more especially in the gallery of antique paintings — in the fashion of the library chamber — and, lastly, in the very peculiar nature of the library's contents — there is more than sufficient evidence to warrant the belief.

The recollections of my earliest years are connected with that chamber, and with its volumes — of which latter I will say no more. Here died my mother. Herein was I born. But it is mere idleness to say that I had not lived before — that the soul has no previous existence. You deny it? — let us not argue the matter. Convinced myself, I seek not to convince. There is, however, a remembrance of aërial forms — of spiritual and meaning eyes — of sounds, musical yet sad; a remembrance which will not be excluded; a memory like a shadow — vague, variable, indefinite, unsteady; and like a shadow, too, in the impossibility of my getting rid of it while the sunlight of my reason shall exist.

In that chamber was I born. Thus awakening from the long night of what seemed, but was not, nonentity, at once into the very regions of fairy land — into a palace of imagination — into the wild dominions of monastic thought and erudition — it is not singular that I gazed around me with a startled and ardent eye — that I loitered away my boyhood in books, and dissipated my youth in revery; but it *is* singular, that as years rolled away, and the noon of manhood found me still in the mansion of my fathers — it *is* wonderful what a stagnation there fell upon the springs of my life — wonderful how total an inversion took place in the character of my commonest thought. The realities of the world affected me as visions, and as visions only, while the wild ideas of the land of dreams became, in turn, not the material of my every-day existence, but in very deed that existence utterly and solely in itself.

Berenice and I were cousins, and we grew up together in my paternal halls. Yet differently we grew — I, ill of health, and buried in gloom — she, agile, graceful, and overflowing with energy; hers the ramble on the hillside — mine, the studies of the cloister; I, living within my own heart, and addicted, body and soul, to the most intense and painful meditation — she, roaming carelessly through life, with no thought of the shadows in her path, or the silent flight of the raven-winged hours. Berenice! — I call upon her name — Berenice! — and from the gray ruins of memory a thousand tumultuous recollections are startled at the sound! Ah, vividly is her image before me now, as in the early days of her light-heartedness and joy! Oh, gorgeous yet fantastic beauty! Oh, sylph amid the shrubberies of Arnheim! Oh, Naiad among its fountains! And then — then all is mystery and terror, and a tale which should not be told. Disease — a fatal disease, fell like the simoon upon her frame; and even, while I gazed upon her, the spirit of change swept over her, pervading her mind, her habits, and her character, and, in a manner the most subtle and terrible, disturbing even the identity of her person! Alas! the destroyer came and went! — and the victim — where is she? I knew her not — or knew her no longer as Berenice!

Among the numerous train of maladies superinduced by that fatal and primary one which effected a revolution of so horrible a kind in the moral and physical being of my cousin, may be mentioned as the most distressing and obstinate in its nature, a species of epilepsy not unfrequently terminating in *trance* itself — trance very nearly resembling positive dissolution, and from which her manner of recovery was, in most instances, startlingly abrupt. In the meantime, my own disease — for I have been told that I should call it by no other appellation — my own disease, then, grew rapidly upon me, and assumed finally a monomaniac character of a novel and extraordinary form — hourly and momently gaining vigour — and at length obtaining over me the most incomprehensible ascendency. This monomania, if I must so term it, consisted in a morbid irritability of those properties of the mind in metaphysical science termed the *attentive*. It is more than probable that I am not understood; but I fear, indeed, that it is in no manner possible to convey to the mind of the merely general reader, an adequate idea of that nervous *intensity of interest* with which, in my case, the powers of meditation (not to speak technically) busied and buried themselves, in the contemplation of even the most ordinary objects of the universe.

To muse for long unwearied hours, with my attention riveted to some frivolous device on the margin or in the typography of a book; to become absorbed, for the better part of a summer's day, in a quaint shadow falling aslant upon the tapestry or upon the floor; to lose myself, for an entire night, in watching the steady flame of a lamp, or the embers of a fire; to dream away whole days over the perfume of a flower; to repeat, monotonously, some common word, until the sound, by dint of frequent repetition, ceased to convey any idea whatever to the mind; to lose all sense of motion or physical existence, by means of absolute bodily quiescence long and obstinately persevered in: such were a few of the most common and least pernicious vagaries induced by a condition of the mental faculties, not, indeed, altogether unparalleled, but certainly bidding defiance to any thing like analysis or explanation.

Yet let me not be misapprehended. The undue, earnest, and morbid attention thus excited by objects in their own nature frivolous, must not be confounded in character with that ruminating propensity common to all mankind, and more especially indulged in by persons of ardent imagination. It was not even, as might be at first supposed, an extreme condition, or exaggeration of such propensity, but primarily and essentially distinct and different. In the one instance, the dreamer, or enthusiast, being interested by an object usually *not* frivolous, imperceptibly loses sight of this object in a wilderness of deductions and suggestions issuing there-from, until, at the conclusion of a day-dream *often replete with luxury*, he finds the *incitamentum*, or first cause of his musings, entirely vanished and forgotten. In my case, the primary object was *invariably frivolous*, although assuming, through the medium of my distempered vision, a refracted and unreal importance. Few deductions, if any, were made; and those few pertinaciously returning in upon the original object as a centre. The meditations were *never* pleasurable; and at the termination of the revery, the first cause, so far from being out of sight, had attained that supernaturally exaggerated interest which was the prevailing feature of the disease. In a word, the powers of mind more particularly exercised were, with me, as I have said before, the *attentive*, and are, with the day-dreamer, the *speculative*.

My books, at this epoch, if they did not actually serve to irritate the disorder, partook, it will be perceived, largely, in their imaginative and inconsequential nature, of the characteristic qualities of the disorder itself. I well remember, among others, the treatise of the noble Italian, Cœlius Secundus Curio, *De Amplitudine Beati Regni Dei*; St Austin's great work, *The City of God*; and Tertullian's *De Carne Christi*, in which the paradoxical sentence, '*Mortuus est Dei filius; credibile est quia ineptum est; et sepultus resurrexit; certum est quia impossible est,*' occupied my undivided time, for many weeks of laborious and fruitless investigation.

Thus it will appear that, shaken from its balance only by trivial things, my reason bore resemblance to that ocean-crag spoken of by Ptolemy Hephestion, which steadily resisting the attacks of human violence, and the fiercer fury of the waters and the winds, trembled only to the touch of the flower called Asphodel. And although, to a careless thinker, it might appear a matter beyond doubt, that the alteration produced by her unhappy malady, in the *moral* condition of Berenice, would afford me many objects for the exercise of that intense and abnormal meditation whose nature I have been at some trouble in explaining, yet such was not in any degree the case. In the lucid intervals of my infirmity, her calamity, indeed, gave me pain, and, taking deeply to heart that total wreck of her fair and gentle life, I did not fail to ponder, frequently and bitterly, upon the wonder-working means by which so strange a revolution had been so suddenly brought to pass. But these reflections partook not of the idiosyncrasy of my disease, and were such as would have occurred, under similar circumstances, to the ordinary mass of mankind. True to its own character, my disorder revelled in the less important but more startling changes wrought in the *physical* frame of Berenice—in the singular and most appalling distortion of her personal identity.

During the brightest days of her unparalleled beauty, most surely I had never loved her. In the strange anomaly of my existence, feelings with me, *had never been* of the heart, and my passions *always were* of the mind. Through the gray of the early morning—among the trellised shadows of the forest at noonday—and in the silence of my library at night—she had flitted by my eyes, and I had seen her—not as the living and breathing Berenice, but as the Berenice of a dream; not as a being of the earth, earthy, but as the abstraction of such a being; not as a thing to admire, but to analyze; not as an object of love, but as the theme of the most abstruse although desultory speculation. And *now*—now I shuddered in her presence, and grew pale at her approach; yet, bitterly lamenting her fallen and desolate condition, I called to mind that she had loved me long, and, in an evil moment, I spoke to her of marriage.

And at length the period of our nuptials was approaching, when, upon an afternoon in the winter of the year—one of

those unseasonably warm, calm, and misty days which are the nurse of the beautiful Halcyon,[1] — I sat (and sat, as I thought, alone) in the inner apartment of the library. But, uplifting my eyes, I saw that Berenice stood before me.

Was it my own excited imagination — or the misty influence of the atmosphere — or the uncertain twilight of the chamber — or the gray draperies which fell around her figure — that caused in it so vacillating and indistinct an outline? I could not tell. She spoke no word; and I — not for worlds could I have uttered a syllable. An icy chill ran through my frame; a sense of insufferable anxiety oppressed me; a consuming curiosity pervaded my soul; and, sinking back upon the chair, I remained for some time breathless and motionless, with my eyes riveted upon her person. Alas! its emaciation was excessive, and not one vestige of the former being lurked in any single line of the contour. My burning glances at length fell upon the face.

The forehead was high, and very pale, and singularly placid; and the once jetty hair fell partially over it, and overshadowed the hollow temples with innumerable ringlets, now of a vivid yellow, and jarring discordantly, in their fantastic character, with the reigning melancholy of the countenance. The eyes were lifeless, and lustreless, and seemingly pupilless, and I shrank involuntarily from their glassy stare to the contemplation of the thin and shrunken lips. They parted; and in a smile of peculiar meaning, *the teeth* of the changed Berenice disclosed themselves slowly to my view. Would to God that I had never beheld them, or that, having done so, I had died!

The shutting of a door disturbed me, and looking up, I found that my cousin had departed from the chamber. But from the disordered chamber of my brain, had not, alas! departed, and would not be driven away, the white and ghastly *spectrum* of the teeth. Not a speck on their surface — not a shade on their enamel — not an indenture in their edges — but what that brief period of her smile had sufficed to brand in upon my memory. I saw them *now* even more unequivocally than I beheld them *then*. The teeth! — the teeth! — they were here, and there, and everywhere, and visibly and palpably before me; long, narrow, and excessively white, with the pale lips writhing about them, as in the very moment of their first terrible development. Then came the full fury of my *monomania*, and I struggled in vain against its strange and irresistible influence. In the multiplied objects of the external world I had no thoughts but for the teeth. For these I longed with a frenzied desire. All other matters and all different interests became absorbed in their single contemplation. They — they alone were present to the mental eye, and they, in their sole individuality, became the essence of my mental life. I held them in every light. I turned

them in every attitude. I surveyed their characteristics. I dwelt upon their peculiarities. I pondered upon their conformation. I mused upon the alteration in their nature. I shuddered as I assigned to them, in imagination, a sensitive and sentient power, and, even when unassisted by the lips, a capability of moral expression. Of Mademoiselle Salle it has been well said: *'Que tous ses pas étaient des sentiments,'* and of Berenice I more seriously believed *que tous ses dents étaient des idées. Des idées!* — ah, here was the idiotic thought that destroyed me! *Des idées!* — ah, *therefore* it was that I coveted them so madly! I felt that their possession could alone ever restore me to peace, in giving me back to reason.

And the evening closed in upon me thus — and then the darkness came, and tarried, and went — and the day again dawned — and the mists of a second night were now gathering around — and still I sat motionless in that solitary room — and still I sat buried in meditation — and still the *phantasma* of the teeth maintained its terrible ascendancy, as, with the most vivid and hideous distinctness, it floated about amid the changing lights and shadows of the chamber. At length there broke in upon my dreams a cry as of horror and dismay; and thereunto, after a pause, succeeded the sound of troubled voices, intermingled with many low moanings of sorrow or of pain. I arose from my seat, and throwing open one of the doors of the library, saw standing out in the antechamber a servant maiden, all in tears, who told me that Berenice was — no more! She had been seized with epilepsy in the early morning, and now, at the closing in of the night, the grave was ready for its tenant, and all the preparations for the burial were completed.

I found myself sitting in the library, and again sitting there alone. It seemed to me that I had newly awakened from a confused and exciting dream. I knew that it was now midnight, and I was well aware, that since the setting of the sun, Berenice had been interred. But of that dreary period which intervened I had no positive, at least no definite, comprehension. Yet its memory was replete with horror — horror more horrible from being vague, and terror more terrible from ambiguity. It was a fearful page in the record of my existence, written all over with dim, and hideous, and unintelligible recollections. I strived to decipher them, but in vain; while ever and anon, like the spirit of a departed sound, the shrill and piercing shriek of a female voice seemed to be ringing in my ears. I had done a deed — what was it? I asked myself the question aloud, and the whispering echoes of the chamber answered me — *'What was it?'*

On the table beside me burned a lamp, and near it lay a little box. It was of no remarkable character, and I had seen in frequently before, for it was the property of the family physician; but how came it *there*, upon my table, and why did I shudder in regarding it? These things were in no manner to

[1] For as Jove, during the winter season, gives twice seven days of warmth, men have called this clement and temperate time the nurse of the beautiful Halcyon. — *Simonides.*

be accounted for, and my eyes at length dropped to the open pages of a book, and to a sentence underscored therein. The words were the singular but simple ones of the poet Ebn Zaiat: — *'Dicebant mihi sodales si sepulchrum amicæ visitarem, curas meas aliquantulum fore levatas.'* Why, then, as I perused them, did the hairs of my head erect themselves on end, and the blood of my body become congealed within my veins?

There came a light tap at the library door — and, pale as the tenant of a tomb, a menial entered upon tiptoe. His looks were wild with terror, and he spoke to me in a voice tremulous, husky, and very low. What said he? — some broken sentences I heard. He told of a wild cry disturbing the silence of the night — of the gathering together of the household — of a search in the direction of the sound; and then his tones grew thrillingly distinct as he whispered to me of a violated grave — of a disfigured body enshrouded, yet still breathing — still palpitating — *still alive!*

He pointed to my garments; they were muddy and clotted with gore. I spoke not, and he took me gently by the hand: it was indented with the impress of human nails. He directed my attention to some object against the wall. I looked at it for some minutes: it was a spade. With a shriek I bounded to the table, and grasped the box that lay upon it. But I could not force it open; and, in my tremor, it slipped from my hands, and fell heavily, and burst into pieces; and from it, with a rattling sound, there rolled out some instruments of dental surgery, intermingled with thirty-two small, white, and ivory-looking substances that were scattered to and fro about the floor.

THE FALL
OF THE HOUSE OF USHER

Son coeur est un luth suspendu;
Sitôt qu'on le touche il résonne.
— De Béranger

DURING the whole of a dull, dark, and soundless day in the autumn of the year, when the clouds hung oppressively low in the heavens, I had been passing alone, on horseback, through a singularly dreary tract of country, and at length found myself, as the shades of the evening drew on, within view of the melancholy House of Usher. I know not how it was — but, with the first glimpse of the building, a sense of insufferable gloom pervaded my spirit. I say insufferable; for the feeling was unrelieved by any of that half-pleasurable, because poetic, sentiment with which the mind usually receives even the sternest natural images of the desolate or terrible. I looked upon the scene before me — upon the mere house, and the simple landscape features of the domain — upon the bleak walls — upon the vacant eye-like windows — upon a few rank sedges — and upon a few white trunks of decayed trees — with an utter depression of soul which I can compare to no earthly sensation more properly than to the after-dream of the reveller upon opium — the bitter lapse into every-day life — the hideous dropping off of the veil. There was an iciness, a sinking, a sickening of the heart — an unredeemed dreariness of thought which no goading of the imagination could torture into aught of the sublime. What was it — I paused to think — what was it that so unnerved me in the contemplation of the House of Usher? It was a mystery all insoluble; nor could I grapple with the shadowy fancies that crowded upon me as I pondered. I was forced to fall back upon the unsatisfactory conclusion, that while, beyond doubt, there *are* combinations of very simple natural objects which have the power of thus affecting us, still the analysis of this power lies among considerations beyond our depth. It was possible, I reflected, that a mere different arrangement of the particulars of the scene, of the details of the picture, would be sufficient to modify, or perhaps to annihilate its capacity for sorrowful impression; and, acting upon this idea, I reined my horse to the precipitous brink of a black and lurid tarn that lay in unruffled lustre by the dwelling, and gazed down — but with a shudder even more thrilling than before — upon the remodelled and inverted images of the gray sedge, and the ghastly tree-stems, and the vacant and eye-like windows.

Nevertheless, in this mansion of gloom I now proposed to myself a sojourn of some weeks. Its proprietor, Roderick Usher, had been one of my boon companions in boyhood; but many years had elapsed since our last meeting. A letter, however, had lately reached me in a distant part of the country — a letter from him — which, in its wildly importunate nature, had admitted of no other than a personal reply. The MS gave evidence of nervous agitation. The writer spoke of acute bodily illness — of a mental disorder which oppressed him — and of an earnest desire to see me, as his best and indeed his only personal friend, with a view of attempting, by the cheerfulness of my society, some alleviation of his malady. It was the manner in which all this, and much more, was said — it was the apparent *heart* that went with his request — which allowed me no room for hesitation; and I accordingly obeyed forthwith what I still considered a very singular summons.

Although, as boys, we had been even intimate associates, yet I really knew little of my friend. His reserve had been always excessive and habitual. I was aware, however, that his very ancient family had been noted, time out of mind, for a peculiar sensibility of temperament, displaying itself through long ages, in many works of exalted art, and manifested, of late, in repeated deeds of munificent yet unobtrusive charity, as well as in a passionate devotion to the intricacies, perhaps even more than to the orthodox and easily recognisable beauties, of musical science. I had learned, too, the very remarkable fact, that the stem of the Usher race, all time-honoured as it was, had put forth, at no period, any enduring branch; in other words, that the entire family lay in the direct line of descent, and had always, with very trifling and very temporary variation, so lain. It was this deficiency, I considered, while running over in thought the perfect keeping of the character of the premises with the accredited character of the people, and while speculating upon the possible influence which the one, in the long lapse of centuries, might have exercised upon the other — it was this deficiency, perhaps, of collateral issue, and the consequent undeviating transmission, from sire to son, of the patrimony with the name, which had, at length, so identified the two as to merge the original title of the estate in the quaint and equivocal appellation of the 'House of Usher' — an appellation which seemed to include, in the minds of the peasantry who used it, both the family and the family mansion.

I have said that the sole effect of my somewhat childish experiment — that of looking down within the tarn — had been

to deepen the first singular impression. There can be no doubt that the consciousness of the rapid increase of my superstition—for why should I not so term it?—served mainly to accelerate the increase itself. Such, I have long known, is the paradoxical law of all sentiments having terror as a basis. And it might have been for this reason only, that, when I again uplifted my eyes to the house itself, from its image in the pool, there grew in my mind a strange fancy—a fancy so ridiculous, indeed, that I but mention it to show the vivid force of the sensations which oppressed me. I had so worked upon my imagination as really to believe that about the whole mansion and domain there hung an atmosphere peculiar to themselves and their immediate vicinity—an atmosphere which had no affinity with the air of heaven, but which had reeked up from the decayed trees, and the gray wall, and the silent tarn—a pestilent and mystic vapor, dull, sluggish, faintly discernible, and leaden-hued.

Shaking off from my spirit what *must* have been a dream, I scanned more narrowly the real aspect of the building. Its principal feature seemed to be that of an excessive antiquity. The discoloration of ages had been great. Minute fungi overspread the whole exterior, hanging in a fine tangled web-work from the eaves. Yet all this was apart from any extraordinary dilapidation. No portion of the masonry had fallen; and there appeared to be a wild inconsistency between its still perfect adaptation of parts, and the crumbling condition of the individual stones. In this there was much that reminded me of the specious totality of old wood-work which has rotted for long years in some neglected vault, with no disturbance from the breath of the external air. Beyond this indication of extensive decay, however, the fabric gave little token of instability. Perhaps the eye of a scrutinizing observer might have discovered a barely perceptible fissure, which, extending from the roof of the building in front, made its way down the wall in a zigzag direction, until it became lost in the sullen waters of the tarn.

Noticing these things, I rode over a short causeway to the house. A servant in waiting took my horse, and I entered the Gothic archway of the hall. A valet, of stealthy step, thence conducted me, in silence, through many dark and intricate passages in my progress to the *studio* of his master. Much that I encountered on the way contributed, I know not how, to heighten the vague sentiments of which I have already spoken. While the objects around me—while the carvings of the ceilings, the sombre tapestries of the walls, the ebon blackness of the floors, and the phantasmagoric armorial trophies which rattled as I strode, were but matters to which, or to such as which, I had been accustomed from my infancy—while I hesitated not to acknowledge how familiar was all this—I still wondered to find how unfamiliar were the fancies which ordinary images were stirring up. On one of the staircases, I met

the physician of the family. His countenance, I thought, wore a mingled expression of low cunning and perplexity. He accosted me with trepidation and passed on. The valet now threw open a door and ushered me into the presence of his master.

The room in which I found myself was very large and lofty. The windows were long, narrow, and pointed, and at so vast a distance from the black oaken floor as to be altogether inaccessible from within. Feeble gleams of encrimsoned light made their way through the trellissed panes, and served to render sufficiently distinct the more prominent objects around; the eye, however, struggled in vain to reach the remoter angles of the chamber, or the recesses of the vaulted and fretted ceiling. Dark draperies hung upon the walls. The general furniture was profuse, comfortless, antique, and tattered. Many books and musical instruments lay scattered about, but failed to give any vitality to the scene. I felt that I breathed an atmosphere of sorrow. An air of stern, deep, and irredeemable gloom hung over and pervaded all.

Upon my entrance, Usher rose from a sofa on which he had been lying at full length, and greeted me with a vivacious warmth which had much in it, I at first thought, of an overdone cordiality—of the constrained effort of the *ennuyé* man of the world. A glance, however, at his countenance convinced me of his perfect sincerity. We sat down; and for some moments, while he spoke not, I gazed upon him with a feeling half of pity half of awe. Surely, man had never before so terribly altered, in so brief a period, as had Roderick Usher! It was with difficulty that I could bring myself to admit the identity of the wan being before me with the companion of my early boyhood. Yet the character of his face had been at all times remarkable. A cadaverousness of complexion; an eye large, liquid, and luminous beyond comparison; lips somewhat thin and very pallid but of a surpassingly beautiful curve; a nose of a delicate Hebrew model, but with a breadth of nostril unusual in similar formations; a finely moulded chin, speaking, in its want of prominence, of a want of moral energy; hair of a more than web-like softness and tenuity;—these features, with an inordinate expansion above the regions of the temple, made up altogether a countenance not easily to be forgotten. And now in the mere exaggeration of the prevailing character of these features, and of the expression they were wont to convey, lay so much of change that I doubted to whom I spoke. The now ghastly pallor of the skin, and the now miraculous lustre of the eye, above all things startled and even awed me. The silken hair, too, had been suffered to grow all unheeded, and as, in its wild gossamer texture, it floated rather than fell about the face, I could not, even with effort, connect its Arabesque expression with any idea of simple humanity.

In the manner of my friend I was at once struck with an incoherence—an inconsistency; and I soon found this to arise from a series of feeble and futile struggles to overcome an habitual trepidancy—an excessive nervous agitation. For something of this nature I had indeed been prepared, no less by his letter, than by reminiscences of certain boyish traits, and by conclusions deduced from his peculiar physical confirmation and temperament. His action was alternately vivacious and sullen. His voice varied rapidly from a tremulous indecision (when the animal spirits seemed utterly in abeyance) to that species of energetic concision—that abrupt, weighty, unhurried, and hollow-sounding enunciation—that leaden, self-balanced, and perfectly modulated guttural utterance, which may be observed in the lost drunkard, or the irreclaimable eater of opium, during the periods of his most intense excitement.

It was thus he spoke of the object of my visit, of his earnest desire to see me, and of the solace he expected me to afford him. He entered, at some length, into what he conceived to be the nature of his malady. It was, he said, a constitutional and a family evil, and one for which he despaired to find a remedy—a mere nervous affection, he immediately added, which would undoubtedly soon pass off. It displayed itself in a host of unnatural sensations. Some of these, as he detailed them, interested and bewildered me; although, perhaps, the terms and the general manner of their narration had their weight. He suffered much from a morbid acuteness of the senses; the most insipid food was alone endurable; he could wear only garments of certain texture; the odors of all flowers were oppressive; his eyes were tortured by even a faint light; and there were but peculiar sounds, and these from stringed instruments, which did not inspire him with horror.

To an anomalous species of terror I found him a bounden slave. 'I shall perish,' said he, 'I *must* perish in this deplorable folly. Thus, thus, and not otherwise, shall I be lost. I dread the events of the future, not in themselves, but in their results. I shudder at the thought of any, even the most trivial, incident, which may operate upon this intolerable agitation of soul. I have, indeed, no abhorrence of danger, except in its absolute effect—in terror. In this unnerved, in this pitiable, condition I feel that the period will sooner or later arrive when I must abandon life and reason together, in some struggle with the grim phantasm, FEAR.'

I learned, moreover, at intervals, and through broken and equivocal hints, another singular feature of his mental condition. He was enchained by certain superstitious impressions in regard to the dwelling which he tenanted, and whence, for many years, he had never ventured forth—in regard to an influence whose suppositious force was conveyed in terms too shadowy here to be re-stated—an influence which some peculiarities in the mere form and substance of his family mansion had, by dint of long sufferance, he said, obtained over his spirit—an effect which the *physique* of the gray walls and turrets, and of the dim tarn into which they all looked down, had, at length, brought about upon the *morale* of his existence.

He admitted, however, although with hesitation, that much of the peculiar gloom which thus afflicted him could be traced to a more natural and far more palpable origin—to the severe and long-continued illness—indeed to the evidently approaching dissolution—of a tenderly beloved sister, his sole companion for long years, his last and only relative on earth, 'Her decease,' he said; with a bitterness which I can never forget, 'would leave him (him, the hopeless and the frail) the last of the ancient race of the Ushers.' While he spoke, the lady Madeline (for so was she called) passed through a remote portion of the apartment, and without having noticed my presence, disappeared. I regarded her with an utter astonishment not unmingled with dread; and yet I found it impossible to account for such feelings. A sensation of stupor oppressed me as my eyes followed her retreating steps. When a door, at length, closed upon her, my glance sought instinctively and eagerly the countenance of the brother; but he had buried his face in his hands, and I could only perceive that a far more than ordinary wanness had overspread the emaciated fingers through which trickled many passionate tears.

The disease of the lady Madeline had long baffled the skill of her physicians. A settled apathy, a gradual wasting away of the person, and frequent although transient affections of a partially cataleptical character were the unusual diagnosis. Hitherto she had steadily borne up against the pressure of her malady, and had not betaken herself finally to bed; but on the closing in of the evening of my arrival at the house, she succumbed (as her brother told me at night with inexpressible agitation) to the prostrating power of the destroyer; and I learned that the glimpse I had obtained of her person would thus probably be the last I should obtain—that the lady, at least while living, would be seen by me no more.

For several days ensuing, her name was unmentioned by either Usher or myself; and during this period I was busied in earnest endeavors to alleviate the melancholy of my friend. We painted and read together, or I listened, as if in a dream, to the wild improvisations of his speaking guitar. And thus, as a closer and still closer intimacy admitted me more unreservedly into the recesses of his spirit, the more bitterly did I perceive the futility of all attempt at cheering a mind from which darkness, as if an inherent positive quality, poured forth upon all objects of the moral and physical universe in one unceasing radiation of gloom.

I shall ever bear about me a memory of the many solemn hours I thus spent alone with the master of the House of Usher. Yet I should fail in any attempt to convey an idea of the exact character of the studies, or of the occupations, in which he involved me, or led me the way. An excited and highly distem-

pered ideality threw a sulphureous lustre over all. His long improvised dirges will ring forever in my ears. Among other things, I hold painfully in mind a certain singular perversion and amplification of the wild air of the last waltz of Von Weber. From the paintings over which his elaborate fancy brooded, and which grew, touch by touch, into vaguenesses at which I shuddered the more thrillingly, because I shuddered knowing not why—from these paintings (vivid as their images now are before me) I would in vain endeavor to educe more than a small portion which should lie within the compass of merely written words. By the utter simplicity, by the nakedness of his designs, he arrested and overawed attention. If ever mortal painted an idea, that mortal was Roderick Usher. For me at least, in the circumstances then surrounding me, there arose out of the pure abstractions which the hypochondriac contrived to throw upon his canvas, an intensity of intolerable awe, no shadow of which felt I ever yet in the contemplation of the certainly glowing yet too concrete reveries of Fuseli.

One of the phantasmagoric conceptions of my friend, partaking not so rigidly of the spirit of abstraction, may be shadowed forth, although feebly, in words. A small picture presented the interior of an immensely long and rectangular vault or tunnel, with low walls, smooth, white, and without interruption or device. Certain accessory points of the design served well to convey the idea that this excavation lay at an exceeding depth below the surface of the earth. No outlet was observed in any portion of its vast extent, and no torch or other artificial source of light was discernible; yet a flood of intense rays rolled throughout, and bathed the whole in a ghastly and inappropriate splendour.

I have just spoken of that morbid condition of the auditory nerve which rendered all music intolerable to the sufferer, with the exception of certain effects of stringed instruments. It was, perhaps, the narrow limits to which he thus confined himself upon the guitar which gave birth, in great measure, to the fantastic character of his performances. But the fervid *facility* of his *impromptus* could not be so accounted for. They must have been, and were, in the notes, as well as in the words of his wild fantasias (for he not unfrequently accompanied himself with rhymed verbal improvisations), the result of that intense mental collectedness and concentration to which I have previously alluded as observable only in particular moments of the highest artificial excitement. The words of one of these rhapsodies I have easily remembered. I was, perhaps, the more forcibly impressed with it as he gave it, because, in the under or mystic current of its meaning, I fancied that I perceived, and for the first time, a full consciousness on the part of Usher of the tottering of his lofty reason upon her throne. The verses, which were entitled 'The Haunted Palace,' ran very nearly, if not accurately, thus:-

I

In the greenest of our valleys,
   By good angels tenanted,
Once a fair and stately palace—
   Radiant palace—reared its head.
In the monarch Thought's dominion—
   It stood there!
Never seraph spread a pinion
   Over fabric half so fair.

II

Banners yellow, glorious, golden,
   On its roof did float and flow
(This—all this—was in the olden
   Time long ago);
And every gentle air that dallied,
   In that sweet day,
Along the ramparts plumed and pallid,
   A winged odor went away.

III

Wanderers in that happy valley
   Through two luminous windows saw
Spirits moving musically
   To a lute's well-tuned law;
Round about a throne, where sitting
   (Porphyrogene!)
In state his glory well befitting,
   The ruler of the realm was seen.

IV

And all with pearl and ruby glowing
   Was the fair palace door,
Through which came flowing, flowing, flowing
   And sparkling evermore,
A troop of Echoes whose sweet duty
   Was but to sing,
In voices of surpassing beauty,
   The wit and wisdom of their king.

V

But evil things, in robes of sorrow,
   Assailed the monarch's high estate;
(Ah, let us mourn, for never morrow
   Shall dawn upon him, desolate!)
And, round about his home, the glory
   That blushed and bloomed
Is but a dim-remembered story
   Of the old time entombed.

VI

And travellers now within that valley,
*   Through the red-litten windows see*
Vast forms that move fantastically
*   To a discordant melody;*
While, like a rapid ghastly river,
*   Through the pale door;*
A hideous throng rush out forever,
*   And laugh—but smile no more.*

I well remember that suggestions arising from this ballad led us into a train of thought wherein there became manifest an opinion of Usher's which I mention not so much on account of its novelty (for other men[1] have thought thus), as on account of the pertinacity with which he maintained it. This opinion, in its general form, was that of the sentience of all vegetable things. But, in his disordered fancy, the idea had assumed a more daring character, and trespassed, under certain conditions, upon the kingdom of inorganization. I lack words to express the full extent, or the earnest *abandon* of his persuasion. The belief, however, was connected (as I have previously hinted) with the gray stones of the home of his forefathers. The conditions of the sentence had been here, he imagined, fulfilled in the method of collocation of these stones—in the order of their arrangement, as well as in that of the many *fungi* which overspread them, and of the decayed trees which stood around—above all, in the long undisturbed endurance of this arrangement, and in its reduplication in the still waters of the tarn. Its evidence—the evidence of the sentience—was to be seen, he said (and I here started as he spoke), in the gradual yet certain condensation of an atmosphere of their own about the waters and the walls. The result was discoverable, he added, in that silent yet importunate and terrible influence which for centuries had moulded the destinies of his family, and which made *him* what I now saw him—what he was. Such opinions need no comment, and I will make none.

Our books—the books which, for years, had formed no small portion of the mental existence of the invalid—were, as might be supposed, in strict keeping with this character of phantasm. We pored together over such works as the *Ververt et Chartreuse* of Gresset; the *Belphegor* of Machiavelli; the *Heaven and Hell* of Swedenborg; the *Subterranean Voyage of Nicholas Klimm* of Holberg; the *Chiromancy* of Robert Flud, of Jean D'Indaginé, and of Dela Chambre; the *Journey into the Blue Distance of Tieck*; and the *City of the Sun of Campanella*. One favorite volume was a small octavo edition of the *Directorium Inquisitorium*, by the Dominican Eymeric de Gironne; and there were passages in Pomponius Mela, about the old

African Satyrs and Œgipans, over which Usher would sit dreaming for hours. His chief delight, however, was found in the perusal of an exceedingly rare and curious book in quarto Gothic—the manual of a forgotten church—the *Vigiliæ Mortuorum secundum Chorum Ecclesiæ Maguntinæ*.

I could not help thinking of the wild ritual of this work, and of its probable influence upon the hypochondriac, when, one evening, having informed me abruptly that the lady Madeline was no more, he stated his intention of preserving her corpse for a fortnight (previously to its final interment), in one of the numerous vaults within the main walls of the building. The worldly reason, however, assigned for this singular proceeding, was one which I did not feel at liberty to dispute. The brother had been led to his resolution (so he told me) by consideration of the unusual character of the malady of the deceased, of certain obtrusive and eager inquiries on the part of her medical men, and of the remote and exposed situation of the burial-ground of the family. I will not deny that when I called to mind the sinister countenance of the person whom I met upon the staircase, on the day of my arrival at the house, I had no desire to oppose what I regarded as at best but a harmless, and by no means an unnatural, precaution.

At the request of Usher, I personally aided him in the arrangements for the temporary entombment. The body having been encoffined, we two alone bore it to its rest. The vault in which we placed it (and which had been so long unopened that our torches, half smothered in its oppressive atmosphere, gave us little opportunity for investigation) was small, damp, and entirely without means of admission for light; lying, at great depth, immediately beneath that portion of the building in which was my own sleeping apartment. It had been used, apparently, in remote feudal times, for the worst purposes of a donjon-keep, and, in later days, as a place of deposit for powder, or some other highly combustible substance, as a portion of its floor, and the whole interior of a long archway through which we reached it, were carefully sheathed with copper. The door, of massive iron, had been, also, similarly protected. Its immense weight caused an unusually sharp, grating sound, as it moved upon its hinges.

Having deposited our mournful burden upon tressels within this region of horror, we partially turned-aside the yet unscrewed lid of the coffin, and looked upon the face of the tenant. A striking similitude between the brother and sister now first arrested my attention; and Usher, divining, perhaps, my thoughts, murmured out some few words from which I learned that the deceased and himself had been twins, and that sympathies of a scarcely intelligible nature had always existed between them. Our glances, however, rested not long upon the dead—for we could not regard her unawed. The disease which had thus entombed the lady in the maturity of

[1] Watson, Dr Percival, Spallanzani, and especially the Bishop of Landaff.—See *Chemical Essays* vol. v.

youth, had left, as usual in all maladies of a strictly cataleptical character, the mockery of a faint blush upon the bosom and the face, and that suspiciously lingering smile upon the lip which is so terrible in death. We replaced and screwed down the lid, and, having secured the door of iron, made our way, with toil, into the scarcely less gloomy apartments of the upper portion of the house.

And now, some days of bitter grief having elapsed, an observable change came over the features of the mental disorder of my friend. His ordinary occupations were neglected or forgotten. He roamed from chamber to chamber with hurried, unequal, and objectless step. The pallor of his countenance had assumed, if possible, a more ghastly hue—but the luminousness of his eye had utterly gone out. The once occasional huskiness of his tone was heard no more; and a tremulous quaver, as if of extreme terror, habitually characterized his utterance. There were times, indeed, when I thought his unceasingly agitated mind was laboring with some oppressive secret, to divulge which he struggled for the necessary courage. At times, again, I was obliged to resolve all into the mere inexplicable vagaries of madness, for I beheld him gazing upon vacancy for long hours, in an attitude of the profoundest attention, as if listening to some imaginary sound. It was no wonder that his condition terrified—that it infected me. I felt creeping upon me, by slow yet certain degrees, the wild influences of his own fantastic yet impressive superstitions.

It was, especially, upon retiring to bed late in the night of the seventh or eighth day after the placing of the lady Madeline within the donjon, that I experienced the full power of such feelings. Sleep came not near my couch—while the hours waned and waned away. I struggled to reason off the nervousness which had dominion over me. I endeavored to believe that much, if not all of what I felt, was due to the bewildering influence of the gloomy furniture of the room—of the dark and tattered draperies, which, tortured into motion by the breath of a rising tempest, swayed fitfully to and fro upon the walls, and rustled uneasily about the decorations of the bed. But my efforts were fruitless. An irrepressible tremor gradually pervaded my frame; and, at length, there sat upon my very heart an incubus of utterly causeless alarm. Shaking this off with a gasp and a struggle, I uplifted myself upon the pillows, and, peering earnestly within the intense darkness of the chamber, hearkened—I know not why, except that an instinctive spirit prompted me—to certain low and indefinite sounds which came, through the pauses of the storm, at long intervals, I knew not whence. Overpowered by an intense sentiment of horror, unaccountable yet unendurable, I threw on my clothes with haste (for I felt that I should sleep no more during the night), and endeavored to arouse myself from the pitiable condition into which I had fallen, by pacing rapidly to and fro through the apartment.

I had taken but few turns in this manner, when a light step on an adjoining staircase arrested my attention. I presently recognized it as that of Usher. In an instant afterward he rapped, with a gentle touch, at my door, and entered, bearing a lamp. His countenance was, as usual, cadaverously wan—but, moreover, there was a species of mad hilarity in his eyes—an evidently restrained *hysteria* in his whole demeanor. His air appalled me—but any thing was preferable to the solitude which I had so long endured, and I even welcomed his presence as a relief.

'And you have not seen it?' he said abruptly, after having stared about him for some moments in silence—'you have not then seen it?—but, stay! you shall.' Thus speaking, and having carefully shaded his lamp, he hurried to one of the casements, and threw it freely open to the storm.

The impetuous fury of the entering gust nearly lifted us from our feet. It was, indeed, a tempestuous yet sternly beautiful night, and one wildly singular in its terror and its beauty. A whirlwind had apparently collected its force in our vicinity; for there were frequent and violent alterations in the direction of the wind; and the exceeding density of the clouds (which hung so low as to press upon the turrets of the house) did not prevent our perceiving the life-like velocity with which they flew careering from all points against each other, without passing away into the distance. I say that even their exceeding density did not prevent our perceiving this—yet we had no glimpse of the moon or stars, nor was there any flashing forth of the lightning. But the under surfaces of the huge masses of agitated vapor, as well as all terrestrial objects immediately around us, were glowing in the unnatural light of a faintly luminous and distinctly visible gaseous exhalation which hung about and enshrouded the mansion.

'You must not—you shall not behold this!' said I, shuddering, to Usher, as I led him, with a gentle violence, from the window to a seat. 'These appearances, which bewilder you, are merely electrical phenomena not uncommon—or it may be that they have their ghastly origin in the rank miasma of the tarn. Let us close this casement;—the air is chilling and dangerous to your frame. Here is one of your favorite romances. I will read, and you shall listen:—and so we will pass away this terrible night together.'

The antique volume which I had taken up was the *Mad Trist* of Sir Launcelot Canning; but I had called it a favorite of Usher's more in sad jest than in earnest; for, in truth, there is little in its uncouth and unimaginative prolixity which could have had interest for the lofty and spiritual ideality of my friend. It was, however, the only book immediately at hand; and I indulged a vague hope that the excitement which now agitated the hypochondriac, might find relief (for the history of mental disorder is full of similar anomalies) even in the extremeness of the folly which I should read. Could I have judged, indeed, by the wild overstrained air of vivacity with which he hearkened, or apparently hearkened, to the words of the tale, I might well have congratulated myself upon the success of my design.

I had arrived at that well-known portion of the story where Ethelred, the hero of the Trist, having sought in vain for peaceable admission into the dwelling of the hermit, proceeds to make good an entrance by force. Here, it will be remembered, the words of the narrative run thus:

'And Ethelred, who was by nature of a doughty heart, and who was now mighty withal, on account of the powerfulness of the wine which he had drunken, waited no longer to hold parley with the hermit, who, in sooth, was of an obstinate and maliceful turn, but, feeling the rain upon his shoulders, and fearing the rising of the tempest, uplifted his mace outright, and, with blows, made quickly room in the plankings of the door for his gauntleted hand; and now pulling therewith sturdily, he so cracked, and ripped, and tore all asunder, that the noise of the dry and hollow-sounding wood alarumed and reverberated throughout the forest.'

At the termination of this sentence I started and for a moment, paused; for it appeared to me (although I at once concluded that my excited fancy had deceived me) — it appeared to me that, from some very remote portion of the mansion, there came, indistinctly to my ears, what might have been, in its exact similarity of character, the echo (but a stifled and dull one certainly) of the very cracking and ripping sound which Sir Launcelot had so particularly described. It was, beyond doubt, the coincidence alone which had arrested my attention; for, amid the rattling of the sashes of the casements, and the ordinary commingled noises of the still increasing storm, the sound, in itself, had nothing, surely, which should have interested or disturbed me. I continued the story:

'But the good champion Ethelred, now entering within the door, was sore enraged and amazed to perceive no signal of the maliceful hermit; but, in the stead thereof, a dragon of a scaly and prodigious demeanor, and of a fiery tongue, which sate in guard before a palace of gold, with a floor of silver; and upon the wall there hung a shield of shining brass with this legend enwritten —

Who entereth herein, a conqueror hath bin;
Who slayeth the dragon, the shield he shall win.

And Ethelred uplifted his mace, and struck upon the head of the dragon, which fell before him, and gave up his pesty breath, with a shriek so horrid and harsh, and withal so piercing, that Ethelred had fain to close his ears with his hands against the dreadful noise of it, the like whereof was never before heard.'

Here again I paused abruptly, and now with a feeling of wild amazement — for there could be no doubt whatever that, in this instance, I did actually hear (although from what direction it proceeded I found it impossible to say) a low and apparently distant, but harsh, protracted, and most unusual screaming or grating sound — the exact counterpart of what my fancy had already conjured up for the dragon's unnatural shriek as described by the romancer.

Oppressed, as I certainly was, upon the occurrence of this second and most extraordinary coincidence, by a thousand conflicting sensations, in which wonder and extreme terror were predominant, I still retained sufficient presence of mind to avoid exciting, by any observation, the sensitive nervousness of my companion. I was by no means certain that he had noticed the sounds in question; although, assuredly, a strange alteration had, during the last few minutes, taken place in his demeanor. From a position fronting my own, he had gradually brought round his chair, so as to sit with his face to the door of the chamber; and thus I could but partially perceive his features, although I saw that his lips trembled as if he were murmuring inaudibly. His head had dropped upon his breast — yet I knew that he was not asleep, from the wide and rigid opening of the eye as I caught a glance of it in profile. The motion of his body, too, was at variance with this idea — for he rocked from side to side with a gentle yet constant and uniform sway. Having rapidly taken notice of all this, I resumed the narrative of Sir Launcelot, which thus proceeded:

'And now, the champion, having escaped from the terrible fury of the dragon, bethinking himself of the brazen shield, and of the breaking up of the enchantment which was upon it, removed the carcass from out of the way before him, and approached valorously over the silver pavement of the castle to where the shield was upon the wall; which in sooth tarried not for his full coming, but fell down at his feet upon the silver floor, with a mighty great and terrible ringing sound.'

No sooner had these syllables passed my lips, than — as if a shield of brass had indeed, at the moment, fallen heavily upon a floor of silver — I became aware of a distinct, hollow, metallic, and clangorous, yet apparently muffled, reverberation. Completely unnerved, I leaped to my feet; but the measured rocking movement of Usher was undisturbed. I rushed to the chair in which he sat. His eyes were bent fixedly before him, and throughout his whole countenance there reigned a stony rigidity. But, as I placed my hand upon his shoulder, there came a strong shudder over his whole person; a sickly smile quivered about his lips; and I saw that he spoke in a low, hurried, and gibbering murmur, as if unconscious of my presence. Bending closely over him, I at length drank in the hideous import of his words.

'Now hear it? — yes, I hear it, and *have* heard it. Long — long — long — many minutes, many hours, many days, have I

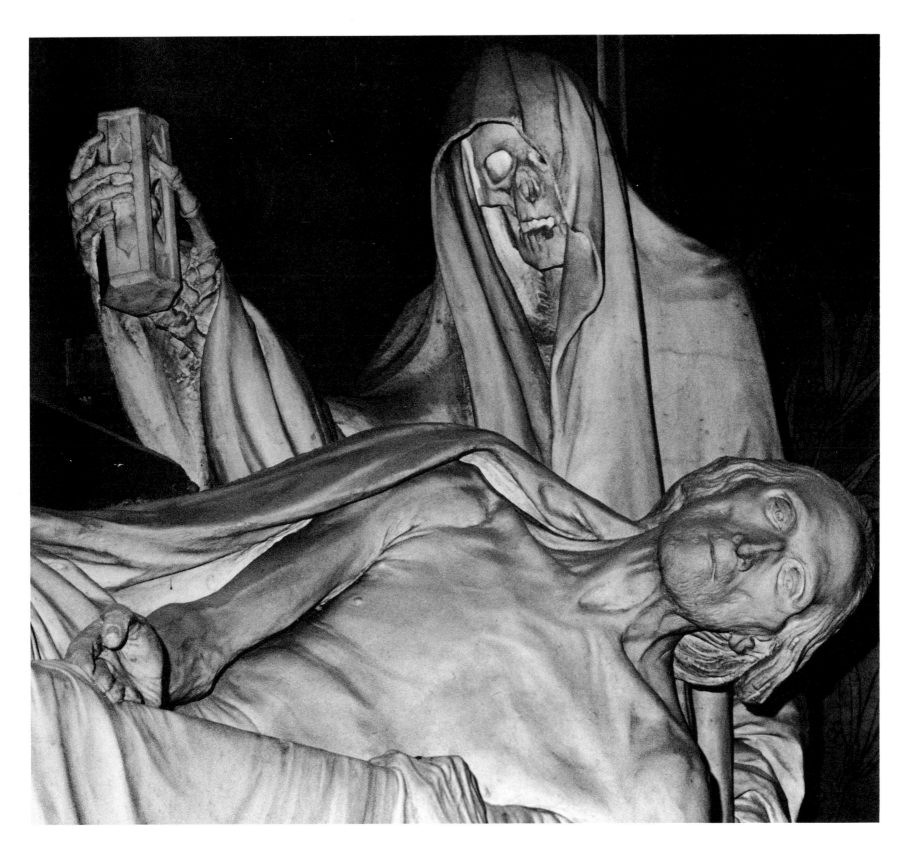

heard it—yet I dared not—oh, pity me, miserable wretch that I am!—I dared not—I *dared* not speak! *We have put her living in the tomb!* Said I not that my senses were acute? I *now* tell you that I heard her first feeble movements in the hollow coffin. I heard them—many, many days ago—yet I dared not—*I dared not speak!* And now—tonight—Ethelred—ha! ha!—the breaking of the hermit's door, and the death-cry of the dragon, and the clangor of the shield—say, rather, the rending of her coffin, and the grating of the iron hinges of her prison, and her struggles within the coppered archway of the vault! Oh! whither shall I fly? Will she not be here anon? Is she not hurrying to upbraid me for my haste? Have I not heard her footstep on the stair? Do I not distinguish that heavy and horrible beating of her heart? Madman!'—here he sprang furiously to his feet, and shrieked out his syllables, as if in the effort he were giving up his soul—'*Madman! I tell you that she now stands without the door!*'

As if in the superhuman energy of his utterance there had been found the potency of a spell, the huge antique panels to which the speaker pointed threw slowly back, upon the instant, their ponderous and ebony jaws. It was the work of the rushing gust—but then without those doors there *did* stand the lofty and enshrouded figure of the lady Madeline of Usher.

There was blood upon her white robes, and the evidence of some bitter struggle upon every portion of her emaciated frame. For a moment she remained trembling and reeling to and fro upon the threshold—then, with a low moaning cry, fell heavily inward upon the person of her brother, and in her violent and now final death-agonies, bore him to the floor a corpse, and a victim to the terrors he had anticipated.

From that chamber, and from that mansion, I fled aghast. The storm was still abroad in all its wrath as I found myself crossing the old causeway. Suddenly there shot along the path a wild light, and I turned to see whence a gleam so unusual could have issued; for the vast house and its shadows were alone behind me. The radiance was that of the full, setting, and blood-red moon, which now shone vividly through that once barely discernible fissure, of which I have before spoken as extending from the roof of the building, in a zigzag direction, to the base. While I gazed, this fissure rapidly widened—there came a fierce breath of the whirlwind—the entire orb of the satellite burst at once upon my sight—my brain reeled as I saw the mighty walls rushing asunder—there was a long tumultuous shouting sound like the voice of a thousand waters—and the deep and dank tarn at my feet closed sullenly and silently over the fragments of the '*House of Usher.*'

THE SPHINX

DURING the dread reign of cholera in New York, I had accepted the invitation of a relative to spend a fortnight with him in the retirement of his *cottage ornée* on the banks of the Hudson. We had here around us all the ordinary means of summer amusement; and what with rambling in the woods, sketching, boating, fishing, bathing, music and books, we should have passed the time pleasantly enough, but for the fearful intelligence which reached us every morning from the populous city. Not a day elapsed which did not bring us news of the decease of some acquaintance. Then, as the fatality increased, we learned to expect daily the loss of some friend. At length we trembled at the approach of every messenger. The very air from the South seemed to us redolent with death. That palsying thought, indeed, took entire possession of my soul. I could neither speak, think, not dream of anything else. My host was of a less excitable temperament, and, although greatly depressed in spirits, exerted himself to sustain my own. His richly philosophical intellect was not at any time affected by unrealities. To the substances of terror he was sufficiently alive, but of its shadows he had no apprehension.

His endeavors to arouse me from the condition of abnormal gloom into which I had fallen, were frustrated, in great measure, by certain volumes which I had found in his library. These were of a character to force into germination whatever seeds of hereditary superstition lay latent in my bosom. I had been reading these books without his knowledge, and thus he was often at a loss to account for the forcible impressions which had been made upon my fancy.

A favourite topic with me was the popular belief in omens — a belief which, at this one epoch of my life, I was almost seriously disposed to defend. On this subject we had long and animated discussions; he maintaining the utter groundlessness of faith in such matters, I contending that a popular sentiment arising with absolute spontaneity — that is to say, without apparent traces of suggestion — had in itself the unmistakable elements of truth, and was entitled to much respect.

The fact is, that soon after my arrival at the cottage there had occurred to myself an incident so entirely inexplicable, and which had in it so much of the portentous character, that I might well have been excused for regarding it as an omen. It appalled, and at the same time so confounded and bewil-dered me, that many days elapsed before I could make up my mind to communicate the circumstance to my friend.

Near the close of an exceedingly warm day, I was sitting, book in hand, at an open window, commanding, through a long vista of the river banks, a view of a distant hill, the face of which nearest my position had been denuded by what is termed a land-slide, of the principal portion of its trees. My thoughts had been long wandering from the volume before me to the gloom and desolation of the neighboring city. Uplifting my eyes from the page, they fell upon the naked face of the hill, and upon an object — upon some living monster of hideous conformation, which very rapidly made its way from the summit to the bottom, disappearing finally in the dense forest below. As this creature first came in sight, I doubted my own sanity — or at least the evidence of my own eyes — and many minutes passed before I succeeded in convincing myself that I was neither mad nor in a dream. Yet when I describe the monster (which I distinctly saw, and calmly surveyed through the whole period of its progress), my readers, I fear, will feel more difficulty in being convinced of these points than even I did myself.

Estimating the size of the creature by comparison with the diameter of the large trees near which it passed — the few giants of the forests which had escaped the fury of the land-slide — I concluded it to be far larger than any ship of the line in existence. I say ship of the line, because the shape of the monster suggested the idea — the hull of one of our seventy-fours might convey a very tolerable conception of the general outline. The mouth of the animal was situated at the extremity of a proboscis some sixty or seventy feet in length, and about as thick as the body of an ordinary elephant. Near the root of this trunk was an immense quantity of black shaggy hair — more than could have been supplied by the coats of a score of buffaloes; and projecting from this hair downwardly and laterally, sprang two gleaming tusks not unlike those of the wild boar, but of infinitely greater dimension. Extending forward, parallel with the proboscis, and on each side of it, was a gigantic staff, thirty or forty feet in length, formed seemingly of pure crystal, and in shape a perfect prism, — it reflected in the most gorgeous manner the rays of the declining sun. The trunk was fashioned like a wedge with the apex to the earth. From it there were outspread two pairs of wings — each wing

nearly one hundred yards in length—one pair being placed above the other, and all thickly covered with metal scales; each scale apparently some ten or twelve feet in diameter. I observed that the upper and lower tiers of wings were connected by a strong chain. But the chief peculiarity of this horrible thing was the representation of a *Death's Head*, which covered nearly the whole surface of its breast, and which was as accurately traced in glaring white, upon the dark ground of the body, as if it had been there carefully designed by an artist. While I regarded this terrific animal, and more especially the appearance on its breast, with a feeling of horror and awe— with a sentiment of forthcoming evil, which I found it impossible to quell by any effort of the reason, I perceived the huge jaws at the extremity of the proboscis suddenly expand themselves, and from them there proceeded a sound so loud and so expressive of woe, that it struck upon my nerves like a knell, and as the monster disappeared at the foot of the hill, I fell at once, fainting, to the floor.

Upon recovering, my first impulse, of course, was to inform my friend of what I had seen and heard—and I can scarcely explain what feeling of repugnance it was which, in the end, operated to prevent me.

At length, one evening, some three or four days after the occurrence, we were sitting together in the room in which I had seen the apparition—I occupying the same seat at the same window, and he lounging on a sofa near at hand. The association of the place and time impelled me to give him an account of the phenomenon. He heard me to the end—at first laughed heartily—and then lapsed into an excessively grave demeanour, as if my insanity was a thing beyond suspicion. At this instant I again had a distinct view of the monster—to which, with a shout of absolute terror, I now directed his attention. He looked eagerly—but maintained that he saw nothing—although I designated minutely the course of the creature, as it made its way down the naked face of the hill.

I was now immeasurably alarmed, for I considered the vision either as an omen of my death, or, worse, as the forerunner of an attack of mania. I threw myself passionately back in my chair, and for some moments buried my face in my hands. When I uncovered my eyes, the apparition was no longer visible.

My host, however, had in some degree resumed the calmness of his demeanour, and questioned me very rigorously in respect to the conformation of the visionary creature. When I had fully satisfied him on this head, he sighed deeply, as if relieved of some intolerable burden, and went on to talk, with what I thought a cruel calmness, of various points of speculative philosophy, which had heretofore formed subject of discussion between us. I remember his insisting very especially (among other things) upon the idea that the principal source of error in all human investigations lay in the liability of the understanding to underrate or to overvalue the importance of an object, through mere misadmeasurement of its propinquity. 'To estimate properly, for example,' he said, 'the influence to be exercised on mankind at large by the thorough diffusion of Democracy, the distance of the epoch at which such diffusion may possibly be accomplished should not fail to form an item in the estimate. Yet can you tell me one writer on the subject of government who has ever thought this particular branch of the subject worthy of discussion at all?'

He here paused for a moment, stepped to a book-case, and brought forth one of the ordinary synopses of Natural History. Requesting me then to exchange seats with him, that he might the better distinguish the fine print of the volume, he took my arm-chair at the window, and, opening the book, resumed his discourse very much in the same tone as before.

'But for your exceeding minuteness,' he said, 'in describing the monster, I might never have had it in my power to demonstrate to you what it was. In the first place, let me read to you a school-boy account of the genus *Sphinx*, of the family *Crepuscularia*, of the order *Lepidoptera*, of the class of *Insecta*— or insects. The account runs thus:

"Four membranous wings covered with little coloured scales of metallic appearance; mouth forming a rolled proboscis, produced by an elongation of the jaws, upon the sides of which are found the rudiments of mandibles and downy palpi; the inferior wings retained to the superior by a stiff hair, antennae in the form of an elongated club, prismatic; abdomen pointed. The Death's-headed Sphinx has occasioned much terror among the vulgar, at times, by the melancholy kind of cry which it utters, and the insignia of death which it wears upon its corslet."'

He here closed the book and leaned forward in the chair, placing himself accurately in the position which I had occupied at the moment of beholding 'the monster.'

'Ah, here it is,' he presently exclaimed—'it is reascending the face of the hill, and a very remarkable looking creature I admit it to be. Still, it is by no means so large or so distant as you imagined it; for the fact is that, as it wriggles its way up this thread, which some spider has wrought along the window-sash, I find it to be about the sixteenth of an inch in its extreme length, and also about the sixteenth of an inch distant from the pupil of my eye.'

ANNABEL LEE

It was many and many a year ago,
　In a kingdom by the sea,
That a maiden there lived whom you may know
　By the name of ANNABEL LEE;
And this maiden she lived with no other thought
　Than to love and be loved by me.

I was a child and *she* was a child,
　In this kingdom by the sea:
But we loved with a love that was more than love—
I and my ANNABEL LEE;
With a love that the winged seraphs of heaven
　Coveted her and me.

And this was the reason that, long ago,
　In this kingdom by the sea,
A wind blew out of a cloud, chilling
　My beautiful ANNABEL LEE;
So that her high-born kinsman came
　And bore her away from me,
To shut her up in a sepulchre
　In this kingdom by the sea.

The angels, not half so happy in heaven,
　Went envying her and me—
Yes!—that was the reason (as all men know,
　In this kingdom by the sea)
That the wind came out of the cloud by night,
　Chilling and killing my ANNABEL LEE.

But our love it was stronger by far than the love
　Of those who were older than we—
　Of many far wiser than we—
And neither the angels in heaven above,
　Nor the demons down under the sea,
Can ever dissever my soul from the soul
　Of the beautiful ANNABEL LEE

For the moon never beams, without bringing me dreams
　Of the beautiful ANNABEL LEE;
And the stars never rise, but I feel the bright eyes
　Of the beautiful ANNABEL LEE;
And so, all the night-tide, I lie down by the side
Of my darling—my darling—my life and my bride,
　In the sepulchre there by the sea,
　In her tomb by the sounding sea.

THE IMP OF THE PERVERSE

IN THE consideration of the faculties and impulses—of the *prima mobilia* of the human soul, the phrenologists have failed to make room for a propensity which, although obviously existing as a radical, primitive, irreducible sentiment, has been equally overlooked by all the moralists who have preceded them. In the pure arrogance of the reason, we have all overlooked it. We have suffered its existence to escape our senses, solely through want of belief—of faith;—whether it be faith in Revelation, or faith in the Kabbala. The idea of it has never occurred to us, simply because of its supererogation. We saw no *need* of the impulse—for the propensity. We could not perceive its necessity. We could not understand, that is to say, we could not have understood, had the notion of this *primum mobile* ever obtruded itself;—we could not have understood in what manner it might be made to further the objects of humanity, either temporal or eternal. It cannot be denied that phrenology and, in great measure, all metaphysicianism have been concocted *a priori*. The intellectual or logical man, rather than the understanding or observant man, set himself to imagine designs—to dictate purposes to God. Having thus fathomed, to his satisfaction, the intentions of Jehovah, out of these intentions he built his innumerable systems of mind. In the matter of phrenology, for example, we first determined, naturally enough, that it was the design of the Deity that man should eat. We then assigned to man an organ of alimentiveness, and this organ is the scourge with which the Deity compels man, will-I nill-I, into eating. Secondly, having settled it to be God's will that man should continue his species, we discovered an organ of amativeness, forthwith. And so with combativeness, with ideality, with causality, with constructiveness,—so, in short, with every organ, whether representing a propensity, a moral sentiment, or a faculty of the pure intellect. And in these arrangements of the *principia* of human action, the Spurzheimites, whether right or wrong, in part, or upon the whole, have but followed, in principle, the footsteps of their predecessors; deducing and establishing every thing from the preconceived destiny of man, and upon the ground of the objects of his Creator.

It would have been wiser, it would have been safer, to classify (if classify we must) upon the basis of what man usually or occasionally did, and was always occasionally doing, rather than upon the basis of what we took it for granted the Deity intended him to do. If we cannot comprehend God in his visible works, how then in his inconceivable thoughts, that call the works into being? If we cannot understand him in his objective creatures, how then in his substantive moods and phases of creation?

Induction, *a posteriori*, would have brought phrenology to admit, as an innate and primitive principle of human action, a paradoxical something, which we may call *perverseness*, for want of a more characteristic term. In the sense I intend, it is, in fact, a *mobile* without motive, a motive not *motiviert*. Through its promptings we act without comprehensible object; or, if this shall be understood as a contradiction in terms, we may so far modify the proposition as to say, that through its promptings we act, for the reason that we should *not*. In theory, no reason can be more unreasonable; but, in fact, there is none more strong. With certain minds, under certain conditions, it becomes absolutely irresistible. I am not more certain that I breathe, than that the assurance of the wrong or error of any action is often the one unconquerable *force* which impels us, and alone impels us to its prosecution. Nor will this overwhelming tendency to do wrong for the wrong's sake, admit of analysis, or resolution into ulterior elements. It is a radical, a primitive impulse—elementary. It will be said, I am aware, that when we persist in acts because we feel we should *not* persist in them, our conduct is but a modification of that which ordinarily springs from the *combativeness* of phrenology. But a glance will show the fallacy of this idea. The phrenological combativeness has for its essence, the necessity of self-defence. It is our safeguard against injury. Its principle regards our well-being; and thus the desire to be well is excited simultaneously with its development. It follows, that the desire to be well must be excited simultaneously with any principle which shall be merely a modification of combativeness, but in the case of that something which I turn *perverseness*, the desire to be well is not only not aroused, but a strongly antagonistical sentiment exists.

An appeal to one's own heart is, after all, the best reply to the sophistry just noticed. No one who trustingly consults and thoroughly questions his own soul, will be disposed to deny the entire radicalness of the propensity in question. It is not more incomprehensible than distinctive. There lives no man

who at some period has not been tormented, for example, by an earnest desire to tantalize a listener by circumlocution. The speaker is aware that he displeases; he has every intention to please; he is usually curt, precise, and clear; the most laconic and luminous language is struggling for utterance upon his tongue; it is only with difficulty that he restrains himself from giving it flow; he dreads and deprecates the anger of him whom he addresses; yet, the thought strikes him, that by certain involutions and parentheses this anger may be engendered. That single thought is enough. The impulse increases to a wish, the wish to a desire, the desire to an uncontrollable longing, and the longing (to the deep regret and mortification of the speaker, and in defiance of all consequences) is indulged.

We have a task before us which must be speedily performed. We know that it will be ruinous to make delay. The most important crisis of our life calls, trumpet-tongued, for immediate energy and action. We glow, we are consumed with eagerness to commence the work, with the anticipation of whose glorious result our whole souls are on fire. It must, it shall be undertaken to-day, and yet we put it off until to-morrow; and why? There is no answer, except that we feel *perverse*, using the word with no comprehension of the principle. To-morrow arrives, and with it a more impatient anxiety to do our duty, but with this very increase of anxiety arrives, also, a nameless, a positively fearful, because unfathomable, craving for delay. This craving gathers strength as the moments fly. The last hour for action is at hand. We tremble with the violence of the conflict within us,—of the definite with the indefinite—of the substance with the shadow. But, if the contest have proceeded thus far, it is the shadow which prevails,—we struggle in vain. The clock strikes, and is the knell of our welfare. At the same time, it is the chanticleer-note to the ghost that has so long overawed us. It flies—it disappears—we are free. The old energy returns. We will labor *now*. Alas, it is *too late!*

We stand upon the brink of a precipice. We peer into the abyss—we grow sick and dizzy. Our first impulse is to shrink from the danger. Unaccountably we remain. By slow degrees our sickness and dizziness and horror become merged in a cloud of unnameable feeling. By gradations, still more imperceptible, this cloud assumes shape, as did the vapour from the bottle out of which arose the genius in the Arabian Nights. But out of this *our* cloud upon the precipice's edge, there grows into palpability, a shape, far more terrible than any genius or any demon of a tale, and yet it is but a thought, although a fearful one, and one which chills the very marrow of our bones with the fierceness of the delight of its horror. It is merely the idea of what would be our sensations during the sweeping precipi-tancy of a fall from such a height. And this fall—this rushing annihilation—for the very reason that it involves that one most ghastly and loathsome of all the most ghastly and loath-

some images of death and suffering which have ever presented themselves to our imagination—for this very cause do we now the most vividly desire it. And because our reason violently deters us from the brink, *therefore* do we the most impetuously approach it. There is no passion in nature so demoniacally impatient, as that of him who, shuddering upon the edge of a precipice, thus meditates a plunge. To indulge, for a moment, in any attempt at *thought*, is to be inevitably lost, for reflection but urges us to forbear, and *therefore* it is, I say, that we *cannot*. If there be no friendly arm to check us, or if we fail in a sudden effort to prostrate ourselves backward from the abyss, we plunge, and are destroyed.

Examine these and similar actions as we will, we shall find them resulting solely from the spirit of the *Perverse*. We perpet-rate them merely because we feel that we should *not*. Beyond or behind this there is no intelligible principle; and we might, indeed, deem this perverseness a direct instigation of the arch-fiend, were it not occasionally known to operate in furtherance of good.

I have said thus much, that in some measure I may answer your question—that I may explain to you why I am here—that I may assign to you something that shall have at least the faint aspect of a cause for my wearing these fetters, and for my tenanting this cell of the condemned. Had I not been thus prolix, you might either have misunderstood me altogether, or, with the rabble, have fancied me mad. As it is, you will easily perceive that I am one of the many uncounted victims of the Imp of the Perverse.

It is impossible that any deed could have been wrought with a more thorough deliberation. For weeks, for months, I pondered upon the means of the murder. I rejected a thousand schemes, because their accomplishment involved a *chance* of detection. At length, in reading some French memoirs, I found an account of a nearly fatal illness that occurred to Madame Pilau, through the agency of a candle accidentally poisoned. The idea struck my fancy at once. I knew my victim's habit of reading in bed. I knew, too, that his apart-ment was narrow and ill-ventilated. But I need not vex you with impertinent details. I need not describe the easy artifices by which I substituted, in his bedroom candle-stand, a wax-light of my own making for the one which I there found. The next morning he was discovered dead in his bed, and the coroner's verdict was—'Death by the visitation of God.'

Having inherited his estate, all went well with me for years. The idea of detection never once entered my brain. Of the remains of the fatal taper I had myself carefully disposed. I had left no shadow of a clew by which it would be possible to convict, or even to suspect, me of the crime. It is inconceiv-able how rich a sentiment of satisfaction arose in my bosom as I reflected upon my absolute security. For a very long period of time I was accustomed to revel in this sentiment. It afforded me more real delight than all the mere wordly advantages accruing from my sin. But there arrived at length an epoch, from which the pleasurable feeling grew, by scarcely perceptible gradations, into a haunting and harassing thought. It harassed because it haunted. I could scarcely get rid of it for an instant. It is quite a common thing to be thus annoyed with the ringing in our ears, or rather in our memories, of the burthen of some ordinary song, or some unimpressive snatches from an opera. Nor will we be the less tormented if the song in itself be good, or the opera air meritorious. In this manner, at last, I would perpetually catch myself pondering upon my security, and repeating, in a low under-tone, the phrase, 'I am safe.'

One day, whilst sauntering along the streets, I arrested myself in the act of murmuring, half aloud, these customary syllables. In a fit of petulance, I re-modelled them thus: 'I am safe—I am safe—yes—if I be not fool enough to make open confession!'

No sooner had I spoken these words, than I felt an icy chill creep to my heart. I had had some experience in these fits of perversity (whose nature I have been at some trouble to explain), and I remembered well that in no instance I had successfully resisted their attacks. And now my own casual self-suggestion, that I might possibly be fool enough to confess the murder of which I had been guilty, confronted me, as if

the very ghost of him whom I had murdered—and beckoned me on to death.

At first, I made an effort to shake off this nightmare of the soul. I walked vigorously—faster—still faster—at length I ran. I felt a maddening desire to shriek aloud. Every succeeding wave of thought overwhelmed me with new terror, for, alas! I well, too well, understood that to *think*, in my situation, was to be lost. I still quickened my pace. I bounded like a madman through the crowded thoroughfares. At length, the populace took the alarm, and pursued me. I felt *then* the consummation of my fate. Could I have torn out my tongue, I would have done it—but a rough voice resounded in my ears—a rougher grasp seized me by the shoulder. I turned—I gasped for breath. For a moment I experienced all the pangs of suffocation; I became blind, and deaf, and giddy; and then some invisible fiend, I thought, struck me with his broad palm upon the back. The long-imprisoned secret burst forth from my soul.

They say that I spoke with a distinct enunciation, but with marked emphasis and passionate hurry, as if in dread of interruption before concluding the brief but pregnant sentences that consigned me to the hangman and to hell.

Having related all that was necessary for the fullest judicial conviction, I fell prostrate in a swoon.

But why shall I say more? To-day I wear these chains, and am *here*! To-morrow I shall be fetterless!—*but where?*

METZENGERSTEIN

Pestis eram vivus — moriens tua mors ero.
— Martin Luther

HORROR and fatality have been stalking abroad in all ages. Why then give a date to the story I have to tell? Let it suffice to say, that at the period of which I speak, there existed, in the interior of Hungary, a settled although hidden belief in the doctrines of the Metempsychosis. Of the doctrines themselves — that is, of their falsity, or of their probability — I say nothing. I assert, however, that much of our incredulity (as La Bruyère says of all our unhappiness) *'vient de ne pouvoir etre seuls.'*[1]

But there were some points in the Hungarian superstition which were fast verging to absurdity. They — the Hungarians — differed very essentially from their Eastern authorities. For example, *'The soul,'* said the former — I give the words of an acute and intelligent Parisian — *'ne demeure qu'une seule fois dans un corps sensible: au reste — un cheval, un chien, un homme même, n'est que la ressemblance peu tangible de ces animaux.'*

The families of Berlifitzing and Metzengerstein had been at variance for centuries. Never before were two houses so illustrious, mutually embittered by hostility so deadly. The origin of this enmity seems to be found in the words of an ancient prophecy — 'A lofty name shall have a fearful fall when, as the rider over his horse, the mortality of Metzengerstein shall triumph over the immortality of Berlifitzing.'

To be sure the words themselves had little or no meaning. But more trivial causes have given rise — and that no long while ago — to consequences equally eventful. Besides, the estates, which were contiguous, had long exercised a rival influence in the affairs of a busy government. Moreover, near neighbours are seldom friends; and the inhabitants of the Castle Berlifitzing might look, from their lofty buttresses, into the very windows of the Palace Metzengerstein. Least of all had the more than feudal magnificence, thus discovered, a tendency to allay the irritable feelings of the less ancient and less wealthy Berlifitzings. What wonder, then, that the words, however silly, of that prediction, should have succeeded in setting and keeping at variance two families already predisposed to quarrel by every instigation of hereditary jealousy? The prophecy seemed to imply — if it implied anything — a final triumph on the part of the already more powerful house; and was of course remembered with the more bitter animosity by the weaker and less influential.

Wilhelm, Count Berlifitzing, although loftily descended, was, at the epoch of this narrative, an infirm and doting old man, remarkable for nothing but an inordinate and inveterate personal antipathy to the family of his rival, and so passionate a love of horses, and of hunting, that neither bodily infirmity, great age, nor mental incapacity, prevented his daily participation in the dangers of the chase.

Frederick, Baron Metzengerstein, was, on the other hand, not yet of age. His father, the Minister G——, died young. His mother, the Lady Mary, followed him quickly. Frederick was, at that time, in his eighteenth year. In a city, eighteen years are no long period; but in a wilderness — in so magnificent a wilderness as that old principality, the pendulum vibrates with a deeper meaning.

From some peculiar circumstances attending the administration of his father, the young Baron, at the decease of the former, entered immediately upon his vast possessions. Such estates were seldom held before by a nobleman of Hungary. His castles were without number. The chief in point of splendour and extent was the 'Palace Metzengerstein.' The boundary line of his dominions was never clearly defined; but his principal park embraced a circuit of fifty miles.

Upon the succession of a proprietor so young, with a character so well known, to a fortune so unparalleled, little speculation was afloat in regard to his probable course of conduct. And, indeed, for the space of three days, the behaviour of the heir out-Heroded Herod, and fairly surpassed the expectations of his most enthusiastic admirers. Shameful debaucheries — flagrant treacheries — unheard-of atrocities — gave his trembling vassals quickly to understand that no servile submission on their part — no punctilios of conscience on his own — were thenceforward to prove any security against the remorseless fangs of a petty Caligula. On the night of the fourth day, the stables of the Castle Berlifitzing were discovered to be on fire; and the unanimous opinion of the neighbourhood added the crime of the incendiary to the already hideous list of the Baron's misdemeanours and enormities.

But during the tumult occasioned by this occurrence, the

[1] Mercier, in *L'an deux mille quatre cents quarante* seriously maintains the doctrines of the Metempsychosis, and J. D'Israeli says that 'no system is so simple and so little repugnant to the understanding.' Colonel Ethan Allen, the 'Green Mountain Boy,' is also said to have been a serious metempsychosist.

young nobleman himself sat apparently buried in meditation, in a vast and desolate upper apartment of the family palace of Metzengerstein. The rich although faded tapestry hangings which swung gloomily upon the walls, represented the shadowy and majestic forms of a thousand illustrious ancestors. *Here*, rich-ermined priests, and pontifical dignitaries, familiarly seated with the autocrat and the sovereign, put a veto on the wishes of a temporal king, or restrained with the fiat of papal supremacy the rebellious sceptre of the Arch-enemy. *There*, the dark, tall statures of the Princes Metzengerstein—their muscular war-coursers plunging over the carcasses of fallen foes—startled the steadiest nerves with their vigorous expression; and *here*, again, the voluptuous and swan-like figures of the dames of days gone by, floated away in the mazes of an unreal dance to the strains of imaginary melody.

But as the Baron listened, or affected to listen, to the gradually increasing uproar in the stables of Berlifitzing—or perhaps pondered upon some more novel, some more decided act of audacity—his eyes were turned unwittingly to the figure of an enormous, and unnaturally coloured horse, represented in the tapestry as belonging to a Saracen ancestor of the family of his rival. The horse itself, in the foreground of the design, stood motionless and statue-like—while, farther back, its discomfited rider perished by the dagger of a Metzengerstein.

On Frederick's lips arose a fiendish expression, as he became aware of the direction which his glance had, without his consciousness, assumed. Yet he did not remove it. On the contrary, he could by no means account for the overwhelming anxiety which appeared falling like a pall upon his senses. It was with difficulty that he reconciled his dreamy and incoherent feelings with the certainty of being awake. The longer he gazed the more absorbing became the spell—the more impossible did it appear that he could ever withdraw his glance from the fascination of that tapestry. But the tumult without becoming suddenly more violent, with a compulsory exertion he diverted his attention to the glare of ruddy light thrown full by the flaming stables upon the windows of the apartment.

The action, however, was but momentary; his gaze returned mechanically to the wall. To his extreme horror and astonishment, the head of the gigantic steed had, in the meantime, altered its position. The neck of the animal, before arched, as if in compassion, over the prostrate body of its lord, was now extended, at full length, in the direction of the Baron. The eyes, before invisible, now wore an energetic and human expression, while they gleamed with a fiery and unusual red; and the distended lips of the apparently enraged horse left in full view his sepulchral and disgusting teeth.

Stupefied with terror, the young nobleman tottered to the door. As he threw it open, a flash of red light, streaming far into the chamber, flung his shadow with a clear outline against the quivering tapestry; and he shuddered to perceive that shadow—as he staggered awhile upon the threshold—assuming the exact position, and precisely filling up the contour, of the relentless and triumphant murderer of the Saracen Berlifitzing.

To lighten the depression of his spirits, the Baron hurried into the open air. At the principal gate of the palace he encountered three equerries. With much difficulty, and at the imminent peril of their lives, they were restraining the convulsive plunges of a gigantic and fiery-coloured horse.

'Whose horse? Where did you get him?' demanded the youth, in a querulous and husky tone, as he became instantly aware that the mysterious steed in the tapestried chamber was the very counterpart of the furious animal before his eyes.

'He is your own property, sire,' replied one of the equerries, 'at least he is claimed by no other owner. We caught him flying, all smoking and foaming with rage, from the burning stables of the Castle Berlifitzing. Supposing him to have belonged to the old Count's stud of foreign horses, we led him back as an estray. But the grooms there disclaim any title to the creature; which is strange, since he bears evident marks of having made a narrow escape from the flames.

'The letters WVB are also branded very distinctly on his forehead,' interrupted a second equerry: 'I supposed them, of course, to be the initials of William Von Berlifitzing—but all at the castle are positive in denying any knowledge of the horse.'

'Extremely singular!' said the young Baron, with a musing air, and apparently unconscious of the meaning of his words. 'He is, as you say, a remarkable horse—a prodigious horse! although, as you very justly observe, of a suspicious and untractable character; let him be mine, however,' he added, after a pause, perhaps a rider like Frederick of Metzengerstein may tame even the devil from the stables of Berlifitzing.'

'You are mistaken, my lord; the horse, as I think we mentioned, is *not* from the stables of the Count. If such had been the case, we know our duty better than to bring him into the presence of a noble of your family.'

'True!' observed the Baron, drily; and at that instant a page of the bed-chamber came from the palace with a heightened colour, and a precipitate step. He whispered into his master's ear an account of the sudden disappearance of a small portion of the tapestry, in an apartment which he designated; entering, at the same time, into particulars of a minute and circumstantial character; but from the low tone of voice in which these latter were communicated, nothing escaped to gratify the excited curiosity of the equerries.

The young Frederick, during the conference, seemed agitated by a variety of emotions. He soon, however, recovered his composure, and an expression of determined malignancy settled upon his countenance, as he gave peremptory orders that the apartment in question should be immediately locked up, and the key placed in his own possession.

'Have you heard of the unhappy death of the old hunter Berlifitzing?' said one of his vassals to the Baron, as, after the departure of the page, the huge steed which that nobleman had adopted as his own, plunged and curveted, with redoubled fury, down the long avenue which extended from the palace to the stables of Metzengerstein.

'No!' said the Baron, turning abruptly toward the speaker, 'dead! say you?'

'It is indeed true, my lord; and, to the noble of your name, will be, I imagine, no unwelcome intelligence.'

A rapid smile shot over the countenance of the listener. 'How died he?'

'In his rash exertions to rescue a favourite portion of the hunting stud, he has himself perished miserably in the flames.'

'I—n—d—e—e—d—!' ejaculated the Baron, as if slowly and deliberately impressed with the truth of some exciting idea.

'Indeed,' repeated the vassal.

'Shocking!' said the youth, calmly, and turned quietly into the palace.

From this date a marked alteration took place in the outward demeanour of the dissolute young Baron Frederick Von Metzengerstein. Indeed, his behaviour disappointed every expectation, and proved little in accordance with the views of many a manœuvring mamma; while his habits and manner, still less than formerly, offered anything congenial with those of the neighbouring aristocracy. He was never to be seen beyond the limits of his own domain, and, in his wide and social world, was utterly companionless—unless, indeed, that unnatural, impetuous, and fiery-coloured horse, which he henceforward continually bestrode, had any mysterious right to the title of his friend.

Numerous invitations on the part of the neighbourhood for a long time, however, periodically came in. 'Will the Baron honor our festivals with his presence?' 'Will the Baron join us in a hunting of the boar?'—'Metzengerstein does not hunt'; 'Metzengerstein will not attend,' were the haughty and laconic answers.

These repeated insults were not to be endured by an imperious nobility. Such invitations became less cordial—less frequent—in time they ceased altogether. The widow of the unfortunate Count Berlifitzing was even heard to express a hope 'that the Baron might be at home when he did not wish to be at home, since he disdained the company of his equals; and ride when he did not wish to ride, since he preferred the society of a horse.' This to be sure was a very silly explosion of hereditary pique; and merely proved how singularly unmeaning our sayings are apt to become, when we desire to be unusually energetic.

The charitable, nevertheless, attributed the alteration in the conduct of the young nobleman to the natural sorrow of a son for the untimely loss of his parents;—forgetting, however, his atrocious and reckless behaviour during the short period immediately succeeding that bereavement. Some there were, indeed, who suggested a too haughty idea of self-consequence and dignity. Others again (among whom may be mentioned the family physician) did not hesitate in speaking of morbid melancholy, and hereditary ill-health; while dark hints, of a more equivocal nature, were current among the multitude.

Indeed, the Baron's perverse attachment to his lately-acquired charger—an attachment which seemed to attain new strength from every fresh example of the animal's ferocious and demon-like propensities—at length became, in the eyes of all reasonable men, a hideous and unnatural fervour. In the glare of noon—at the dead hour of night—in sickness or in health—in calm or in tempest—the young Metzengerstein seemed riveted to the saddle of that colossal horse, whose intractable audacities so well accorded with his own spirit.

There were circumstances, moreover, which, coupled with late events, gave an unearthly and portentous character to the mania of the rider, and to the capabilities of the steed. The space passed over in a single leap had been accurately measured, and was found to exceed, by an astounding difference, the wildest expectations of the most imaginative. The Baron, besides, had no particular *name* for the animal, although all the rest in his collection were distinguished by characteristic appellations. His stable, too, was appointed at a distance from the rest; and with regard to grooming and other necessary offices, none but the owner in person had ventured to officiate, or even to enter the enclosure of that horse's particular stall. It was also to be observed, that although the three grooms, who had caught the steed as he fled from the conflagration at Berlifitzing, had succeeded in arresting his course, by means of a chain-bridle and noose—yet not one of the three could with any certainty affirm that he had, during that dangerous struggle, or at any period thereafter, actually placed his hand upon the body of the beast. Instances of peculiar intelligence in the demeanour of a noble and high-spirited horse are not to be supposed capable of exciting unreasonable attention, but there were certain circumstances which intruded themselves by force upon the most skeptical and phlegmatic; and it is said there were times when the animal caused the gaping crowd who stood around to recoil in horror from the deep and impressive meaning of his terrible stamp—times when the young Metzengerstein turned pale and shrunk away from the rapid and searching expression of his human-looking eye.

Among all the retinue of the Baron, however, none were found to doubt the ardour of that extraordinary affection which existed on the part of the young nobleman for the fiery

qualities of his horse; at least, none but an insignificant and misshapen little page, whose deformities were in everybody's way, and whose opinions were of the least possible importance. He (if his ideas are worth mentioning at all) had the effrontery to assert that his master never vaulted into the saddle without an unaccountable and almost imperceptible shudder; and that, upon his return from every long-continued and habitual ride, an expression of triumphant malignity distorted every muscle in his countenance.

One tempestuous night, Metzengerstein, awaking from a heavy slumber, descended like a maniac from his chamber, and, mounting in hot haste, bounded away into the mazes of the forest. An occurrence so common attracted no particular attention, but his return was looked for with intense anxiety on the part of his domestics, when, after some hours' absence, the stupendous and magnificent battlements of the Palace Metzengerstein, were discovered crackling and rocking to their very foundation, under the influence of a dense and livid mass of ungovernable fire.

As the flames, when first seen, had already made so terrible a progress that all efforts to save any portion of the building were evidently futile, the astonished neighbourhood stood idly around in silent if not pathetic wonder. But a new and fearful object soon riveted the attention of the multitude, and proved how much more intense is the excitement wrought in the feel-ings of a crowd by the contemplation of human agony, than that brought about by the most appalling spectacles of inani-mate matter.

Up the long avenue of aged oaks which led from the forest to the main entrance of the Palace Metzengerstein, a steed, bearing an unbonneted and disordered rider, was seen leaping with an impetuosity which outstripped the very Demon of the Tempest.

The career of the horseman was indisputably, on his own part, uncontrollable. The agony of his countenance, the convulsive struggle of his frame, gave evidence of superhuman exertion: but no sound, save a solitary shriek, escaped from his lacerated lips, which were bitten through and through in the intensity of terror. One instant, and the clattering of hoofs resounded sharply and shrilly above the roaring of the flames and the shrieking of the winds—another, and, clearing at a single plunge the gate-way and the moat, the steed bounded far up the tottering staircases of the palace, and, with its rider, diappeared amid the whirlwind of chaotic fire.

The fury of the tempest immediately died away, and a dead calm sullenly succeeded. A white flame still enveloped the building like a shroud, and, streaming far away into the quiet atmosphere, shot forth a glare of preternatural light; while a cloud of smoke settled heavily over the battlements in the distinct colossal figure of—*a horse.*

THE SLEEPER

At midnight, in the month of June,
I stand beneath the mystic moon.
An opiate vapour, dewy, dim,
Exhales from out her golden rim,
And, softly dripping, drop by drop,
Upon the quiet mountain top,
Steals drowsily and musically
Into the universal valley.
The rosemary nods upon the grave;
The lily lolls upon the wave;
Wrapping the fog about its breast,
The ruin moulders into rest;
Looking like Lethe, see! the lake
A conscious slumber seems to take,
And would not, for the world, awake.
All beauty sleeps! — and lo! where lies
(Her casement open to the skies)
Irene, with her Destinies!

Oh, lady bright! can it be right —
This window open to the night?
The wanton airs, from the tree-top,
Laughingly through the lattice drop —
The bodiless airs, a wizard rout,
Flit through thy chamber in and out,
And wave the curtain canopy
So fitfully — so carefully —
Above the closed and fringed lid
'Neath which thy slumb'ring soul lies hid,
That, o'er the floor and down the wall,
Like ghosts the shadows rise and fall!
Oh, lady dear, hast thou no fear?
Why and what art thou dreaming here?
Sure thou art come o'er far-off seas,
A wonder to these garden trees!

Strange is thy pallor! strange thy dress!
Strange, above all, thy length of tress,
And this all solemn silentness!

The lady sleeps! Oh, may her sleep,
Which is enduring, so be deep!
Heaven have her in its sacred keep!
This chamber changed for one more holy,
This bed for one more melancholy,
I pray to God that she may lie
Forever with unopened eye,
While the dim sheeted ghosts go by!

My love, she sleeps! Oh, may her sleep,
As it is lasting, so be deep!
Soft may the worms about her creep!
Far in the forest, dim and old,
For her may some tall vault unfold —
Some vault that oft hath flung its black
And winged panels fluttering back,
Triumphant, o'er the crested palls,
Of her grand family funerals —
Some sepulchre, remote, alone,
Against whose portal she hath thrown,
In childhood, many an idle stone —
Some tomb from out whose sounding door
She ne'er shall force an echo more,
Thrilling to think, poor child of sin!
It was the dead who groaned within.

THE PREMATURE BURIAL

THERE are certain themes of which the interest is all-absorbing, but which are too entirely horrible for the purposes of legitimate fiction. These the mere romanticist must eschew, if he do not wish to offend, or to disgust. They are with propriety handled only when the severity and majesty of truth sanctify and sustain them. We thrill, for example, with the most intense of 'pleasurable pain' over the accounts of the Passage of the Beresina, of the Earthquake at Lisbon, of the Plague at London, of the Massacre of St Bartholomew, or of the stifling of the hundred and twenty-three prisoners in the Black Hole at Calcutta. But, in these accounts, it is the fact—it is the reality—it is the history which excites. As inventions, we should regard them with simple abhorrence.

I have mentioned some few of the more prominent and august calamities on record; but in these it is the extent, not less than the character of the calamity, which so vividly impresses the fancy. I need not remind the reader that, from the long and weird catalogue of human miseries, I might have selected many individual instances more replete with essential suffering than any of these vast generalities of disaster. The true wretchedness, indeed,—the ultimate woe,—is particular, not diffuse. That the ghastly extremes of agony are endured by man the unit, and never by man the mass—for this let us thank a merciful God!

To be buried while alive is, beyond question, the most terrific of these extremes which has ever fallen to the lot of mere mortality. That it has frequently, very frequently, so fallen will scarcely be denied by those who think. The boundaries which divide Life from Death are at best shadowy and vague. Who shall say where the one ends, and where the other begins? We know that there are diseases in which occur total cessations of all the apparent functions of vitality, and yet in which these cessations are merely suspensions, properly so called. They are only temporary pauses in the incomprehensible mechanism. A certain period elapses, and some unseen mysterious principle again sets in motion the magic pinions and the wizard wheels. The silver cord was not for ever loosed, nor the golden bowl irreparably broken. But where, meantime, was the soul?

Apart, however, from the inevitable conclusion, *a priori* that such causes must produce such effects,—that the well-known occurrence of such cases of suspended animation must naturally give rise, now and then, to premature interments,—apart from this consideration, we have the direct testimony of medical and ordinary experience to prove that a vast number of such interments have actually taken place. I might refer at once, if necessary, to a hundred well-authenticated instances. One of very remarkable character, and of which the circumstances may be fresh in the memory of some of my readers, occurred, not very long ago, in the neighboring city of Baltimore, where it occasioned a painful, intense, and widely-extended excitement. The wife of one of the most respectable citizens—a lawyer of eminence and a member of Congress—was seized with a sudden and unaccountable illness, which completely baffled the skill of her physicians. After much suffering she died, or was supposed to die. No one suspected, indeed, or had reason to suspect, that she was not actually dead. She presented all the ordinary appearances of death. The face assumed the usual pinched and sunken outline. The lips were of the usual marble pallor. The eyes were lustreless. There was no warmth. Pulsation had ceased. For three days the body was preserved unburied, during which it had acquired a stony rigidity. The funeral, in short, was hastened, on account of the rapid advance of what was supposed to be decomposition.

The lady was deposited in her family vault, which, for three subsequent years, was undisturbed. At the expiration of this term it was opened for the reception of a sarcophagus;—but, alas! how fearful a shock awaited the husband, who, personally, threw open the door! As its portals swung outwardly back, some white-apparelled object fell rattling within his arms. It was the skeleton of his wife in her yet unmoulded shroud.

A careful investigation rendered it evident that she had revived within two days after her entombment; that her struggles within the coffin had caused it to fall from a ledge, or shelf, to the floor, where it was so broken as to permit her escape. A lamp which had been accidentally left, full of oil, within the tomb, was found empty; it might have been exhausted, however, by evaporation. On the uppermost of the steps which led down into the dread chamber was a large fragment of the coffin, with which, it seemed that she had endeavored to arrest attention by striking the iron door. While thus

occupied, she probably swooned, or possibly died, through sheer terror; and, in falling, her shroud became entangled in some iron-work which projected interiorly. Thus she remained, and thus she rotted, erect.

In the year 1810, a case of living inhumation happened in France, attended with circumstances which go far to warrant the assertion that truth is, indeed, stranger than fiction. The heroine of the story was a Mademoiselle Victorine Lafourcade, a young girl of illustrious family, of wealth, and of great personal beauty. Among her numerous suitors was Julien Bossuet, a poor *litterateur*, or journalist, of Paris. His talents and general amiability had recommended him to the notice of the heiress, by whom he seems to have been truly beloved; but her pride of birth decided her, finally, to reject him, and to wed a Monsieur Renelle, a banker and a diplomatist of some eminence. After marriage, however, this gentleman neglected, and, perhaps, even more positively ill-treated her. Having passed with him some wretched years, she died—at least her condition so closely resembled death as to deceive every one who saw her. She was buried—not in a vault, but in an ordinary grave in the village of her nativity. Filled with despair, and still inflamed by the memory of a profound attachment, the lover journeys from the capital to the remote province in which the village lies, with the romantic purpose of disinterring the corpse, and possessing himself of its luxuriant tresses. He reaches the grave. At midnight he unearths the coffin, opens it, and is in the act of detaching the hair, when he is arrested by the unclosing of the beloved eyes. In fact, the lady had been buried alive. Vitality had not altogether departed, and she was aroused by the caresses of her lover from the lethargy which had been mistaken for death. He bore her frantically to his lodgings in the village. He employed certain powerful restoratives suggested by no little medical learning. In fine, she revived. She recognized her preserver. She remained with him until, by slow degrees, she fully recovered her original health. Her woman's heart was not adamant, and this last lesson of love sufficed to soften it. She bestowed it upon Bossuet. She returned no more to her husband, but, concealing from him her resurrection, fled with her lover to America. Twenty years afterward, the two returned to France, in the persuasion that time had so greatly altered the lady's appearance that her friends would be unable to recognize her. They were mistaken, however; for, at the first meeting, Monsieur Renelle did actually recognize and make claim to his wife. This claim she resisted, and a judicial tribunal sustained her in her resistance, deciding that the peculiar circumstances, with the long lapse of years, had extinguished not only equitably, but legally, the authority of the husband.

The *Chirurgical Journal* of Leipsic, a periodical of high authority and merit, which some American bookseller would do well to translate and republish, records in a late number a very distressing event of the character in question.

An officer of artillery, a man of gigantic stature and of robust health, being thrown from an unmanageable horse, received a very severe contusion upon the head, which rendered him insensible at once; the skull was slightly fractured, but no immediate danger was apprehended. Trepanning was accomplished successfully. He was bled, and many other of the ordinary means of relief were adopted. Gradually, however, he fell into a more and more hopeless state of stupor, and, finally, it was thought that he died.

The weather was warm, and he was buried with indecent haste in one of the public cemeteries. His funeral took place on Thursday. On the Sunday following, the grounds of the cemetery were, as usual, much thronged with visitors, and about noon an intense excitement was created by the declaration of a peasant that, while sitting upon the grave of the officer, he had distinctly felt a commotion of the earth, as if occasioned by some one struggling beneath. At first little attention was paid to the man's asseveration; but his evident terror, and the dogged obstinacy with which he persisted in his story, had at length their natural effect upon the crowd. Spades were hurriedly procured, and the grave, which was shamefully shallow, was in a few minutes so far thrown open that the head of its occupant appeared. He was then seemingly dead; but he sat nearly erect within his coffin, the lid of which, in his furious struggles, he had partially uplifted.

He was forthwith conveyed to the nearest hospital, and there pronounced to be still living, although in an asphytic condition. After some hours he revived, recognized individuals of his acquaintance, and, in broken sentences spoke of his agonies in the grave.

From what he related, it was clear that he must have been conscious of life for more than an hour, while inhumed, before lapsing into insensibility. The grave was carelessly and loosely filled with an exceedingly porous soil; and thus some air was necessarily admitted. He heard the footsteps of the crowd overhead, and endeavored to make himself heard in turn. It was the tumult within the grounds of the cemetery, he said, which appeared to awaken him from a deep sleep, but no sooner was he awake than he became fully aware of the awful horrors of his position.

This patient, it is recorded, was doing well, and seemed to be in a fair way of ultimate recovery, but fell a victim to the quackeries of medical experiment. The galvanic battery was applied, and he suddenly expired in one of those ecstatic paroxysms which, occasionally, it superinduces.

The mention of the galvanic battery, nevertheless, recalls to my memory a well-known and very extraordinary case in point, where its action proved the means of restoring to animation a young attorney of London, who had been interred for two days. This occurred in 1831, and created, at the time, a very profound sensation wherever it was made the subject of converse.

The patient, Mr Edward Stapleton, had died, apparently, of typhus fever, accompanied with some anomalous symptoms which had excited the curiosity of his medical attendants. Upon his seeming decease, his friends were requested to sanction a *post-mortem* examination, but declined to permit it. As often happens, when such refusals are made, the practitioners resolved to disinter the body and dissect it at leisure, in private. Arrangements were easily effected with some of the numerous corps of body-snatchers with which London abounds; and, upon the third night after the funeral, the supposed corpse was unearthed from a grave eight feet deep, and deposited in the operating chamber of one of the private hospitals.

An incision of some extent had been actually made in the abdomen, when the fresh and undecayed appearance of the subject suggested an application of the battery. One experiment succeeded another, and the customary effects supervened, with nothing to characterize them in any respect, except, upon one or two occasions, a more than ordinary degree of life-likeness in the convulsive action.

It grew late. The day was about to dawn; and it was thought expedient, at length, to proceed at once to the dissection. A student, however, was especially desirous of testing a theory of his own, and insisted upon applying the battery to one of the pectoral muscles. A rough gash was made, and a wire hastily brought in contact; when the patient, with a hurried but quite unconvulsive movement, arose from the table, stepped into the middle of the floor, gazed about him uneasily for a few seconds, and then—spoke. What he said was unintelligible; but words were uttered; the syllabification was distinct. Having spoken, he fell heavily to the floor.

For some moments all were paralyzed with awe—but the urgency of the case soon restored them their presence of mind. It was seen that Mr Stapleton was alive, although in a swoon. Upon exhibition of ether he revived and was rapidly restored to health, and to the society of his friends—from whom, however, all knowledge of his resuscitation was withheld, until a relapse was no longer to be apprehended. Their wonder—their rapturous astonishment—may be conceived.

The most thrilling peculiarity of this incident, nevertheless, is involved in what Mr S himself asserts. He declares that at no period was he altogether insensible—that, dully and confusedly, he was aware of everything which happened to him, from the moment in which he was pronounced *dead* by his physicians, to that in which he fell swooning to the floor of the hospital. 'I am alive,' were the uncomprehended words which, upon recognizing the locality of the dissecting-room, he had endeavored, in his extremity, to utter.

It were an easy matter to multiply such histories as these—but I forbear—for, indeed, we have no need of such to establish the fact that premature interments occur. When we reflect how very rarely, from the nature of the case, we have it in our power to detect them, we must admit that they may *frequently* occur without our cognizance. Scarcely, in truth, is a graveyard ever encroached upon, for any purpose, to any great extent, that skeletons are not found in postures which suggest the most fearful of suspicions.

Fearful indeed the suspicion—but more fearful the doom! It may be asserted, without hesitation, that *no* event is so terribly well adapted to inspire the supremeness of bodily and of mental distress, as is burial before death. The unendurable oppression of the lungs—the stifling fumes of the damp earth—the clinging to the death garments—the rigid embrace of the narrow house—the blackness of the absolute Night—the silence like a sea that overwhelms—the unseen but palpable presence of the Conqueror Worm—these things, with the thoughts of the air and grass above, with memory of dear friends who would fly to save us if but informed of our fate, and with consciousness that of this fate they can *never* be informed—that our hopeless portion is that of the really dead—these considerations, I say, carry into the heart, which still palpitates, a degree of appalling and intolerable horror from which the most daring imagination must recoil. We know of nothing so agonizing upon Earth—we can dream of nothing half so hideous in the realms of the nethermost Hell. And thus all narratives upon this topic have an interest profound; an interest, nevertheless, which, through the sacred awe of the topic itself, very properly and very peculiarly depends upon our conviction of the *truth* of the matter narrated. What I have now to tell is of my own actual knowledge—of my own positive and personal experience.

For several years I had been subject to attacks of the singular disorder which physicians have agreed to term catalepsy, in default of a more definite title. Although both the immediate and the predisposing causes, and even the actual diagnosis, of this disease are still mysterious, its obvious and apparent character is sufficiently well understood. Its variations seem to be chiefly of degree. Sometimes the patient lies, for a day only, or even for a shorter period, in a species of exaggerated lethargy. He is senseless and externally motionless; but the pulsation of the heart is still faintly perceptible; some traces of warmth remain; a slight color lingers within the centre of the cheek; and, upon application of a mirror to the lips, we can detect a torpid, unequal, and vacillating action of the lungs. Then again the duration of the trance is for weeks—even for months; while the closest scrutiny, and the most rigorous medical tests, fail to establish any material distinction between the state of the sufferer and what we conceive of absolute death. Very usually he is saved from premature interment solely by the knowledge of his friends that he has been previously subject to catalepsy, by the consequent suspicion excited, and, above all, by the non-appearance of decay. The advances of the malady are, luckily, gradual. The first manifestations, although marked, are unequivocal. The fits grow successively more and more distinctive, and endure each for a longer term than the preceding. In this lies the principal security from inhumation. The unfortunate whose *first* attack should be of the extreme character which is occasionally seen, would almost inevitably be consigned alive to the tomb.

My own case differed in no important particular from those mentioned in medical books. Sometimes, without any apparent cause, I sank, little by little, into a condition of semi-syncope, or half swoon; and, in this condition, without pain, without ability to stir, or, strictly speaking, to think, but with a dull lethargic consciousness of life and of the presence of those who surrounded my bed, I remained, until the crisis of the disease restored me, suddenly, to perfect sensation. At other times I was quickly and impetuously smitten. I grew sick, and numb, and chilly, and dizzy, and so fell prostrate at once. Then, for weeks, all was void, and black, and silent, and Nothing became the universe. Total annihilation could be no more. From these latter attacks I awoke, however, with a gradation slow in proportion to the suddenness of the seizure. Just as the day dawns to the friendless and houseless beggar who roams the streets throughout the long desolate winter night—just so tardily—just so wearily—just so cheerily came back the light of the Soul to me.

Apart from the tendency to trance, however, my general health appeared to be good; nor could I perceive that it was at all affected by the one prevalent malady—unless, indeed, an idiosyncrasy in my ordinary *sleep* may be looked upon as superinduced. Upon awaking from slumber, I could never gain, at once, thorough possession of my senses, and always remained, for many minutes, in much bewilderment and perplexity—the mental faculties in general, but the memory in especial, being in a condition of absolute abeyance.

In all that I endured there was no physical suffering, but of moral distress an infinitude. My fancy grew charnel. I talked 'of worms, of tombs, and epitaphs.' I was lost in reveries of death, and the idea of premature burial held continual possession of my brain. The ghastly Danger to which I was subjected haunted me day and night. In the former, the torture of meditation was excessive; in the latter, supreme. When the grim Darkness overspread the Earth, then, with every horror of thought, I shook—shook as the quivering plumes upon the hearse. When Nature could endure wakefulness no longer, it was with a struggle that I consented to sleep—for I shuddered to reflect that, upon awaking, I might find myself the tenant of a grave. And when, finally, I sank into slumber, it was only to rush at once into a world of phantasms, above which, with

vast, sable, overshadowing wings, hovered, predominant, the one sepulchral Idea.

From the innumerable images of gloom which thus oppressed me in dreams, I select for record but a solitary vision. Methought I was immersed in a cataleptic trance of more than usual duration and profundity. Suddenly there came an icy hand upon my forehead, and an impatient gibbering voice whispered the word 'Arise!' within my ear.

I sat erect. The darkness was total. I could not see the figure of him who had aroused me. I could call to mind neither the period at which I had fallen into the trance, nor the locality in which I then lay. While I remained motionless, and busied in endeavours to collect my thoughts, the cold hand grasped me fiercely by the wrist, shaking it petulantly, while the gibbering voice said again:

'Arise! did I not bid thee arise?'

'And who,' I demanded, 'art thou?'

'I have no name in the regions which I inhabit,' replied the voice, mournfully; 'I was mortal, but am fiend. I was merciless, but am pitiful. Thou dost feel that I shudder. My teeth chatter as I speak, yet it is not with the chilliness of the night—of the night without end. But this hideousness is insufferable. How canst *thou* tranquilly sleep? I cannot rest for the cry of these great agonies. These sights are more than I can bear. Get thee up! Come with me into the outer Night, and let me unfold to thee the graves. Is not this a spectacle of woe?—Behold!'

I looked; and the unseen figure, which still grasped me by the wrist, had caused to be thrown open the graves of all mankind; and from each issued the faint phosphoric radiance of decay; so that I could see into the innermost recesses, and there view the shrouded bodies in their sad and solemn slumbers with the worm. But alas! the real sleepers were fewer, by many millions, than those who slumbered not at all; and there was a feeble struggling; and there was a general and sad unrest; and from out the depths of the countless pits there came a melancholy rustling from the garments of the buried. And of those who seemed tranquilly to repose, I saw that a vast number had changed, in a greater or less degree, the rigid and uneasy position in which they had originally been entombed. And the voice again said to me as I gazed:

'Is it not—oh! is it *not* a pitiful sight?' But, before I could find words to reply, the figure had ceased to grasp my wrist, the phosphoric lights expired, and the graves were closed with a sudden violence, while from out them arose a tumult of despairing cries, saying again: 'Is it not—O, God! is it *not* a very pitiful sight?'

Phantasies such as these, presenting themselves at night, extended their terrific influence far into my waking hours. My nerves became thoroughly unstrung, and I fell a prey to perpetual horror. I hesitated to ride, or to walk, or to indulge

in any exercise that would carry me from home. In fact, I no longer dared trust myself out of the immediate presence of those who were aware of my proneness to catalepsy, lest, falling into one of my usual fits, I should be buried before my real condition could be ascertained. doubted the care, the fidelity of my dearest friends. I dreaded that, in some trance of more than customary duration, they might be prevailed upon to regard me as irrecoverable. I even went so far as to fear that, as I occasioned much trouble, they might be glad to consider any very protracted attack as sufficient excuse for getting rid of me altogether. It was in vain they endeavored to reassure me by the most solemn promises. I exacted the most sacred oaths, that under no circumstances they would bury me until decomposition had so materially advanced as to render further preservation impossible. And, even then, my mortal terrors would listen to no reason — would accept no consolation. I entered into a series of elaborate precautions. Among other things, I had the family vault so remodelled as to admit of being readily opened from within. The slightest pressure upon a long lever that extended far into the tomb would cause the iron portals to fly back. There were arrangements also for the free admission of air and light, and convenient receptacles for food and water, within immediate reach of the coffin intended for my reception. This coffin was warmly and softly padded, and was provided with a lid, fashioned upon the principle of the vault-door, with the addition of springs so contrived that the feeblest movement of the body would be sufficient to set it at liberty. Besides all this, there was suspended from the roof of the tomb, a large bell, the rope of which, it was designed, should extend through a hole in the coffin, and so be fastened to one of the hands of the corpse. But, alas! what avails the vigilance against the Destiny of man? Not even these well-contrived securities sufficed to save from the uttermost agonies of living inhumation, a wretch to these agonies foredoomed!

There arrived an epoch — as often before there had arrived — in which I found myself emerging from total unconsciousness into the first feeble and indefinite sense of existence. Slowly — with a tortoise gradation — approached the faint gray dawn of the psychal day. A torpid uneasiness. An apathetic endurance of dull pain. No care — no hope — no effort. Then, after a long interval, a ringing in the ears; then, after a lapse still longer, a pricking or tingling sensation in the extremities; then a seemingly eternal period of pleasurable quiescence, during which the awakening feelings are struggling into thought; then a brief re-sinking into nonentity; then a sudden recovery. At length the slight quivering of an eyelid, and immediately thereupon, an electric shock of a terror, deadly and indefinite, which sends the blood in torrents from the temples to the heart. And now the first positive effort to think. And now the first endeavor to remember. And now a partial

and evanescent success. And now the memory has so far regained its dominion, that, in some measure, I am cognizant of my state. I feel that I am not awaking from ordinary sleep. I recollect that I have been subject to catalepsy. And now, at last, as if by the rush of an ocean, my shuddering spirit is overwhelmed by the one grim Danger — by the one spectral and ever-prevalent idea.

For some minutes after this fancy possessed me, I remained without motion. And why? I could not summon courage to move. I dared not make the effort which was to satisfy me of my fate — and yet there was something at my heart which whispered me *it was sure.* Despair — such as no other species of wretchedness ever calls into being — despair alone urged me, after long irresolution, to uplight the heavy lids of my eyes. I uplifted them. It was dark — all dark. I knew that the fit was over. I knew that the crisis of my disorder had long passed. I knew that I had now fully recovered the use of my visual faculties — and yet it was dark — all dark — the intense and utter raylessness of the Night than endureth for evermore.

I endeavored to shriek; and my lips and my parched tongue moved convulsively together in the attempt — but no voice issued from the cavernous lungs, which, oppressed as if by the weight of some incumbent mountain, gasped and palpitated, with the heart, at every elaborate and struggling inspiration.

The movement of the jaws, in this effort to cry aloud, showed me that they were bound up, as is usual with the dead. I felt, too, that I lay upon some hard substance; and by something similar my sides were, also, closely compressed. So far, I had not ventured to stir any of my limbs — but now I violently threw up my arms, which had been lying at length, with the wrists crossed. They struck a solid wooden substance, which extended above my person at an elevation of not more than six inches from my face. I could no longer doubt that I reposed within a coffin at last.

And now, amid all my infinite miseries, came sweetly the cherub Hope — for I thought of my precautions. I writhed, and made spasmodic exertions to force open the lid: it would not move. I felt my wrists for the bell-rope: it was not to be found. And now the Comforter fled for ever, and a still sterner Despair reigned triumphant; for I could not help perceiving the absence of the paddings which I had so carefully prepared — and then, too, there came suddenly to my nostrils the strong peculiar odor of moist earth. The conclusion was irresistible. I was *not* within the vault. I had fallen into a trance while absent from home — while among strangers — when, or how, I could not remember — and it was they who had buried me as a dog — nailed up in some common coffin — and thrust, deep, deep, and for ever, into some ordinary and nameless *grave.*

As this awful conviction forced itself, thus, into the innermost chambers of my soul, I once again struggled to cry aloud.

And in this second endeavor I succeeded. A long, wild, and continuous shriek, or yell, of agony, resounded through the realms of the subterranean Night.

'Hillo! hillo, there!' said a gruff voice, in reply.

'What the devil's the matter now!' said a second.

'Get out o' that!' said a third.

'What do you mean by yowling in that ere kind of style, like a cattymount?' said a fourth; and hereupon I was seized and shaken without ceremony, for several minutes, by a junto of very rough-looking individuals. They did not arouse me from my slumber — for I was wide-awake when I screamed — but they restored me to the full possession of my memory.

This adventure occurred near Richmond, in Virginia. Accompanied by a friend, I had proceeded, upon a gunning expedition, some miles down the banks of the James River. Night approached, and we were overtaken by a storm. The cabin of a small sloop lying at anchor in the stream, and laden with garden mould, afforded us the only available shelter. We made the best of it, and passed the night on board. I slept in one of the only two berths in the vessel — and the berths of a sloop of sixty or seventy tons need scarcely be described. That which I occupied had no bedding of any kind. Its extreme width was eighteen inches. The distance of its bottom from the deck overhead was precisely the same. I found it a matter of exceeding difficulty to squeeze myself in. Nevertheless, I slept soundly; and the whole of my vision — for it was no dream, and no nightmare — arose naturally from the circumstances of my position — from my ordinary bias of thought — and from the difficulty, to which I have alluded, of collecting my senses, and especially of regaining my memory, for a long time after awaking from slumber. The men who shook me were the crew of the sloop, and some laborers engaged to unload it. From the load itself came the earthy smell. The bandage about the jaws was a silk handkerchief in which I had bound up my head, in default of my customary nightcap.

The tortures endured, however, were indubitably quite equal, for the time, to those of actual sepulture. They were fearfully — they were inconceivably hideous; but out of Evil proceeded Good; for their very excess wrought in my spirit an inevitable revulsion. My soul acquired tone — acquired temper. I went abroad. I took vigorous exercise. I breathed the free air of Heaven. I thought upon other subjects than Death. I discarded my medical books. 'Buchan' I burned. I read no 'Night Thoughts' — no fustian about church-yards — no bugaboo tales — *such as this*. In short I became a new man, and lived a man's life. From that memorable night, I dismissed forever my charnel apprehensions, and with them vanished the cataleptic disorder, of which, perhaps, they had been less the consequence than the cause.

There are moments when, even to the sober eye of Reason, the world of our sad Humanity may assume the semblance of a Hell — but the imagination of man is no Carathis, to explore with impunity its every cavern. Alas! the grim legion of sepulchral terrors cannot be regarded as altogether fanciful — but, like the Demons in whose company Afrasiab made his voyage down the Oxus, they must sleep, or they will devour us — they must be suffered to slumber, or we perish.

THE BELLS

I

Hear the sledges with the bells—
Silver bells!
What a world of merriment their melody foretells!
How they tinkle, tinkle, tinkle,
In the icy air of night!
While the stars that oversprinkle
All the heavens seem to twinkle
With a crystalline delight;
Keeping time, time, time,
In a sort of Runic rhyme,
To the tintinnabulation that so musically wells
From the bells, bells, bells, bells,
Bells, bells, bells—
From the jingling and the tinkling of the bells.

II

Hear the mellow wedding bells,
Golden bells!
What a world of happiness their harmony foretells!
Through the balmy air of night
How they ring out their delight!
From the molten-golden notes,
And all in tune,
What a liquid ditty floats
To the turtle-dove that listens, while she gloats
On the moon!
Oh, from out the sounding cells
What a gush of euphony voluminously wells!
How it swells!
How it dwells
On the Future! how it tells
Of the rapture that impels
To the swinging and the ringing
Of the bells, bells, bells, bells,
Bells, bells, bells—
To the rhyming and the chiming of the bells!

III

Hear the loud alarum bells—
Brazen bells!
What a tale of terror, now, their turbulency tells!
In the startled ear of night
How they scream out their affright!
Too much horrified to speak,
They can only shriek, shriek,
Out of tune,
In a clamorous appealing to the mercy of the fire,
In a mad expostulation with the deaf and frantic fire,
Leaping higher, higher, higher,
With a desperate desire,
And a resolute endeavour
Now—now to sit, or never,
By the side of the pale-faced moon.
Oh, the bells, bells, bells!
What a tale their terror tells
Of despair!
How they clang, and clash, and roar!
What a horror they outpour
On the bosom of the palpitating air!
Yet the ear it fully knows,
By the twanging,
And the clanging,
How the danger ebbs and flows;
Yet the ear distinctly tells,
In the jangling,
And the wrangling,
How the danger sinks and swells,
By the sinking or the swelling in the anger of the bells—
Of the bells—
Of the bells, bells, bells, bells,
Bells, bells, bells—
In the clamour and the clangour of the bells!

IV

Hear the tolling of the bells—
Iron bells!
What a world of solemn thought their melody compels!
In the silence of the night,
How we shiver with affright
At the melancholy menace of their tone!
For every sound that floats
From the rust within their throats
Is a groan.
And the people—ah, the people—
They that dwell up in the steeple,
All alone,
And who tolling, tolling, tolling,
In that muffled monotone,
Feel a glory in so rolling
On the human heart a stone—
They are neither man nor woman—
They are neither brute nor human—
They are Ghouls:
And their king it is who tolls;
And he rolls, rolls, rolls,
Rolls
A pæan from the bells!
And his merry bosom swells
With the pæan of the bells!
And he dances, and he yells;
Keeping time, time, time,
In a sort of Runic rhyme,
To the pæan of the bells—
Of the bells:
Keeping time, time, time,
In a sort of Runic rhyme,
To the throbbing of the bells—
Of the bells, bells, bells—
To the sobbing of the bells;
Keeping time, time, time,
As he knells, knells, knells,
In a happy Runic rhyme,
To the rolling of the bells—
Of the bells, bells bells—
To the tolling of the bells,
Of the bells, bells, bells, bells—
Bells, bells, bells—
To the moaning and the groaning of the bells.

THE SYSTEM OF DOCTOR TARR
AND PROFESSOR FETHER

DURING the autumn of 18—, while on a tour through the extreme southern provinces of France, my route led me within a few miles of a certain *Maison de Santé* or private mad-house, about which I had heard much, in Paris, from my medical friends. As I had never visited a place of the kind, I thought the opportunity too good to be lost; and so proposed to my travelling companion (a gentleman with whom I had made casual acquaintance a few days before), that we should turn aside, for an hour or so, and look through the establishment. To this he objected—pleading haste, in the first place, and, in the second, a very usual horror at the sight of a lunatic. He begged of me, however, not to let any mere courtesy toward himself interfere with the gratification of my curiosity, and said that he would ride on leisurely, so that I might overtake him during the day, or, at all events, during the next. As he bade me good-by, I bethought me that there might be some difficulty in obtaining access to the premises, and mentioned my fears on this point. He replied that, in fact, unless I had personal knowledge of the superintendent, Monsieur Maillard, or some credential in the way of a letter, a difficulty might be found to exist, as the regulations of these private mad-houses were more rigid than the public hospital laws. For himself, he added, he had, some years since, made the acquaintance of Maillard, and would so far assist me as to ride up to the door and introduce me; although his feelings on the subject of lunacy would not permit of his entering the house.

I thanked him, and, turning from the main road, we entered a grassgrown by-path, which, in half an hour, nearly lost itself in a dense forest, clothing the base of a mountain. Through this dank and gloomy wood we rode some two miles, when the *Maison de Santé* came in view. It was a fantastic *château*, much dilapidated, and indeed scarcely tenantable through age and neglect. Its aspect inspired me with absolute dread, and, checking my horse, I half resolved to turn back. I soon, however, grew ashamed of my weakness, and proceeded.

As we rode up to the gate-way, I perceived it slightly open, and the visage of a man peering through. In an instant afterward, this man came forth, accosted my companion by name, shook him cordially by the hand, and begged him to alight. It was Monsieur Maillard himself. He was a portly, fine-looking gentleman of the old school, with a polished manner, and a certain air of gravity, dignity, and authority which was very impressive.

My friend, having presented me, mentioned my desire to inspect the establishment, and received Monsieur Maillard's assurance that he would show me all attention, now took leave, and I saw him no more.

When he had gone, the superintendent ushered me into a small and exceedingly neat parlour, containing, among other indications of refined taste, many books, drawings, pots of flowers, and musical instruments. A cheerful fire blazed upon the hearth. At a piano, singing an aria from Bellini, sat a young and very beautiful woman, who, at my entrance, paused in her song, and received me with graceful courtesy. Her voice was low, and her whole manner subdued. I thought, too, that I perceived the traces of sorrow in her countenance, which was excessively, although to my taste, not unpleasingly, pale. She was attired in deep mourning, and excited in my bosom a feeling of mingled respect, interest, and admiration.

I had heard, at Paris, that the institution of Monsieur Maillard was managed upon what is vulgarly termed the 'system of soothing'—that all punishments were avoided—that even confinement was seldom resorted to—that the patients, while secretly watched, were left much apparent liberty, and that most of them were permitted to roam about the house and grounds in the ordinary apparel of persons in right mind.

Keeping these impressions in view, I was cautious in what I said before the young lady; for I could not be sure that she was sane; and, in fact, there was a certain restless brilliancy about her eyes which half led me to imagine she was not. I confined my remarks, therefore, to general topics, and to such as I thought would not be displeasing or exciting even to a lunatic. She replied in a perfectly rational manner to all that I said; and even her original observations were marked with the soundest good sense; but a long acquaintance with the metaphysics of *mania*, had taught me to put no faith in such evidence of sanity, and I continued to practise, throughout the interview, the caution with which I commenced it.

Presently a smart footman in livery brought in a tray with fruit, wine, and other refreshments, of which I partook, the lady soon afterward leaving the room. As she departed I turned my eyes in an inquiring manner toward my host.

'No,' he said, 'oh, no—a member of my family—my niece, and a most accomplished woman,'

'I beg a thousand pardons for the suspicion,' I replied, 'but of course you will know how to excuse me. The excellent administration of your affairs here is well understood in Paris, and I thought it just possible, you know—'

'Yes, yes—say no more—or rather it is myself who should thank you for the commendable prudence you have displayed. We seldom find so much of forethought in young men; and, more than once, some unhappy *contre-temps* has occurred in consequence of thoughtlessness on the part of our visitors. While my former system was in operation, and my patients were permitted the privilege of roaming to and fro at will, they were often aroused to a dangerous frenzy by injudicious persons who called to inspect the house. Hence I was obliged to enforce a rigid system of exclusion; and none obtained access to the premises upon whose discretion I could not rely.'

'While your *former* system was in operation!' I said, repeating his words—'do I understand you, then, to say that the "soothing system" of which I have heard so much is no longer in force?'

'It is now,' he replied, 'several weeks since we have concluded to renounce it forever.'

'Indeed! you astonish me!'

'We found it, sir,' he said, with a sigh, 'absolutely necessary to return to the old usages. The *danger* of the soothing system was, at all times, appalling; and its advantages have been much overrated. I believe, sir, that in this house it has been given a fair trial, if ever in any. We did every thing that rational humanity could suggest. I am sorry that you could not have paid us a visit at an earlier period, that you might have judged for yourself. But I presume you are conversant with the soothing practice—with its details.'

'Not altogether. What I have heard has been at third or fourth hand.'

'I may state the system, then, in general terms, as one in which the patients were *ménagés*—humoured. We contradicted *no* fancies which entered the brains of the mad. On the contrary, we not only indulged but encouraged them; and many of our most permanent cures have been thus effected. There is no argument which so touches the feeble reason of the madman as the *reductio ad absurdum*. We have had men, for example, who fancied themselves chickens. The cure was, to insist upon the thing as a fact —to accuse the patient of stupidity in not sufficiently perceiving it to be a fact—and thus to refuse him any other diet for a week than that which properly appertains to a chicken. In this manner a little corn and gravel were made to perform wonders.'

'But was this species of acquiescence all?'

'By no means. We put much faith in amusements of a simple kind, such as music, dancing, gymnastic exercises generally, cards, certain classes of books, and so forth. We affected to treat each individual as if for some ordinary physical disorder;

and the word "lunacy" was never employed. A great point was to set each lunatic to guard the actions of all the others. To repose confidence in the understanding or discretion of a madman, is to gain him body and soul. In this way we were enabled to dispense with an expensive body of keepers.'

'And you had no punishments of any kind?'

'None.'

'And you never confined your patients?.'

'Very rarely. Now and then, the malady of some individual growing to a crisis, or taking a sudden turn of fury, we conveyed him to a secret cell, lest his disorder should infect the rest, and there kept him until we could dismiss him to his friends—for with the raging maniac we have nothing to do. He is usually removed to the public hospitals.'

'And you have now changed all this—and you think for the better?'

'Decidedly. The system had its disadvantages, and even its dangers. It is now, happily, exploded throughout all the *Maisons de Santé* of France.'

'I am very much surprised,' I said, 'at what you tell me; for I made sure that, at this moment, no other method of treatment for mania existed in any portion of the country.'

'You are young yet, my friend,' replied my host, 'but the time will arrive when you will learn to judge for yourself of what is going on in the world, without trusting to the gossip of others. Believe nothing you hear, and only one half that you see. Now about our *Maisons de Santé*, it is clear that some ignoramus has misled you. After dinner, however, when you have sufficiently recovered from the fatigue of your ride, I will be happy to take you over the house, and introduce to you a system which, in my opinion, and in that of every one who has witnessed its operation, is incomparably the most effectual as yet devised.'

'Your own?' I inquired—'one of your own invention?'

'I am proud,' he replied, 'to acknowledge that it is—at least in some measure.'

In this manner I conversed with Monsieur Maillard for an hour or two, during which he showed me the gardens and conservatories of the place.

'I cannot let you see my patients,' he said, 'just at present. To a sensitive mind there is always more or less of the shocking in such exhibitions; and I do not wish to spoil your appetite for dinner. We will dine. I can give you some veal *à la St. Menehoult*, with cauliflowers in *velouté* sauce —after that a glass of *Clos de Vougeôt*—then your nerves will be sufficiently steadied.'

At six, dinner was announced; and my host conducted me into a large *salle à manger*, where a very numerous company were assembled—twenty-five or thirty in all. They were, apparently, people of rank—certainly of high breeding—although their habiliments, I thought, were extravagantly rich,

partaking somewhat too much of the ostentatious finery of the *ville cour*. I noticed that at least two thirds of these guests were ladies; and some of the latter were by no means accoutred in what a Parisian would consider good taste at the present day. Many females, for example, whose age could not have been less than seventy, were bedecked with a profusion of jewelry, such as rings, bracelets, and ear-rings, and wore their bosoms and arms shamefully bare. I observed, too, that very few of the dresses were well made — or, at least, that very few of them fitted the wearers. In looking about, I discovered the interesting girl to thom Monsieur Maillard had presented me in the little parlour; but my surprise was great to see her wearing a hoop and farthingale, with high-heeled shoes, and a dirty cap of Brussels lace, so much too large for her that it gave her face a ridiculously diminutive expression. When I had first seen her, she was attired, most becomingly, in deep mourning. There was an air of oddity, in short, about the dress of the whole party, which, at first, caused me to recur to my original idea of the 'soothing system,' and to fancy that Monsieur Maillard had been willing to deceive me until after dinner, that I might experience no uncomfortable feelings during the repast, at finding myself dining with lunatics; but I remembered having been informed, in Paris, that the southern provincialists were a peculiarly eccentric people, with a vast number of antiquated notions; and then, too, upon conversing with several members of the company, my apprehensions were immediately and fully dispelled.

The dining-room itself, although perhaps sufficiently comfortable and of good dimensions, had nothing too much of elegance about it. For example, the floor was uncarpeted; in France, however, a carpet is frequently dispensed with. The windows, too, were without curtains; the shutters, being shut, were securely fastened with iron bars, applied diagonally, after the fashion of our shop-shutters. The apartment, I observed, formed, in itself, a wing of the *château*, and thus the windows were on three sides of the parallelogram, the door being at the other. There were no less than ten windows in all.

The table was superbly set out. It was loaded with plate, and more than loaded with delicacies. The profusion was absolutely barbaric. There were meats enough to have feasted the Anakim. Never, in all my life, had I witnessed so lavish, so wasteful an expenditure of the good things of life. There seemed very little taste, however, in the arrangements; and my eyes, accustomed to quiet lights, were sadly offended by the prodigious glare of a multitude of wax candles, which, in silver *candelabra*, were deposited upon the table, and all about the room, wherever it was possible to find a place. There were several active servants in attendance; and, upon a large table, at the farther end of the apartment, were seated seven or eight people with fiddles, fifes, trombones, and a drum. These fellows annoyed me very much, at intervals, during the repast,

by an infinite variety of noises, which were intended for music, and which appeared to afford much entertainment to all present, with the exception of myself.

Upon the whole, I could not help thinking that there was much of the *bizarre* about every thing I saw — but then the world is made up of all kinds of persons, with all modes of thought, and all sorts of conventional customs. I had travelled, too, so much, as to be quite an adept at the *nil admirari*; so I took my seat very coolly at the right hand of my host, and, having an excellent appetite, did justice to the good cheer set before me.

The conversation, in the meantime, was spirited and general. The ladies, as usual, talked a great deal. I soon found that nearly all the company were well-educated; and my host was a world of good-humored anecdote in himself. He seemed quite willing to speak of his position as superintendent of a *Maison de Santé*; and, indeed, the topic of lunacy was, much to my surprise, a favourite one with all present. A great many amusing stories were told, having reference to the *whims* of the patients.

'We had a fellow here once,' said a fat little gentleman, who sat at my right, — 'a fellow that fancied himself a tea-pot; and by the way, is it not especially singular how often this particular crotchet has entered the brain of the lunatic? There is scarcely an insane asylum in France which cannot supply a human tea-pot. *Our* gentleman was a Britannia-ware tea-pot, and was careful to polish himself every morning with buckskin and whiting.'

'And then,' said a tall man just opposite, 'we had here, not long ago, a person who had taken it into his head that he was a donkey — which, allegorically speaking, you will say, was quite true. He was a troublesome patient; and we had much ado to keep him within bounds. For a long time he would eat nothing but thistles; but of this idea we soon cured him by insisting upon his eating nothing else. Then he was perpetually kicking out his heels — so — so'

'Mr De Kock! I will thank you to behave yourself!' here interrupted an old lady, who sat next to the speaker. 'Please keep your feet to yourself! You have spoiled my brocade! Is it necessary, pray, to illustrate a remark in so practical a style? Our friend here can surely comprehend you without all this. Upon my word, you are nearly as great a donkey as the poor unfortunate imagined himself. Your acting is very natural, as I live.'

'Mille pardons! Ma'm'selle!' replied Monsieur De Kock, thus addressed — 'a thousand pardons! I had no intention of offending. M'am'selle Laplace — Monsieur De Kock will do himself the honour of taking wine with you.'

Here Monsieur De Kock bowed low, kissed his hand with much ceremony, and took wine with Ma'm'selle Laplace.

'Allow me, *mon ami*.' now said Monsieur Maillard, addressing myself, 'allow me to send you a morsel of this veal *à la St. Menehoult*—you will find it particularly fine.'

At this instant three sturdy waiters had just succeeded in depositing safely upon the table an enormous dish, or trencher, containing what I supposed to be the *monstrum, horrendum, informe, ingens, cui lumen ademptum.* A closer scrutiny assured me, however, that it was only a small calf roasted whole, and set upon its knees, with an apple in its mouth, as is the English fashion of dressing a hare.

'Thank you, no,' I replied; 'to say the truth, I am not particularly partial to veal *à la St.*—what is it?—for I do not find that it altogether agrees with me. I will change my plate, however, and try some of the rabbit.'

There were several side-dishes on the table, containing what appeared to be the ordinary French rabbit—a very delicious *morceau*, which I can recommend.

'Pierre,' cried the host, 'change this gentleman's plate, and give him a side-piece of this rabbit *au-chat.*'

'This what?' said I.

'This rabbit *au-chat.*'

'Why, thank you–upon second thoughts, no. I will just help myself to some of the ham.'

There is no knowing what one eats, thought I to myself, at the tables of these people of the province. I will have none of their rabbit *au-chat*—and, for the matter of that, none of their *cat-au-rabbit* either.

'And then,' said a cadaverous-looking personage, near the foot of the table, taking up the thread of the conversation where it had been broken off,—'and then, among other oddities, we had a patient, once upon a time, who very pertinaciously maintained himself to be a Cordova cheese, and went about, with a knife in his hand, soliciting his friends to try a small slice from the middle of his leg.'

'He was a great fool, beyond doubt,' interposed some one, 'but not to be compared with a certain individual whom we all know, with the exception of this strange gentleman. I mean the man who took himself for a bottle of champagne, and always went off with a pop and a fizz, in this fashion.'

Here the speaker, very rudely, as I thought, put his right thumb in his left cheek, withdrew it with a sound resembling the popping of a cork, and then, by a dexterous movement of the tongue upon the teeth, created a sharp hissing and fizzing, which lasted for several minutes, in imitation of the frothing of champagne. This behaviour, I saw plainly, was not very pleasing to Monsieur Maillard; but that gentleman said nothing, and the conversation was resumed by a very lean little man in a big wig.

'And then there was an ignoramus,' said he, 'who mistook himself for a frog; which, by the way, he resembled in no little degree. I wish you could have seen him, sir,'—here the speaker addressed myself,—'it would have done your heart good to see

the natural airs that he put on. Sir, if that man was *not* a frog, I can only observe that it is a pity he was not. His croak thus—o-o-o-o-gh—o-o-o-o-gh! was the finest note in the world—B flat; and when he put his elbows upon the table thus—after taking a glass or two of wine—and distended his mouth, thus, and rolled up his eyes, thus, and winked them with excessive rapidity, thus, why then, sir, I take it upon myself to say, positively, that you would have been lost in admiration of the genius of the man.'

'I have no doubt of it,' I said.

'And then,' said somebody else, 'then there was Petit Gaillard, who thought himself a pinch of snuff, and was truly distressed because he could not take himself between his own finger and thumb.'

'And then there was Jules Desoulières, who was a very singular genius, indeed, and went mad with the idea that he was a pumpkin. He persecuted the cook to make him up into pies—a thing which the cook indignantly refused to do. For my part, I am by no means sure that a pumpkin pie *à la Desoulières* would not have been very capital eating indeed!'

'You astonish me!' said I; and I looked inquisitively at Monsieur Maillard.

'Ha! ha! ha!' said that gentleman,—'he! he! he!—hi! hi! hi!—ho! ho! ho!—hu! hu! hu!—very good indeed! You must not be astonished, *mon ami*; our friend here is a wit—*a drôle*—you must not understand him to the letter.'

'And then,' said some other one of the party,—'then there was Bouffon Le Grand—another extraordinary personage in his way. He grew deranged through love, and fancied himself possessed of two heads. One of these he maintained to be the head of Cicero; the other he imagined a composite one, being Demosthenes' from the top of the forehead to the mouth, and Lord Brougham's from the mouth to the chin. It is not impossible that he was wrong; but he would have convinced you of his being in the right; for he was a man of great eloquence. He had an absolute passion for oratory, and could not refrain from display. For example, he used to leap upon the dinner-table thus, and—and—.'

Here a friend, at the side of the speaker, put a hand upon his shoulder and whispered a few words in his ear; upon which he ceased talking with great suddenness, and sank back within his chair.

'And then,' said the friend who had whispered, 'there was Boullard, the tee-totum. I call him the tee-totum because, in fact, he was seized with the droll, but not altogether irrational, crotchet, that he had been converted into a tee-totum. You would have roared with laughter to see him spin. He would turn around upon one heel by the hour, in this manner—so—'

Here the friend whom he had just interrupted by a whisper, performed an exactly similar office for himself.

'But then,' cried an old lady, at the top of her voice, 'your

Monsieur Boullard was a madman, and a very silly madman at best; for who, allow me to ask you, ever heard of a human tee-totum? The thing is absurd. Madame Joyeuse was a more sensible person, as you know. She had a crotchet, but it was instinct with common sense, and gave pleasure to all who had the honour of her acquaintance. She found, upon mature deliberation, that, by some accident, she had been turned into a chicken-cock; but, as such, she behaved with propriety. She flapped her wings with prodigious effect — so — so — so — and, as for her crow, it was delicious! Cock-a-doodle-doo! — cock-a-doodle-doo! — cock-a-doodle-de-doo-doo-dooo-do-o-o-o-o-o!

'Madame Joyeuse, I will thank you to behave yourself! here interrupted our host, very angrily. 'you can either conduct yourself as a lady should do, or you can quit the table forthwith — take your choice.'

The lady (whom I was much astonished to hear addressed as Madame Joyeuse, after the description of Madame Joyeuse she had just given) blushed up to the eyebrows, and seemed exceedingly abashed at the reproof. She hung down her head, and said not a syllable in reply. But another and younger lady resumed the theme. It was my beautiful girl of the little parlor.

'Oh, Madame Joyeuse *was* a fool!' she exclaimed, 'but there was really much sound sense, after all, in the opinion of Eugénie Salsafette. She was a very beautiful and painfully modest young lady, who thought the ordinary mode of habiliment indecent, and wished to dress herself, always, by getting outside instead of inside of her clothes. It is a thing very easily done, after all. You have only to do so — and then so — so — so — and then so — so — so — and then — '

'*Mon dieu!* Ma'm'selle Salsafette!' here cried a dozen voices at once. 'What *are* you about? — forbear! — that is sufficient! — we see, very plainly, how it is done! — hold! hold!' and several persons were already leaping from their seats to withhold Ma'm'selle Salsafette from putting herself upon a par with the Medicean Venus, when the point was very effectually and suddenly accomplished by a series of loud screams, or yells, from some portion of the main body of the *château*.

My nerves were very much affected, indeed, by these yells; but the rest of the company I really pitied. I never saw any set of reasonable people so thoroughly frightened in my life. They all grew as pale as so many corpses, and, shrinking within their seats, sat quivering and gibbering with terror, and listening for a repetition of the sound. It came again — louder and seemingly nearer — and then a third time *very* loud, and then a fourth time with a vigour evidently diminished. At this apparent dying away of the noise, the spirits of the company were immediately regained, and all was life and anecdote as before. I now ventured to inquire the cause of the disturbance.

'A mere *bagatelle*,' said Monsieur Maillard. 'We are used to these things, and care really very little about them. The lunatics, every now and then, get up a howl in concert; one starting another, as is sometimes the case with a bevy of dogs at night. It occasionally happens, however, that the *concerto* yells are succeeded by a simultaneous effort at breaking loose; when, of course, some little danger is to be apprehended.'

'And how many have you in charge?'

'At present we have not more than ten, all together.'

'Principally females, I presume?'

'Oh, no — every one of them men, and stout fellows, too, I can tell you.'

'Indeed! I have always understood that the majority of lunatics were of the gentler sex.'

'It is generally so, but not always. Some time ago, there were about twenty-seven patients here; and, of that number, no less than eighteen were women; but lately, matters have changed very much, as you see.'

'Yes — have changed very much, as you see.' here interrupted the gentleman who had broken the shins of Ma'm'selle Laplace.

'Yes — have changed very much, as you see!' chimed in the whole company at once.

'Hold your tongues, every one of you! said my host, in a great rage. Whereupon the whole company maintained a dead silence for nearly a minute. As for one lady, she obeyed Monsieur Maillard to the letter, and thrusting out her tongue, which was an excessively long one, held it very resignedly, with both hands, until the end of the entertainment.

'And this gentlewoman,' said I, to Monsieur Maillard, bending over and addressing him in a whisper — 'this good lady who has just spoken, and who gives us the cock-a-doodle-de-doo — she, I presume, is harmless — quite harmless, eh?'

'Harmless!' ejaculated he, in unfeigned surprise, 'why — why, what *can* you mean?'

'Only slightly touched?' said I, touching my head. 'I take it for granted that she is not particularly — not dangerously affected, eh?'

'*Mon dieu!* what *is* it you imagine? This lady, my particular old friend, Madame Joyeuse, is as absolutely sane as myself. She has her little eccentricities, to be sure — but then, you know, all old women — all *very* old women — are more or less eccentric!'

'To be sure,' said I, — 'to be sure — and then the rest of these ladies and gentlemen — '

'Are my friends and keepers,' interrupted Monsieur Maillard, drawing himself up with *hauteur*, — 'my very good friends and assistants.'

'What! all of them?' I asked, — 'the women and all?'

'Assuredly,' he said, — 'we could not do at all without the women; they are the best lunatic nurses in the world; they have a way of their own, you know; their bright eyes have a marvellous effect — something like the fascination of the snake, you know.'

'To be sure,' said I, — 'to be sure! They behave a little odd, eh? — they are a little *queer*, eh? — don't you think so?'

'Odd! — queer! — why, do you *really* think so? We are not very prudish, to be sure, here in the South — do pretty much as we please — enjoy life, and all that sort of thing, you know — '

'To be sure,' said I, — 'to be sure.'

'And then, perhaps, this *Clos de Vougeôt* is a little heady, you know — a little *strong* — you understand, eh?'

'To be sure,' said I, — 'to be sure. By the by, Monsieur, did I understand you to say that the system you have adopted, in place of the celebrated soothing system, was one of very rigorous severity?'

'By no means. Our confinement is necessarily close; but the treatment — the medical treatment, I mean — is rather agreeable to the patients than otherwise.'

'And the new system is one of your own invention?'

'Not altogether. Some portions of it are referable to Professor Tarr, of whom you have, necessarily, heard; and, again, there are modifications in my plan which I am happy to acknowledge as belonging of right to the celebrated Fether, with whom, if I mistake not, you have the honor of an intimate acquaintance.'

'I am quite ashamed to confess,' I replied, 'that I have never even heard the names of either gentleman before.'

'Good heavens!' ejaculated my host, drawing back his chair abruptly, and uplifting his hands. 'I surely do not hear you aright! You did not intend to say, eh? that you had never *heard* either of the learned Doctor Tarr, or of the celebrated Professor Fether?'

'I am forced to acknowledge my ignorance,' I replied; 'but the truth should be held inviolate above all things. Nevertheless, I feel humbled to the dust, not to be acquainted with the works of these, no doubt, extraordinary men. I will seek out their writings forthwith, and peruse them with deliberate care. Monsieur Maillard, you have really — I must confess it — you have *really* — made me ashamed of myself!'

And this was the fact.

'Say no more, my good young friend,' he said kindly, pressing my hand, — 'join me now in a glass of Sauterne.'

We drank. The company followed our example without stint. They chatted — they jested — they laughed — they perpetrated a thousand absurdities — the fiddles shrieked — the drum row-de-dowed — the trombones bellowed like so many brazen bulls of Phalaris — and the whole scene, growing gradually worse and worse, as the wines gained the ascendancy, became at length a sort of pandemonium *in petto*. In the meantime, Monsieur Maillard and myself, with some bottles of Sauterne and Vougeôt between us, continued our conversation at the top of the voice. A word spoken in an ordinary key stood no more chance of being heard than the voice of a fish from the bottom of Niagara Falls.

'And, sir,' said I, screaming in his ear, 'you mentioned something before dinner about the danger incurred in the old system of soothing. How is that?'

'Yes,' he replied, 'there was, occasionally, very great danger indeed. There is no accounting for the caprices of madmen; and, in my opinion, as well as in that of Dr Tarr and Professor Fether, it is *never* safe to permit them to run at large unattended. A lunatic may be "soothed," as it is called, for a time, but, in the end, he is very apt to become obstreperous. His cunning, too, is proverbial and great. If he has a project in view, he conceals his design with a marvellous wisdom; and the dexterity with which he counterfeits sanity, presents, to the metaphysician, one of the most singular problems in the study of mind. When a madman appears *thoroughly* sane, indeed, it is high time to put him in a strait-jacket.'

'But the *danger*, my dear sir, of which you were speaking — in your own experience — during your control of this house — have you had practical reason to think liberty hazardous in the case of a lunatic?'

'Here? — in my own experience? — why, I may say, yes. For example: — no *very* long while ago, a singular circumstance occurred in this very house. The "soothing system", you know, was then in operation, and the patients were at large. They behaved remarkably well — especially so, — any one of sense might have known that some devilish scheme was brewing from that particular fact, that the fellows behaved so *remarkably* well. And, sure enough, one fine morning the keepers found themselves pinioned hand and foot, and thrown into the cells, where they were attended, as if *they* were the lunatics, by the lunatics themselves, who had usurped the offices of the keepers'.

'You don't tell me so! I never heard of any thing so absurd in my life!'

'Fact — it all came to pass by means of a stupid fellow — a lunatic — who, by some means, had taken it into his head that he had invented a better system of government than any ever heard of before — of lunatic government, I mean. He wished to give his invention a trial, I suppose, and so he persuaded the rest of the patients to join him in a conspiracy for the overthrow of the reigning powers.'

'And he really succeeded?'

'No doubt of it. The keepers and kept were soon made to exchange places. Not that exactly either, for the madmen had been free, but the keepers were shut up in cells forthwith, and treated, I am sorry to say, in a very cavalier manner.'

'But I presume a counter-revolution was soon effected. This condition of things could not have long existed. The country people in the neighborhood — visitors coming to see the establishment — would have given the alarm'.

'There you are out. The head rebel was too cunning for that. He admitted no visitors at all — with the exception, one day, of a very stupid looking young gentleman of whom he

had no reason to be afraid. He let him in to see the place — just by way of variety, — to have a little fun with him. As soon as he had gammoned him sufficiently, he let him out, and sent him about his business.'

'And *how* long, then, did the madmen reign?'

'Oh, a very long time, indeed — a month certainly — how much longer I can't precisely say. In the meantime, the lunatics had a jolly season of it — that you may swear. They doffed their own shabby clothes, and made free with the family wardrobe and jewels. The cellars of the *château* were well stocked with wine; and these madmen are just the devils that know how to drink it. They lived well, I can tell you.'

'And the treatment — what was the particular species of treatment which the leader of the rebels put into operation?'

'Why, as for that, a madman is not necessarily a fool, as I have already observed; and it is my honest opinion that his treatment was a much better treatment than that which it superseded. It was a very capital system indeed — simple — neat — no trouble at all — in fact it was delicious — it was — '

Here my host's observations were cut short by another series of yells, of the same character as those which had previously disconcerted us. This time, however, they seemed to proceed from persons rapidly approaching.

'Gracious heavens!' I ejaculated — 'the lunatics have most undoubtedly broken loose.'

'I very much fear it is so,' replied Monsieur Maillard, now becoming excessively pale. He had scarcely finished the sentence, before loud shouts and imprecations were heard beneath the windows; and, immediately afterward, it became evident that some persons outside were endeavouring to gain entrance in to the room. The door was beaten with what appeared to be a sledge-hammer, and the shutters were wrenched and shaken with prodigious violence.

A scene of the most terrible confusion ensued. Monsieur Maillard, to my excessive astonishment, threw himself under the sideboard. I had expected more resolution at his hands. The members of the orchestra, who, for the last fifteen minutes, had been seemingly too much intoxicated to do duty, now sprang all at once to their feet and to their instruments, and, scrambling upon their table, broke out, with one accord, into, 'Yankee Doodle,' which they performed, if not exactly in tune, at least with an energy superhuman, during the whole of the uproar.

Meantime, upon the main dining-table, among the bottles and glasses, leaped the gentleman who, with such difficulty, had been restrained from leaping there before. As soon as he fairly settled himself, he commenced an oration, which, no doubt, was a very capital one, if it could only have been heard. At the same moment, the man with the tee-totum predilection, set himself to spinning around the apartment, with immense energy, and with arms outstretched at right angles

with his body; so that he had all the air of a tee-totum in fact, and knocked everybody down that happened to get in his way. And now, too, hearing an incredible popping and fizzing of champagne, I discovered at length, that it proceeded from the person who performed the bottle of that delicate drink during dinner. And then, again, the frog-man croaked away as if the salvation of his soul depended upon every note that he uttered. And, in the midst of all this, the continuous braying of a donkey arose over all. As for my old friend, Madame Joyeuse, I really could have wept for the poor lady, she appeared se terribly perplexed. All she did, however, was to stand up in a corner, by the fireplace, and sing out incessantly at the top of her voice, 'Cock-a-doodle-de-dooooooh!'

And now came the climax — the catastrophe of the drama. As no resistance, beyond whooping and yelling and cock-a-doodling, was offered to the encroachments of the party without, the ten windows were very speedily, and almost simultaneously, broken in. But I shall never forget the emotions of wonder and horror with which I gazed, when, leaping through these windows, and down among us *pêle-mêle*, fighting, stamping, scratching, and howling, there rushed a perfect army of what I took to be chimpanzees, ourang-outangs, or big black baboons of the Cape of Good Hope.

I received a terrible beating — after which I rolled under a sofa and lay still. After lying there some fifteen minutes, however, during which time I listened with all my ears to what was going on in the room, I came to some satisfactory *dénouement* of this tradgedy. Monsieur Maillard, it appeared, in giving me the account of the lunatic who had excited his fellows to rebellion, had been merely relating his own exploits. This gentleman had, indeed, some two or three years before, been the superintendent of the establishment; but grew crazy himself, and so became a patient. This fact was unknown to the travelling companion who introduced me. The keepers, ten in number, having been suddenly overpowered, were first well tarred, then carefully feathered, and then shut up in underground cells. They had been so imprisoned for more than a month, during which period Monsieur Maillard had generously allowed them not only the tar and feathers (which constituted his 'system',) but some bread and abundance of water. The latter was pumped on them daily. At length, one escaping through a sewer, gave freedom to all the rest.

The 'soothing system,' with important modifications, has been resumed at the *château*; yet I cannot help agreeing with Monsieur Maillard, that his own 'treatment' was a very capital one of its kind. As he justly observed, it was 'simple — neat — and gave no trouble at all — not the least.'

I have only to add that, although I have searched every library in Europe for the works of Doctor *Tarr* and Professor *Fether*, I have, up to the present day, utterly failed in my endeavors to procure a copy.

SILENCE — A FABLE

Ένδουοιν ρορεων χοδ'υψαι τε χαι ψαραγγες
Πρνεςπ τε χαι χαραδραι   — Alcman

'The mountain pinnacles slumber; valleys, crags, and caves *are silent.*'

LISTEN TO ME,' said the Demon, as he placed his hand upon my head. 'The region of which I speak is a dreary region in Libya, by the borders of the river Zaïre, and there is no quiet there, nor silence.

'The waters of the river have a saffron and sickly hue; and they flow not onward to the sea, but palpitate forever and forever beneath the red eye of the sun with a tumultuous and convulsive motion. For many miles on either side of the river's oozy bed is a pale desert of gigantic water-lilies. They sigh one unto the other in that solitude, and stretch toward the heavens their long and ghastly necks, and nod to and fro their everlasting heads. And there is an indistinct murmur which cometh out from among them like the rushing of subterrene water. And they sigh one unto the other.

'But there is a boundary to their realm — the boundary of the dark, horrible, lofty forest. There, like the waves about the Hebrides, the low underwood is agitated continually. But there is no wind throughout the heaven. And the tall primeval trees rock eternally hither and thither with a crashing and mighty sound. And from their high summits, one by one, drop everlasting dews. And at the roots strange poisonous flowers lie writhing in perturbed slumber. And overhead, with a rustling and loud noise, the gray clouds rush westwardly forever, until they roll, a cataract, over the fiery wall of the horizon. But there is no wind throughout the heaven. And by the shores of the river Zaïre there is neither quiet nor silence.

'It was night, and the rain fell; and, falling, it was rain, but, having fallen, it was blood. And I stood in the morass among the tall lilies, and the rain fell upon my head — and the lilies sighed one unto the other in the solemnity of their desolation.

'And, all at once, the moon arose through the thin ghastly mist, and was crimson in colour. And mine eyes fell upon a huge gray rock which stood by the shore of the river, and was lighted by the light of the moon. And the rock was gray, and ghastly, and tall, — and the rock was gray. Upon its front were characters engraven in the stone; and I walked through the morass of water-lilies, until I came close unto the shore, that I might read the characters upon the stone. But I could not decipher them. And I was going back into the morass, when the moon shone with a fuller red, and I turned and looked again upon the rock and upon the characters; and the characters were DESOLATION.

'And I looked upward, and there stood a man upon the summit of the rock; and I hid myself among the water-lilies that I might discover the actions of the man. And the man was tall and stately in form, and was wrapped up from his shoulders to his feet in the toga of old Rome. And the outlines of his figure were indistinct — but his features were the features of a deity; for the mantle of the night, and of the mist, and of the moon, and of the dew, had left uncovered the features of his face. And his brow was lofty with thought, and his eye wild with care; and in the few furrows upon his cheek I read the fables of sorrow, and weariness, and disgust with mankind, and a longing after solitude.

'And the man sat upon the rock, and leaned his head upon his hand, and looked out upon the desolation. He looked down into the low unquiet shrubbery, and up into the tall primeval trees, and up higher at the rustling heaven, and into the crimson moon. And I lay close within shelter of the lilies, and observed the actions of the man. And the man trembled in the solitude; — but the night waned, and he sat upon the rock.

'And the man turned his attention from the heaven, and looked out upon the dreary river Zaïre, and upon the yellow ghastly waters, and upon the pale legions of the water-lilies. And the man listened to the sighs of the water-lilies, and to the murmur that came up from among them. And I lay close within my covert and observed the actions of the man. And the man trembled in the solitude; — but the night waned and he sat upon the rock.

'Then I went down into the recesses of the morass and waded afar in among the wilderness of lilies, and called upon the hippopotami which dwelt among the fens in the recesses of the morass. And the hippopotami heard my call, and came, with the behemoth, unto the foot of the rock, and roared loudly and fearfully beneath the moon. And I lay close within my covert and observed the actions of the man. And the man trembled in the solitude; — but the night waned and he sat upon the rock.

'Then I cursed the elements with the curse of the tumult; and a frightful tempest gathered in the heaven, where, before, there had been no wind. And the heaven became livid with the violence of the tempest — and the rain beat upon the head

of the man—and the floods of the river came down—and the river was tormented into foam—and the water-lilies shrieked within their beds—and the forest crumbled before the wind—and the thunder rolled—and the lightning fell—and the rock rocked to its foundation. And I lay close within my covert and observed the actions of the man. And the man trembled in the solitude;—but the night waned and he sat upon the rock.

'Then I grew angry and cursed, with the curse of *silence*, the river, and the lilies, and the wind, and the forest, and the heaven, and the thunder, and the sighs of the water-lilies. And they became accursed, and *were still*. And the moon ceased to totter up its pathway to heaven—and the thunder died away—and the lightning did not flash—and the clouds hung motionless—and the waters sunk to their level and remained—and the trees ceased to rock—and the water-lilies sighed no more—and the murmur was heard no longer from among them, nor any shadow of sound throughout the vast illimitable desert. And I looked upon the characters of the rock, and they were changed; and the characters were SILENCE.

'And mine eyes fell upon the countenance of the man, and his countenance was wan with terror. And, hurriedly, he raised his head from his hand, and stood forth upon the rock and listened. But there was no voice throughout the vast illimitable desert, and the characters upon the rock were SILENCE. And the man shuddered, and turned his face away, and fled afar off, in haste, so that I beheld him no more'.

* * *

Now there are fine tales in the volumes of the Magi— in the iron-bound, melancholy volumes of the Magi. Therein, I say, are glorious histories of the Heaven, and of the Earth, and of the mighty sea—and of the Genii that overruled the sea, and the earth, and the lofty heaven. There was much lore too in the sayings which were said by the Sibyls; and holy, holy things were heard of old by the dim leaves that trembled around Dodona—but, as Allah liveth, that fable which the demon told me as he sat by my side in the shadow of the tomb, I hold to be the most wonderful of all! And as the Demon made an end of his story, he fell back within the cavity of the tomb and laughed. And I could not laugh with the Demon, and he cursed me because I could not laugh. And the lynx which dwelleth forever in the tomb, came out therefrom, and lay down at the feet of the Demon, and looked at him steadily in the face.

LIGEIA

And the will therein lieth, which dieth not. Who knoweth the mysteries of the will, with its vigour? For God is but a great will pervading all things by nature of its intentness. Man doth not yield himself to the angels, nor unto death utterly, save only through the weakness of his feeble will.

— Joseph Glanvill

I CANNOT, for my soul, remember how, when, or even precisely where, I first became acquainted with the lady Ligeia. Long years have since elapsed, and my memory is feeble through much suffering. Or, perhaps, I cannot *now* bring these points to mind, because, in truth, the character of my beloved, her rare learning, her singular yet placid cast of beauty, and the thrilling and enthralling eloquence of her low musical language, made their way into my heart by paces so steadily and stealthily progressive, that they have been unnoticed and unknown. Yet I believe that I met her first and most frequently in some large, old, decaying city near the Rhine. Of her family — I have surely heard her speak. That it is of a remotely ancient date cannot be doubted. Ligeia! Ligeia! Buried in studies of a nature more than all else adapted to deaden impressions of the outward world, it is by that sweet word alone — by Ligeia — that I bring before mine eyes in fancy the image of her who is no more. And now, while I write, a recollection flashes upon me that I have *never known* the paternal name of her who was my friend and my betrothed, and who became the partner of my studies, and finally the wife of my bosom. Was it a playful charge on the part of my Ligeia? or was it a test of my strength of affection, that I should institute no inquiries upon this point? or was it rather a caprice of my own — a wildly romantic offering on the shrine of the most passionate devotion? I but indistinctly recall the fact itself — what wonder that I have utterly forgotten the circumstances which originated or attended it? And, indeed, if ever that spirit which is entitled *Romance* — if ever she, the wan and the misty-winged *Ashtophet* of idolatrous Egypt, presided, as they tell, over marriages ill-omened, then most surely she presided over mine.

There is one dear topic, however, on which my memory fails me not. It is the *person* of Ligeia. In stature she was tall, somewhat slender, and, in her latter days, even emaciated. I would in vain attempt to portray the majesty, the quiet ease of her demeanour, or the incomprehensible lightness and elasticity of her footfall. She came and departed as a shadow. I was never made aware of her entrance into my closed study, save by the dear music of her low sweet voice, as she placed her marble hand upon my shoulder. In beauty of face no maiden ever equalled her. It was the radiance of an opium-dream — an airy and spirit-lifting vision more wildly divine than the phantasies which hovered about the slumbering souls of the daughters of Delos. Yet her features were not of that regular mould which we have been falsely taught to worship in the classical labours of the heathen. 'There is no exquisite beauty,' says Bacon, Lord Verulam, speaking truly of all the forms and *genera* of beauty, 'without some *strangeness* in the proportion.' Yet, although I saw that the features of Ligeia were not of a classic regularity — although I perceived that her loveliness was indeed 'exquisite,' and felt that there was much of 'strangeness' pervading it, yet I have tried in vain to detect the irregularity and to trace home my own perception of 'the strange.' I examined the contour of the lofty and pale forehead — it was faultless — how cold indeed that word when applied to a majesty so divine! — the skin rivalling the purest ivory, the commanding extent and repose, the gentle prominence of the regions above the temples; and then the raven-black, the glossy, the luxuriant, and naturally-curling tresses, setting forth the full force of the Homeric epithet, 'hyacinthine!' I looked at the delicate outlines of the nose — and nowhere but in the graceful medallions of the Hebrews had I beheld a similar perfection. There were the same luxurious smoothness of surface, the same scarcely perceptible tendency to the aquiline, the same harmoniously curved nostrils speaking the free spirit. I regarded the sweet mouth. Here was indeed the triumph of all things heavenly — the magnificent turn of the short upper lip — the soft, voluptuous slumber of the under — the dimples which sported, and the colour which spoke — the teeth glancing back, with a brilliancy almost startling, every ray of the holy light which fell upon them in her serene and placid yet most exultingly radiant of all smiles. I scrutinized the formation of the chin — and, here too, I found the gentleness of breadth, the softness and the majesty, the fulness and the spirituality, of the Greek — the contour which the god Apollo revealed but in a dream, to Cleomenes, the son of the Athenian. And then I peered into the large eyes of Ligeia.

For eyes we have no models in the remotely antique. It might have been, too, that in these eyes of my beloved lay the secret to which Lord Verulam alludes. They were, I must believe, far larger than the ordinary eyes of our own race. They were even fuller than the fullest of the gazelle eyes of the tribe of the valley of Nourjahad. Yet it was only at intervals — in

moments of intense excitement — that this peculiarity became more than slightly noticeable in Ligeia. And at such moments was her beauty — in my heated fancy thus is appeared perhaps — the beauty of beings either above or apart from the earth — the beauty of the fabulous Houri of the Turk. The hue of the orbs was the most brilliant of black, and, far over them, hung jetty lashes of great length. The brows, slightly irregular in outline, had the same tint. The 'strangeness,' however, which I found in the eyes was of a nature distinct from the formation, or the colour, or the brilliancy of the features, and must, after all, be referred to the *expression*. Ah, word of no meaning! behind whose vast latitude of mere sound we intrench our ignorance of so much of the spiritual. The expression of the eyes of Ligeia! How for long hours have I pondered upon it! How have I, through the whole of a midsummer night, struggled to fathom it! What was it — that something more profound than the well of Democritus — which lay far within the pupils of my beloved? What *was* it? I was possessed with a passion to discover. Those eyes! those large, those shining, those divine orbs! they became to me twin stars of Leda, and I to them devoutest of astrologers.

There is no point, among the many incomprehensible anomalies of the science of mind, more thrillingly exciting than the fact — never, I believe, noticed in the schools — that in our endeavours to recall to memory something long forgotten, we often find ourselves *upon the very verge* of remembrance, without being able, in the end, to remember. And thus how frequently, in my intense scrutiny of Ligeia's eyes, have I felt approaching the full knowledge of their expression — felt it approaching — yet not quite be mine — and so at length entirely depart! And (strange, oh, strangest mystery of all!) I found, in the commonest objects of the universe, a circle of analogies to that expression. I mean to say that, subsequently to the period when Ligeia's beauty passed into my spirit, there dwelling as in a shrine, I derived, from many existences in the material world, a sentiment such as I felt always around, within me, by her large and luminous orbs. Yet not the more could I define that sentiment, or analyze, or even steadily view it. I recognized it, let me repeat, sometimes in the survey of a rapidly growing vine — in the contemplation of a moth, a butterfly, a chrysalis, a stream of running water. I have felt it in the ocean — in the falling of a meteor. I have felt it in the glances of unusually aged people. And there are one or two stars in heaven (one especially, a star of the sixth magnitude, double and changeable, to be found near the large star in Lyra) in a telescopic scrutiny of which I have been made aware of the feeling. I have been filled with it by certain sounds from stringed instruments, and not unfrequently by passages from books. Among innumerable other instances, I well remember something in a volume of Joseph Glanvill, which (perhaps merely from its quaintness — who shall say?) never failed to inspire me with the sentiment: 'And the will therein lieth, which dieth not. Who knoweth the mysteries of the will, with its vigour? For God is but a great will pervading all things by nature of its intentness. Man doth not yield him to the angels, nor unto death utterly, save only through the weakness of his feeble will.'

Length of years and subsequent reflection have enabled me to trace, indeed, some remote connection between this passage in the English moralist and a portion of the character of Ligeia. An *intensity* in thought, action, or speech was possibly, in her, a result, or at least an index, of that gigantic volition which during our long intercourse, failed to give other and more immediate evidence of its existence. Of all the women who I have ever known, she, the outwardly calm, the ever-placid Ligeia, was the most violently a prey to the tumultuous vultures of stern passion. And of such passion I could form no estimate, save by the miraculous expansion of those eyes which at once so delighted and appalled me, — by the almost magical melody, modulation, distinctness, and placidity of her very low voice, — and by the fierce energy (rendered doubly effective by contrast with her manner of utterance) of the wild words which she habitually uttered.

I have spoken of the learning of Ligeia: it was immense — such as I have never known in woman. In the classical tongues was she deeply proficient, and as far as my own acquaintence extended in regard to the modern dialects of Europe, I have never known her at fault. Indeed upon any theme of the most admired because simply the most abstruse of the boasted erudition of the Academy, have I *ever* found Ligeia at fault? How singularly — how thrillingly, this one point in the nature of my wife has forced itself, at this late period only, upon my attention! I said her knowledge was such as I have never known in woman — but where breathes the man who has traversed, and successfully, *all* the wide areas of moral, physical, and mathematical science? I saw not then what I now clearly perceive, that the acquisitions of Ligeia were gigantic, were astounding; yet I was sufficiently aware of her infinite supremacy to resign myself, with a child-like confidence, to her guidance through the chaotic world of metaphysical investigation at which I was most busily occupied during the earlier years of our marriage. With how vast a triumph — with how vivid a delight — with how much of all that is ethereal in hope did I *feel*, as she bent over me in studies but little sought — but less known, — that delicious vista by slow degrees expanding before me, down whose long, gorgeous, and all untrodden path, I might at length pass onward to the goal of a wisdom too divinely precious not to be forbidden!

How poignant, then, must have been the grief with which, after some years, I beheld my well-grounded expectations take wings to themsleves and fly away! Without Ligeia I was but as a child groping benighted. Her presence, her readings alone, rendered vividly luminous the many mysteries of the transcendentalism in which we were immersed. Wanting the radiant lustre of her eyes, letters, lambent and golden, grew duller than Saturnian lead. And now those eyes shone less and less frequently upon the pages over which I pored. Ligeia grew ill. The wild eyes blazed with a too—too glorious effulgence; the pale fingers became of the transparent waxen hue of the grave; and the blue veins upon the lofty forehead swelled and sank impetuously with the tides of the most gentle emotion. I saw that she must die—and I struggled desperately in spirit with the grim Azrael. And the struggles of the passionate wife were, to my astonishment, even more energetic than my own. There had been much in her stern nature to impress me with the belief that, to her, death would have come withouts its terrors; but not so. Words are impotent to convey any just idea of the fierceness of resistance with which she wrestled with the Shadow. I groaned in anguish at the pitiable spectacle. I would have soothed—I would have reasoned; but in the intensity of her wild desire for life—for life—*but* for life—solace and reason were alike the uttermost of folly. Yet not until the last instance, amid the most convulsive writhings of her fierce spirit, was shaken the external placidity of her demeanour. Her voice grew more gentle—grew more low—yet I would not wish to dwell upon the wild meaning of the quietly uttered words. My brain reeled as I hearkened, entranced to a melody more than mortal—to assumptions and aspirations which mortality had never before known.

That she loved me I should not have doubted; and I might have been easily aware that, in a bosom such as hers, love would have reigned no ordinary passion. But in death only was I fully impressed with the strength of her affection. For long hours, detaining my hand, would she pour out before me the overflowing of a heart whose more than passionate devotion amounted to idolatry. How had I deserved to be so blessed by such confessions—how had I deserved to be so cursed with the removal of my beloved in the hour of my making them? But upon this subject I cannot bear to dilate. Let me say only, that in Ligeia's more than womanly abandonment to a love, alas! all unmerited, all unworthily bestowed, I at length recognized the principle of her longing, with so wildly earnest a desire, for the life which was now fleeing so rapidly away. It is this wild longing—it is this eager vehemence of desire for life—*but* for life—that I have no power to portray—no utterance capable of expressing.

At high noon of the night in which she departed, beckoning me, peremptorily, to her side, she bade me repeat certain verses composed by herself not many days before. I obeyed her. They were these:—

Lo! 'tis a gala night
    Within the lonesome latter years!
An angel throng, bewinged, bedight
    In veils, and drowned in tears,
Sit in a theatre, to see
    A play of hopes and fears,
While the orchestra breathes fitfully
    The music of the spheres.

Mimes, in the form of God on high,
    Mutter and mumble low,
And hither and thither fly;
    Mere puppets they, who come and go
At bidding of vast formless things
    That shift the scenery to and fro,
Flapping from out their condor wings
    Invisible Woe!

That motley drama!—oh, be sure
    It shall not be forgot!
With its Phantom chased for evermore,
    By a crowd that seize it not,
Through a circle that ever returneth in
    To the self-same spot;
And much of Madness, and more of Sin
And Horror, the soul of the plot!

But see, amid the mimic rout
    A crawling shape intrude!
A blood-red thing that writhes from out
    The scenic solitude!
It writhes!—it writhes!—with mortal pangs
    The mimes become its food,
And the seraphs sob at vermin fangs
    In human gore imbued.

Out—out are the lights—out all!
    And over each quivering form,
The curtain, a funeral pall,
    Comes down with the rush of a storm—
And the angels, all pallid and wan,
    Uprising, unveiling, affirm
That the play is the tragedy, 'Man,'
    And its hero, the conqueror Worm.

'O God!' half shrieked Ligeia, leaping to her feet and extending her arms aloft with a spasmodic movement, as I made an end of these lines—'O God! O Divine Father!—shall

these things be undeviatingly so? — shall this conqueror be not once conquered? Are we not part and parcel in Thee? — who knoweth the mysteries of the will with its vigour? Man doth not yield him to the angels, *nor unto death utterly*, save only through the weakness of his feeble will.'

And now, as if exhausted with emotion, she suffered her white arms to fall, and returned solemnly to her bed of death. And as she breathed her last sighs, there came mingled with them a low murmur from her lips. I bent to them my ear, and distinguished, again, the concluding words of the passage in Glanvill: '*Man doth not yield him to the angels, nor unto death utterly, save only through the weakness of his feeble will.*'

She died: and I, crushed into the very dust with sorrow, could no longer endure the lonely desolation of my dwelling in the dim and decaying city by the Rhine. I had no lack of what the world calls wealth. Ligeia had brought me far more, very far more, than ordinarily falls to the lot of mortals. After a few months, therefore, of weary and aimless wandering, I purchased and put in some repair, an abbey, which I shall not name, in one of the wildest and least frequented portions of fair England. The gloomy and dreary grandeur of the building, the almost savage aspect of the domain, the many melancholy and time-honored memories connected with both, had much in unison with the feelings of utter abandonment which had driven me into that remote and unsocial region of the country. Yet although the external abbey, with its verdant decay hanging about it, suffered but little alteration, I gave way, with a child-like perversity, and perchance with a faint hope of alleviating my sorrows, to a display of more than regal magnificence within. For such follies, even in childhood, I had imbibed a taste, and now they came back to me as if in the dotage of grief. Alas, I feel how much even of incipient madness might have been discovered in the gorgeous and fantastic draperies, in the solemn carvings of Egypt, in the wild cornices and furniture, in the Bedlam patterns of the carpets of tufted gold! I had become a bounden slave in the trammels of opium, and my labors and my orders had taken a colouring from my dreams. But these absurdities I must not pause to detail. Let me speak only of that one chamber, ever accursed, whither, in a moment of mental alienation, I led from the altar as my bride — as the successor of the unforgotten Ligeia — the fair-haired and blue-eyed Lady Rowena Trevanion, of Tremaine.

There is no individual portion of the architecture and decoration of that bridal chamber which is not now visibly before me. Where were the souls of the haughty family of the bride, when, through thirst of gold, they permitted to pass the threshold of an apartment *so* bedecked, a maiden and a daughter so beloved? I have said, that I minutely remember the details of the chamber — yet I am sadly forgetful on topics of deep moment; and here there was no system, no keeping, in the fantastic display, to take hold upon the memory. The room lay in a high turret of the castellated abbey, was pentagonal in shape, and of capacious size. Occupying the whole southern face of the pentagon was the sole window — an immense sheet of unbroken glass from Venice — a single pane, and tinted of a leaden hue, so that the rays of either the sun or moon passing through it, fell with a ghastly lustre on the objects within. Over the upper portion of this huge window, extended the trellis-work of an aged vine, which clambered up the massy walls of the turret. The ceiling, of gloomy-looking oak, was excessively lofty, vaulted, and elaborately fretted with the wildest and most grotesque specimens of a semi-Gothic, semi-Druidical device. From out the most central recess of this melancholy vaulting, depended, by a single chain of gold with long links, a huge censer of the same metal, Saracenic in pattern, and with many perforations so contrived that there writhed in and out of them, as if endued with a serpent vitality, a continual succession of parti-coloured fires.

Some few ottomans and golden candelabra, of Eastern figure, were in various stations about; and there was the couch, too — the bridal couch — of an Indian model, and low, and sculptured of solid ebony, with a pall-like canopy above. In each of the angles of the chamber stood on end a gigantic sarcophagus of black granite, from the tombs of the kings over against Luxor, with their aged lids full of immemorial sculpture. But in the draping of the apartment lay, alas! the chief phantasy of all. The lofty walls, gigantic in height — even unproportionably so — were hung from summit to foot, in vast folds, with a heavy and massive-looking tapestry — tapestry of a material which was found alike as a carpet on the floor, as a covering for the ottomans and the ebony bed, as a canopy for the bed and as the gorgeous volutes of the curtains which partially shaded the window. The material was the richest cloth of gold. It was spotted all over, at irregular intervals, with arabesque figures, about a foot in diameter, and wrought upon the cloth in patterns of the most jetty black. But these figures partook of the true character of the arabesque only when regarded from a single point of view. By a contrivance now common, and indeed traceable to a very remote period of antiquity, they were made changeable in aspect. To one entering the room, they bore the appearance of simple monstrosities: but upon a farther advance, this appearance gradually departed; and, step by step, as the visitor moved his station in the chamber, he saw himself surrounded by an endless succession of the ghastly forms which belong to the superstition of the Norman, or arise in the guilty slumbers of the monk. The phantasmagoric effect was vastly heightened by the artificial introduction of a strong continual current of wind behind the draperies — giving a hideous and uneasy animation to the whole.

In halls such as these — in a bridal chamber such as this — I passed, with the Lady of Tremaine, the unhallowed hours of the first month of our marriage — passed them with but little disquietude. That my wife dreaded the fierce moodiness of my temper — that she shunned me, and loved me but little — I could not help perceiving; but it gave me rather pleasure than otherwise. I loathed her with a hatred belonging more to demon than to man. My memory flew back (oh, with what intensity of regret!) to Ligeia, the beloved, the august, the beautiful, the entombed. I revelled in recollections of her purity, of her wisdom, of her lofty — her ethereal nature, of her passionate, her idolatrous love. Now, then, did my spirit fully and freely burn with more than all the fires of her own. In the excitement of my opium dreams (for I was habitually fettered in the shackles of the drug), I would call aloud upon her name, during the silence of the night, or among the sheltered recesses of the glens by day, as if, through the wild eagerness, the solemn passion, the consuming ardour of my longing for the departed, I could restore her to the pathways she had abandoned — ah, *could* it be for ever? — upon the earth.

About the commencement of the second month of the marriage, the Lady Rowena was attacked with sudden illness, from which her recovery was slow. The fever which consumed her rendered her nights uneasy; and in her perturbed state of half-slumber, she spoke of sounds, and of motions, in and about the chamber of the turret, which I concluded had no origin save in the distemper of her fancy, or perhaps in the phantasmagoric influences of the chamber itself. She became at length convalescent — finally, well. Yet but a brief period elapsed, ere a second more violent disorder again threw her upon a bed of suffering; and from this attack her frame, at all times feeble, never altogether recovered. Her illnesses were, after this epoch, of alarming character, and of more alarming recurrence, defying alike the knowledge and the great exertions of her physicians. With the increase of the chronic disease, which had thus, apparently, taken too sure hold upon her constitution to be eradicated by human means, I could not fail to observe a similar increase in the nervous irritation of her temperament, and in her excitability by trivial causes of fear. She spoke again, and now more frequently and pertinaciously, of the sounds — of the slight sounds — and of the unusual motions among the tapestries, to which she had formerly alluded.

One night, near the closing in of September, she pressed this distressing subject with more than usual emphasis upon my attention. She had just awakened from an unquiet slumber, and I had been watching, with feelings half of anxiety, half of vague terror, the workings of her emaciated countenance. I sat by the side of her ebony bed, upon one of the ottomans of India. She partly arose, and spoke, in an earnest low whisper, of sounds which she *then* heard, but which I could not hear — of motions which she *then* saw, but which I could not perceive. The wind was rushing hurriedly behind the tapestries, and I wished to show her (what, let me confess it, I could not *all* believe) that those almost inarticulate breathings, and those very gentle variations of the figures upon the wall, were but the natural efects of that customary rushing of the wind. But a deadly pallor, overspreading her face, had proved to me that my exertions to reassure her would be fruitless. She appeared to be fainting, and no attendants were within call. I remembered where was deposited a decanter of light wine which had been ordered by her physicians, and hastened across the chamber to procure it. But, as I stepped beneath the light of the censer, two circumstances of a startling nature attracted my attention. I had felt that some palpable although invisible object had passed lightly by my person; and I saw that there lay upon the golden carpet, in the very middle of the rich lustre thrown from the censer, a shadow — a faint, indefinite shadow of angelic aspect — such as might be fancied for the shadow of a shade. But I was wild with the excitement of an immoderate dose of opium, and heeded these things but little, nor spoke of them to Rowena. Having found the wine, I recrossed the chamber, and poured out a gobletful, which I held to the lips of the fainting lady. She had now partially recovered, however, and took the vessel herself, while I sank upon an ottoman near me, with my eyes fastened upon her person. It was then that I became distinctly aware of a gentle foot-fall upon the carpet, and near the couch; and in a second thereafter, as Rowena was in the act of raising the wine to her lips, I saw, or may have dreamed that I saw, fall within the goblet, as if from some invisible spring in the atmosphere of the room, three or four large drops of a brilliant and ruby colored fluid. If this I saw — not so Rowena. She swallowed the wine unhesitatingly, and I forbore to speak to her of a circumstance which must, after all, I considered, have been but the suggestion of a vivid imagination, rendered morbidly active by the terror of the lady, by the opium, and by the hour.

Yet I cannot conceal it from my own perception that, immediately subsequent to the fall of ruby-drops, a rapid change for the worse took place in the disorder of my wife; so that, on the third subsequent night, the hands of her menials prepared her for the tomb, and on the fourth, I sat alone, with her shrouded body, in that fantastic chamber which had received her as my bride. Wild visions, opium-engendered, flitted, shadow-like, before me. I gazed with unquiet eye upon the sarcophagi in the angles of the room, upon the varying figures of the drapery, and upon the writhing of the parti-colored fires in the censer overhead. My eyes then fell, as I called to mind the circumstances of a former night, to the spot beneath the glare of the censer where I had seen the faint traces of the shadow. It was there, however, no longer; and breathing with greater freedom, I turned my glances to the pallid and rigid figure upon the bed. Then rushed upon me a thousand memories of Ligeia—and then came back upon my heart, with the turbulent violence of a flood, the whole of that unutterable woe with which I had regarded *her* thus enshrouded. The night waned; and still, with a bosom full of bitter thoughts of the one only and supremely beloved, I remained gazing upon the body of Rowena.

It might have been midnight, or perhaps earlier, or later, for I had taken no note of time, when a sob, low, gentle, but very distinct, startled me from my revery. I *felt* that it came from the bed of ebony—the bed of death. I listened in an agony of superstitious terror—but there was no repetition of the sound. I strained my vision to detect any motion in the corpse—but there was not the slightest perceptible. Yet I could not have been deceived. I *had* heard the noise, however faint, and my soul was awakened within me. I resolutely and perseveringly kept my attention riveted upon the body. Many minutes elapsed before any circumstance occurred tending to throw light upon the mystery. At length it became evident that a slight, a very feeble, and barely noticeable tinge of color had flushed up within the cheeks, and along the sunken small veins of the eye-lids. Through a species of unutterable horror and awe, for which the language of mortality has no sufficiently energetic expression, I felt my heart cease to beat, my limbs grow rigid where I sat. Yet a sense of duty finally operated to restore my self-possession. I could no longer doubt that we had been precipitate in our preparations—that Rowena still lived. It was necessary that some immediate exertion be made; yet the turret was altogether apart from the portion of the abbey tenanted by the servants—there were none within call—I had no means of summoning them to my aid without leaving the room for many minutes—and this I could not venture to do. I therefore struggled alone in my endeavours to call back the spirit still hovering. In a short period it was certain, however, that a relapse had taken place; the colour disappeared from both eyelid and cheek, leaving a wanness even more than that of marble; the lips became doubly shrivelled and pinched up in the ghastly expression of death; a repulsive clamminess and coldness overspread rapidly the surface of the body; and all the usual rigorous stiffness immediately supervened. I fell back with a shudder upon the couch from which I had been so startlingly aroused, and again gave myself up to passionate waking visions of Ligeia.

An hour thus elapsed, when (could it be possible?) I was a second time aware of some vague sound issuing from the region of the bed. I listened—in extremity of horror. The sound came again—it was a sigh. Rushing to the corpse, I saw—distinctly saw—a tremor upon the lips. In a minute afterward they relaxed, disclosing a bright line of the pearly teeth. Amazement now struggled in my bosom with the profound awe which

had hitherto reigned there alone. I felt that my vision grew dim, that my reason wandered; and it was only by a violent effort that I at length succeeded in nerving myself to the task which duty thus once more had pointed out. There was now a partial glow upon the forehead and upon the cheek and throat; a perceptible warmth pervaded the whole frame; there was even a slight pulsation at the heart. The lady *lived*; and with redoubled ardour I betook myself to the task of restoration. I chafed and bathed the temples and the hands, and used every exertion which experience, and no little medical reading, could suggest. But in vain. Suddenly, the colour fled, the pulsation ceased, the lips resumed the expression of the dead, and, in an instant afterward, the whole body took upon itself the icy chilliness, the livid hue, the intense rigidity, the sunken outline, and all the loathsome peculiarities of that which has been, for many days, a tenant of the tomb.

And again I sunk into visions of Ligeia—and again (what marvel that I shudder while I write?), *again* there reached my ears a low sob from the region of the ebony bed. But why shall I minutely detail the unspeakable horrors of that night? Why shall I pause to relate how, time after time, until near the period of the gray dawn, this hideous drama of revivification was repeated; how each terrific relapse was only into a sterner and apparently more irredeemable death; how each agony wore the aspect of a struggle with some invisible foe; and how each struggle was succeeded by I know not what of wild change in the personal appearance of the corpse? Let me hurry to a conclusion.

The greater part of the fearful night had worn away, and she who had been dead once again stirred—and now more vigorously than hitherto, although arousing from a dissolution more appalling in its utter hopelessness than any. I had long ceased to struggle or to move, and remained sitting rigidly upon the ottoman, a helpless prey to a whirl of violent emotions, of which extreme awe was perhaps the least terrible, the least consuming. The corpse, I repeat, stirred, and now more vigorously than before. The hues of life flushed up with unwonted energy into the countenance—the limbs relaxed—and, save that the eyelids were yet pressed heavily together, and that the bandages and draperies of the grave still imparted their charnel character to the figure, I might have dreamed that Rowena had indeed shaken off, utterly, the fetters of Death. But if this idea was not, even then, altogether adopted, I could at least doubt no longer, when, arising from the bed, tottering, with feeble steps, with closed eyes, and with the manner of one bewildered in a dream, the thing that was enshrouded advanced boldly and palpably into the middle of the apartment.

I trembled not—I stirred not—for a crowd of unutterable fancies connected with the air, the stature, the demeanour, of the figure, rushing hurriedly through my brain, had

paralyzed — had chilled me into stone. I stirred not — but gazed upon the apparition. There was a mad disorder in my thoughts — a tumult unappeasable. Could it, indeed, be the *living* Rowena who confronted me? Could it, indeed, be Rowena *at all* — the fair-haired, the blue-eyed Lady Rowena Trevanion of Tremaine? Why, *why* should I doubt it? The bandage lay heavily about the mouth — but then might it not be the mouth of the breathing Lady of Tremaine? And the cheeks — there were the roses as in her noon of life — yes, these might indeed be the fair cheeks of the living Lady of Tremaine. And the chin, with its dimples, as in health, might it not be hers? — but *had she then grown taller since her malady?* What inexpressible madness seized me with that thought? One bound, and I had reached her feet! Shrinking from my touch, she let fall from her head, unloosened, the ghastly cerements which had confined it, and there streamed forth into the rushing atmosphere of the chamber huge masses of long and dishevelled hair; *it was blacker than the raven wings of midnight?* And now slowly opened *the eyes* of the figure which stood before me. 'Here then, at least,' I shrieked aloud, 'can I never — can I never be mistaken — these are the full, and the black, and the wild eyes — of my lost love — of the Lady — of the LADY LIGEIA.'

A DREAM WITHIN A DREAM

Take this kiss upon the brow!
And, in parting from you now,
Thus much let me avow—
You are not wrong, who deem
That my days have been a dream;
Yet if hope has flown away
In a night, or in a day,
In a vision, or in none,
Is it therefore the less *gone?*
All that we see or seem
Is but a dream within a dream.

I stand amid the roar
Of a surf-tormented shore,
And I hold within my hand
Grains of the golden sand—
How few! yet how they creep
Through my fingers to the deep,
While I weep—while I weep!
O God! can I not grasp
Them with a tighter clasp?
O God! can I not save
One from the pitiless wave?
Is *all* that we see or seem
But a dream within a dream?

ACKNOWLEDGEMENTS

MY THANKS are due to the following for their inspiration and help in compiling this book: Patsy Wilson, Conrad Pommerlau and Pat O'Brien, Lord and Lady Rosse, Jeff Jerome, Muffy Burns, Lord Patrick Conyngham, Vic Giolitto, David Larcher, Duncan McLaren, The Countess of St Germans, Alexander Rose and Delian Bower.

A special thank you to my wife Cassie who helped and encouraged me through good times and bad and who also shares my respect and empathy for Poe.

NB   As several of the houses included in this book are private and are not open to the public, the author asks that the reader respects their privacy.

LIST OF ILLUSTRATIONS

PICTURE CREDITS

BBC Hulton Picture Library   9
Edgar Allan Poe Museum of the Poe Foundation Inc, Richmond, Virginia   6, 8
International Museum of Photography at George Eastman House   Frontispiece